A RAVEL OF WATERS

GEOFFREY JENKINS was born in Port Elizabeth, South Africa, and educated in the Transvaal, where he wrote his first book – a local history – at the age of seventeen. After leaving school he worked as a sub-editor in what was then Rhodesia, later becoming a newspaperman both in Britain and South Africa.

His first novel, *A Twist of Sand*, was published in 1959 and immediately became a bestseller; it was later filmed. Since then he has written ten more successful novels which have sold over five million copies in twenty-three different languages.

Geoffrey Jenkins and his wife Eve Palmer – also an author – live near Pretoria.

GEOFFREY JENKINS

A Ravel of
Waters

FONTANA/Collins

First published in Great Britain by
William Collins Sons & Co. Ltd 1981
First issued in Fontana Paperbacks 1982
Second impression August 1982
Third impression September 1982
Fourth impression November 1984

Made and printed in Great Britain by
William Collins Sons & Co. Ltd, Glasgow

Whatever ravelled waters rise and fall
Or stormy silver fret the gold of day

W. B. Yeats

Author's Foreword

Jetwind, the fully automated, computer-controlled, space-age windjammer which is the centrepiece of my story, is not my invention. It is an actual design project on the boards of the Institut für Schiffbau of the University of Hamburg, evolved after a decade and a half of intensive aerodynamic and hydrodynamic testing. I wish to thank the Institut for its open-handed technical assistance to me, especially Mr H. H. W. Thieme, who was intimately involved in the project. My thanks also go to Captain S. A. Azad of the Department of Maritime Studies, Liverpool Polytechnic, and to the National Maritime Museum, Greenwich, London.

The monster Antarctic iceberg, Trolltunga, is likewise not imaginary. Details of its origin, age, drift and size – measured by satellite – have been generously given to me by Captain A. Blackham, of Noble, Denton and Associates, London, who also supplied me with invaluable expertise regarding the unique Weather Routing Service which operates from Bracknell, England.

PROLOGUE:
War, 1980s Style

Classified: Top Secret. Red Code.

Office of Issue: Task Force 24, Atlantic Fleet HQ, Norfolk, Virginia. Monitored exchange of final signals between Orion T-3 on maximum-range search of Southern Ocean and Commander, US Naval Securities Group Activities, South Atlantic, Sector T-G-F South (Tristan da Cunha).

Location of missing aircraft: Uncertain. Last position and intended movement reported on entering Southern Ocean Air-Launched Acoustical Reconnaissance Zone SSI on an effective air path of 220 degrees (true) between Lat. 44° South and Long. 14° West, approx. 850 sea miles SSW Tristan da Cunha.

Time: 21/2/81

Mission: Top Secret. Acoustic Intelligence.

Crew: 12

Report Orders: Special visual flight rules. Air reports in plain language.

Weather at time of loss: Force 9 gale, severe maritime polar air mass (analysis by National Oceanic and Atmospheric Agency). Course, directional controlled automatic meteorological (special Antarctic compensations). Visibility, poor.

Intercept Tracking and Control Group: Detached unit, US Naval Securities Group Activities, Tristan da Cunha.

Surface Observation Report immediately prior to loss:
Yacht in full sail, mysterious type of rig. No Mayday

Evaluation of loss: Possible enemy underwater-to-air missile.

MONITOR:
Tape input begins.
The following is a verbatim reel of the cockpit tape of missing Orion T-3, the last flight deck conversations between Captain Bill Werner and his crew, as well as verbal reports by Captain Werner to Commander, US Naval Securities Group on the island of Tristan da Cunha, South Atlantic.

Reel commences ————
'Hello, NSGA, Bill Werner reporting, Orion T-3. Do you hear me?'
'I hear you, Bill. Readability, strength and tone okay. Shoot.'
'Fine. Fine. Time 0100 GMT. Estimated position 850 miles southsouthwest of Tristan, approximately 600 miles southsouthwest of Gough Island.'
'What the hell's wrong with your navigation, Bill? Can't you do better than that? Be exact. You could be anywhere.'
'Maybe I am, fellah. You should be here. I'm flying blind, dead blind. I reckon the top of the overcast could be anything up to 30,000 feet. There's a 50-knot gale. I'm plugging right into the teeth of it. Air speed is down to 200 knots – plane's guzzling gas.'
'What's your visibility?'
'Nil. I couldn't see another plane if it came into me. It's nine hours since take-off· and this ship can stay in the air for seventeen. Not at this rate though.'
'You're not going to crap out of the mission because of that, are you, Bill?'
'Who said I was crapping out? You should be here to see for yourself. This is one hell of a cockamamie search – acoustical reconnaissance, Jeez! All the

acoustics I can hear is the sound of the goddam gale!'

'Nothing on your anti-sub plot? No malfunction of your electronic data-gathering gear? No intercept?'

'You're making my co-pilot piss himself laughing, fellah. I said, you should be here. This sort of flying is poker with everything wild. There isn't a damn thing from here to Cape Horn. Not a ship, not an island – nothing! It's all sea and gale and icebergs. As for a Red sub . . .!'

'What is your estimated time to the turn, Bill?'

'Could be anything. Depends on how much gas she consumes how far south I get. I'm at 10,000 feet now. I've been right down to 2000 and up to 20,000 looking for easier conditions. It don't make much difference to the gale. *Hey, wait a moment . . .!*'

MONITOR:

Crew report. Surface radar and navigation operator to pilot.

Pilot's voice resumes.

'I've got a surface intercept on the radar! Can you believe it! Out here!'

'You sure, Bill? It's not a radar angel – an iceberg?'

'No. We're holding the image. It's a ship, for sure! Looks like a small one.'

'Maybe it's a sub sail, Bill?'

'I'm going down to investigate. Keep the line open, fellah!'

'For sure.'

MONITOR:

This section of the tape has been shortened. It covers the descent of the Orion through heavy overcast with nil visibility and Force 9 gale to zero altitude above sea surface. There are no reports of instrument or mechanical failure from the aircraft.

Pilot's voice resumes.

'Three hundred feet – two fifty – two hundred – cloud's clearing – it's clear – Holy Mother of God!'

'What is it, Bill? *What is it, man!*'

'It's enough to blow your mind – I've never seen anything like this!'

'Bill! Report, for Chrissake!'

'Sorry. It took my breath away. I'm at 200 feet. As far as I can see the water looks like calf slobber – there are icebergs everywhere! Like huge meringues! Every goddam iceberg you ever saw! Whole clusters of 'em! There's also one hell of a berg – yeah, it's all one berg – it goes back clean to the horizon . . .'

'You're crazy, Bill! *One berg that big!*'

'I'm flying alongside it now – it's higher than our altitude – the top of it is lost in the overcast . . .'

'What do you estimate its size to be, Bill?'

'I can't.'

'Whadderyemean, you can't?'

'See here, fellah, I've never seen a sea like this. The whole ocean's like a vast Shivering Liz pudding made out of icebergs – the sea's all slushy in between – it's steaming mist and fog – and I'm manoeuvring round the shoulder of this great berg now – there it is! Surface observation, visual! It's a sub sail . . . no, hold it! *It is a boat! A yacht!* A yacht, do you hear? Here! She's travelling fast, too. She's planing down the waves like a rollercoaster – I can see her wake – I'll be over her in a moment. Say, there's something wrong! I can spot the sea through her sails – they're not ordinary sails – they're sails with slits in 'em – looks like a kinda Venetian blind turned wrong way up . . .'

MONITOR:

What follows is a flight deck conversation between pilot and crew.

'Captain! Captain! Visual! There! Starboard!

Coming up out of the sea . . . !'
'Captain here! Missile alert! Stand by everyone!
Emergency evasive drill! Underwater-to-air missile
tracking radar on! Jesus! It's too late! We've bought
the farm! It's going to catch us right up the ass . . . !'

MONITOR:
Tape returns to zero. No further contact.

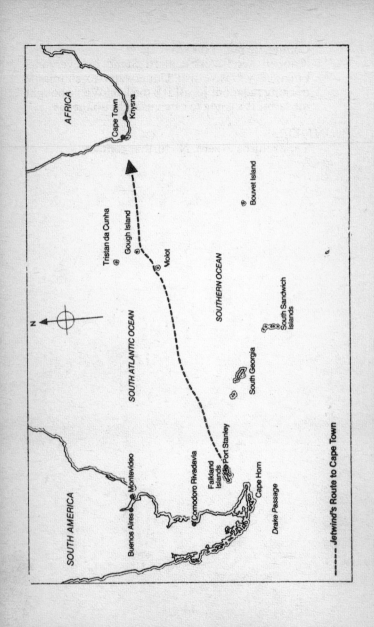

AFRICA

Cape Town

Knysna

Tristan da Cunha

Gough Island

Molot

Bouvet Island

SOUTH ATLANTIC OCEAN

SOUTHERN OCEAN

N

South Sandwich Islands

South Georgia

SOUTH AMERICA

Buenos Aires

Montevideo

Comodoro Rivadavia

Falkland Islands

Port Stanley

Cape Horn

Drake Passage

----- *Jetwind*'s Route to Cape Town

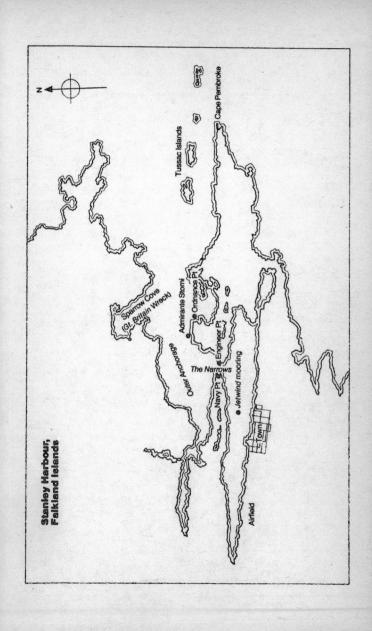

Stanley Harbour,
Falkland Islands

N

Cape Pembroke

Tussac Islands

Admirante Storni

Ordnance Pt

Sparrow Cove
(Gt. Britain Wreck)

Engineer Pt

Outer Anchorage

The Narrows

Navy Pt

Jetwind mooring

Town

Airfield

Chapter 1

Windeater. That should have been her name.

Her sails were six pairs of lips, parted now like a woman's in passion. Six on the main, six on the jib. Each pair seemed to drink in the wind, swallow it and, by some magic of aerodynamics, regurgitate it as energy to thrust the yacht's lean hull through the sea at speeds unheard of by conventional rigs.

Both sails, the main and the jib, were, unlike any others, split into segments lengthwise to the top of the mast. Each strip had transverse battens fixed at intervals to make for easy handling.

This was a space-age rig. Named the Venetian Rig, in memory of the Venetian Republic's great sailing past. Into the design of the wind-filled dacron segments above my head had gone all that man had learned of aerodynamics. Solar energy, in the form of wind, was being converted into thrust in a way which made the conventional sail as out of date as the Wright Brothers' first aeroplane compared to a Concorde.

Those dozen cross-battened strips of dacron had gunned me from Cape Horn to the Cape of Good Hope in record time for a single-handed sailor: 4200 sea-miles in twenty-six days – an average speed of seven knots.

Now *Albatros* and I were at the end of our journey. At about 10.30 in the morning, I looked up, the way I had checked those newfangled sails a thousand times during my race across the world's wildest ocean. Suddenly, the high rocky cliffs of the coast-line, backed by bush-covered hills, opened like a gate. About a mile away, bearing about ten degrees, was my landfall, my home-coming from an epic journey. These were the Heads of Knysna, entrance to the small port on the Cape's southern coast where *Albatros* had first taken the water. She was the third sailing ship to carry the famous name. The first had been a schooner which had brought a family of boat-builders, the Thesens, from Norway to Knysna over a century before. The second had been a Cape-to-Rio yacht race winner. But my *Albatros* had proved to be the fastest sailing boat afloat between Cape Horn and the Cape.

The narrow, dangerous entrance needed all my concentration. It would not have done to pile *Albatros* up on her home cliffs. Ahead lay a tricky outer and inner bar to negotiate, further complicated by the peculiarities of the Venetian Rig. Its principal virtue was excellence in heavy weather. Below the towering cliffs the sails would be blanketed from the fresh southeaster and I marvelled again, as I had done so many times on the voyage, at the paradoxical sight of *Albatros*'s burgee streaming in one direction, forward, while tufts of rope in the lee of the sail streamed in the opposite direction, against the wind. It was the embodiment of the aerodynamic magic of the Venetian Rig.

Breakers threw up a menacing line of white between the towering head-lands guarding the entrance channel. In a moment I was among them. The strong thrust of the wind disappeared below the cliffs. It became fluky, bouncing from high point to high point. I held on, however, and then I was over the inner bar to where the narrow channel led into the lagoon beyond.

I was in the process of lining up the yacht's sea-stained white hull for the last turn into the anchorage when I was deafened by the blast of horns. Hundreds of cars which I had not noticed before because of my concentration lined the eastern head-land and the road flanking my route. It seemed as if the whole population of Knysna had turned out – hooting, shouting, waving, cheering. Then a fleet of motor-boats appeared from nowhere. Men and women in holiday wear came alongside shouting congratulations and gawping at *Albatros*'s sea-swept cockpit and the salt stains trailing from the sail battens, mute witnesses to half a dozen furious encounters with the Roaring Forties. In my dark clothes and my unkempt month-old beard, I felt like the Flying Dutchman himself.

The motor-boats began sheep-dogging *Albatros* down-channel past Leisure Island, a paradise of luxury homes and gardens standing among dark milkwood trees. It seemed to me that not only *Albatros*'s home port but the whole country was waiting when I stepped ashore on the jetty at Thesen's Yard, where *Albatros* had been built. There was a barrage of press camera flashes, TV and movie cameras. Microphones were thrust in front of my face; I was assaulted by scores of questions. The Venetian Rig – what was its secret? Speed? Best day's run? From all the shaking of well-wishers' hands my arm felt as if I had pumped out *Albatros*'s bilges for a week.

Then, after a brief respite, Knysna's pride in *Albatros* and its hospitality overflowed at an official luncheon. More interviews. Endless handshakes. The blur of friendly, anonymous, admiring faces. Inevitably a local beauty queen found her way into a picture pose with me.

Finally, in the late afternoon, I was the house guest of the reception committee's chairman, a yachting enthusiast named Don Mackay. I was thankful to be whisked away from the never-ending congratulations to his home on the summit of Eastern Head from which I overlooked the entrance channel I had sailed through that morning.

Don was apologetic about the place.

'It's only the old Pilot House,' he explained. 'But I wanted the view. When the harbour was still functioning commercially, it used to be the spot from which the pilots could see what ships were approaching Knysna – from any direction.' It had a wood-panelled room whose octagonal sides consisted entirely of glass as high as the waist. The panorama of ocean and mountain landwards was stupendous. A telescope on a stand, clipper ship prints on the walls, a full-rigged model in a glass càse, mounted scenic charts of the coast, and a flagstaff on the so-green lawn beyond the windows made the Pilot House comfortably suburban-nautical.

Don's whisky felt good. I was exhausted. I felt more like ninety years old than twenty-seven. Every muscle, every nerve-ending, was tired. My mind was as flat as a sail in the doldrums.

Don, a sunburned, red-headed giant of a man, held out the whisky bottle for me to inspect. 'Like it?' he asked.

I looked at the label in surprise. 'I thought it was genuine Scotch.'

'No, South African. Good as the original heather brew. "Three Ships" – the name seemed appropriate for the occasion.'

'I hope the occasion's done. I couldn't stand much more of it.' I wanted more than anything to be alone, like a drunk with his bottle.

I said gruffly, 'I hope you're not throwing another party for me now.'

Don looked uncomfortable and glanced at his watch. 'Not a party. Just one other guest.'

'Friend of yours?'

Don hesitated. 'His name is Axel Thomsen. He jetted in early this morning and motored over to Knysna from the airfield at George. He collected a speeding fine on the way because he was so keen not to miss your arrival. He got here literally in a jib-boom ahead of *Albatros*.'

'What's the rush?'

Don was cagey. 'He'll tell you himself. He's late.'

Sheila, Don's wife, appeared and saved him from further questions. Any woman looks beautiful after you've been a month alone at sea but Sheila didn't need that distorted view to boost her good looks.

'Peter,' she said to me, 'I'll show you to your room if you'd like to clean up before Mr Thomsen arrives.'

'My room?'

'You're staying, surely?'

I tried to laugh off their disappointment. 'A fakir likes to get back to his bed of nails. I think I'd rather sleep aboard *Albatros* tonight. I'll come some other time, if I may.'

'We'll keep you to that,' she said.

Just then a car drew up on the driveway. There was

something in the glance that Don shot in my direction which puzzled me.

'Here comes Axel Thomsen. I hope you'll like him.'

He came forward, and without any preliminaries, took my hand.

'Congratulations, Captain Rainier,' he said. He had the most compelling pair of eyes I had ever seen. He held my hand in a strong grip. There was power in it, power about the man himself. He would draw people to himself like iron filings to a magnet. His scrutiny of me was as keen as a wind off the Drake Passage. He was of medium height only, and looked about forty. The clothes he wore – light blue casual slacks and a kind of matching battle blouse – emphasized his leanness. A Chinese white silk choker was secured at his throat by a yellow diamond pin.

He seemed to miss, or simply override, my resentment.

'I was in one of the boats that came to cheer you on completing your magnificent feat. I saw you bring your ship through that tricky entrance. I didn't think it possible to manoeuvre any craft with the mainboom centred without adjustment to the sheets.'

'I hope you're now satisfied that it's possible,' I retorted.

'I think it must be because there are vents from the high pressure to the low pressure sides of the sail at such short intervals that the air flow turns round the back and still gives a high degree of lift even when it's well beyond what would be the stall angle in a normal sail.'

I realized how near the limit of fatigue I was when I heard myself rasp, 'What are you trying to prove?'

Thomsen threw me a keen up-and-under glance. His reply was conciliatory. 'Nothing – except one must understand what one is up against. I have a rig which works better.'

Chapter 2

Thomsen stood there, rocking on the balls of his feet as if inviting me to hit him verbally. His eyes were searching mine, assessing me. Then he pulled out a gold and black pack of Perilly's Private Blend and offered me one, lighting it and his own with a tiny gold lighter in the shape of a dolphin.

I answered him, repeating it by rote – I was too tired to be original – 'The Venetian Rig is the first major advance in sail design for centuries. It was invented by Dr Glauco Corbellini, an Italian engineer . . .'

Thomsen made an impatient sweep with his cigarette. 'I know all that. What I want to know is, how does it work?'

'The answer is on the board – twenty-six days, four thousand, two hundred miles.'

'That doesn't say *how*.'

'It handles easily. It's ideal for one man sailing alone. It is simple. It is fast. It is highly efficient – in strong winds.'

'How fast?'

Thomsen had a curious empathy which made me continue. Now I explained. 'I'll tell you. Right at the beginning of my run I struck a lucky slant just east of the Horn . . .'

He seemed to draw the story out of me. 'What do you call a lucky slant?'

Sheila, who had been present for the introductions, slipped away when the conversation became technical. Don stood by, drinking it in.

'A gale sprang up out of nowhere, as it does near the Horn. It hit fifty knots before I realized what was happening. It was the first big test for the Venetian Rig. It turned out to be a winner. *Albatros* was going like a bomb, surfing up to twenty-five knots on the bigger rollers. I shortened sail, which was easy, even in those conditions, because each sail is a separate strip and there are quick-release expansion buttons to facilitate things – no reefing like ordinary sails. The anenometer touched sixty knots shortly after. That's its maximum calibration. It was, in fact, gusting higher – seventy-five knots, perhaps. So, in order to make the best time, I took *Albatros* through the Strait of Le Maire. With the wind and tide-rips in her favour, I managed another four knots over the ground. *Albatros* was really moving. However, I had to get clear of the Strait before the tide changed or else I'd have been in trouble. As it was, I made it by a whisker. I managed with half an hour to spare.'

Thomsen was still eyeing me. 'The Strait of Le Maire is the most bloody dangerous place in the world. In any craft. Most of all in a small yacht.'

It may have been the whisky, or perhaps the way Thomsen seemed to relate to *Albatros*'s achievements, but I continued to talk, describing how I'd cut through the Jasons and the prevailing conditions which I admitted were fairly rough. The man was showing so much interest in my account, often interrupting me to put a very knowledgeable question to me, that he began to intrigue me – as did the reason for his presence. I was particularly intrigued as to why he should know so much about the Falklands and about a short cut through a group of remote, gale-lashed islands at the other side of the earth, of interest only to penguin fanciers and environmentalists.

Thomsen brought his right fist into his left palm with a smack.

'Hell's teeth! You were as close to Port Stanley in the Falklands as the Jasons! And I didn't know it!'

He strode across to one of the big windows overlooking the anchorage. The lagoon, in the last light of the midsummer's day, was incomparably soft and lovely, pearl-grey and other-world against a back-drop of blue peaks and green forested slopes of the soaring Outeniqua mountains.

Catching the mood, Don said, 'At this time of day a flock of wild ostriches comes down from the Belvedere side and feeds on the prawns in the shallows. They stay until the tide rises up to their bellies.'

Thomsen, however, had eyes only for *Albatros* at anchor.

'She looks very small.'

'Big enough, when you're only one. Bigger than a house when she pitchpoled and fell on top of me.'

He took another drink from Don. 'Arse over tip! What happened?'

'Listen, I'm tired . . .' I began, when a thought struck me. 'I appreciate your enthusiasm and interest in *Albatros*. I don't know anything about you beyond your name. What's it all about?'

Don looked uncomfortable. 'Mr Thomsen is from the Aaland Isles.' As if that explained everything.

Thomsen laughed. 'You can't expect him to know anything as civilized as the Aalands.' He grinned at me. 'The Aalands are a group in the Baltic between Finland and Sweden. I am a Finn. I was born in Mariehamn, the Aalands capital. So was Gustav Erickson, the last great windjammer ship-owner before World War II. He had some magnificent ships – like the *Herzogin Cecile*, for one. Even today people remember her.'

Thomsen's amused glance at me was the sort that professionals swap in the company of amateurs. 'Finished up on the rocks in Cornwall.

'Erickson was a relation of mine, on my mother's side. Seamanship goes back centuries in the Aalanders' blood. Erickson drew his splendid crews mainly from the Aaland Isles. Even the advent of steam hasn't quite killed their love for sail. There are still crews to be had there who would rather man a windjammer than a steamer.'

Thomsen did not look like a dreamer to me. Yet today windjammers are the stuff that dreams are made of.

Don interrupted. 'Aaland is the home of the International Association of Cape Horners – men and women who have rounded the Horn in sail.'

'Don't forget to join the fraternity, Rainier,' Thomsen added, a little ironically. He resumed in a different tone. 'It is true, the Aaland Isles are the last resort of what few windjammers remain in the nuclear age. We Aalanders still hanker after sail for sail's sake, although our reason and our pockets tell us it is dead.'

'There are still people who love dinosaurs,' I remarked.

He downed his drink – he drank it on the rocks – in a gulp. 'It is a good comparison, that. The dinosaur was a complex creature. Complex and cumbersome. He lacked mobility, which means speed. Nowadays, speed is equated with evolution. The windjammer died because it was complex and cumbersome.'

'Sail has a place, even if a limited place, today still . . .' I began.

'*Albatros* has proved what I am trying to say,' he broke in. 'The Venetian Rig is simple; it has speed. Corbellini had a touch of genius.'

'No,' I said. 'You are trying to equate two things which cannot be compared – the yacht and the commercial sailing vessel. Let's face it, the cargo-carrying windjammer is dead. Dead as the dinosaur. What works for a small yacht doesn't necessarily work in a scaled-up version in a big ship.'

Thomsen paused a long while before replying. Then he said decisively, as if he had made up his mind about something – or someone, 'The Venetian Rig is not the only modern development in sail. There is another, which technically functions in exactly the opposite way in almost every respect. Nor is the windjammer dead. I have taken a twenty million dollar gamble to prove it is not.'

Chapter 3

All the circuits in my brain meshed, like a switch-board in which suddenly the right connections have been made. I knew now who Thomsen was. I knew why he was interested in sail. If I had not been so punch-drunk with fatigue I should have been wise to his identity earlier.

'*Jetwind*,' I said. 'You're the man who built *Jetwind*.'

'Right. That's me.'

Now that the wraps were off his mystery guest, Don became vocal. 'Mr Thomsen was visiting Cape Town. He was dead keen to meet you. A mutual yachting friend put us in touch.'

Thomsen brushed aside Don's courtesies. Sail was what mattered in his scheme of things, not social niceties. The latent power I had noticed about the man was more in evidence now.

He said, almost declaiming the facts, '*Jetwind* is a seventeen thousand tonnes, six-masted sailing ship of the most revolutionary design that has ever appeared on the high seas. She bears no resemblance to the old-time clipper or windjammer. The only thing she has in common with them is being powered by sail. Even her sails are not sails in the accepted sense. They are aerodynamically perfect aerofoils. There is no rigging, no old-time spider's web of ropes. The masts are special alloy, unstayed and stream-lined, actuated by hydraulic servo-mechanisms or locked in trim by a push-button on her bridge. A single operator only is needed. There is roller-type automatic sail furling and reefing. It works by means of stainless steel runners along the yards. Every operation aboard *Jetwind* is automated. Computers determine her optimum sailing angle and yard trim. The design has been evolved over years and tested by the

Institut für Schiffbau in Hamburg. Thousands of wind-tunnel tests went into the final design.'

'They call her the nuclear-age marvel,' interjected Don.

'She is that,' Thomsen agreed. 'Everything – and more. On passage she is weather routed to utilize the most favourable winds on her ongoing course. Data is fed by satellite twice a day into her computers. Conventional navigation went overboard with all the rest of the old-fashioned junk surrounding windjammers. Push-button prints from computers do it all. At any moment of the day or night she can establish her position – to within half a mile – on any ocean. All the captain has to do is to press a button and read a dial.'

'The sea isn't licked by push-buttons and computers,' I observed. 'The same goes for *Jetwind*'s unsupported masts and yards. Fifty-two metres high! I'll withhold judgement until I've seen how *Jetwind* performs in a Southern Ocean blow.'

Thomsen met my scepticism with obvious self-control. '*Jetwind* is as radical in construction as in conception. We brought in aircraft manufacturers for the long, lightweight masts. Their experience in assembling wing structures and understanding the stresses involved was what we needed, not old-fashioned ship-building methods. We reduced overhead costs by using off-the-shelf aircraft mountings for the masts and yards as well.'

'It sounds like science fiction to me. But seeing is believing!'

Thomsen did not raise his voice, but the power which had brought *Jetwind* to reality in the face of the sceptics and scoffers and put sail back on the high seas pulsed through his reply.

'I am not a dreamer, get that clear. I am a business-man, a ship-owner. Nor is *Jetwind* my brain child. First and foremost, my stake in *Jetwind* is money. The dream part belonged to a German engineer named Wilhelm Prolss. That dream began a long time ago, before World War II. Prolss was attending a dry-as-dust business conference in Hamburg. The board room overlooked the harbour. Prolss

27

was trying to keep awake through a dull discussion. Then, under the window, a tug went by towing an old four-masted barque to the scrap yard. It was a sight to make a sailor sad, but Prolss wasn't a sailor. Yet it triggered something deep inside his brain. Ten thousand years of man's skill and endeavour to conquer the sea lay behind that pathetic old ship going to the knackers, he told himself. Was the sailing ship really so inefficient? Did man's use of the wind have to end tragically like that?'

Don refilled our glasses. The twilight over the serene sweep of waters below us was as softly melancholy as the sight of Prolss's doomed windjammer must have been.

Thomsen enmeshed us in his narrative. 'From that day, for twenty-one long years, the idea of wind-power incubated in Prolss's mind. Finally, he took his ideas to the Institut für Schiffbau in Hamburg. The experts became sold on the idea. For ten years scientists wind-tunnel tested, examined, redesigned, perfected. They made models – radical, space-age-looking structures – of masts, yards, sails, hulls, hydraulic machinery for furling the sails and trimming the masts and yards. Finally they came up with the design that became *Jetwind* – a space-age sailing ship of seventeen thousand tonnes, one hundred and fifty metres long, masts fifty-two metres high, and a gigantic sail area of nine thousand, four hundred and thirty square metres. There had never been a ship like it before.'

'So you've rescued an endangered species,' I said. 'The new-age windjammer arises, phoenix-like, from the Aaland Isles.'

'You mock, like the others have,' retorted Thomsen vehemently. 'You think I am a sentimentalist, with sail in my genes. I repeat, I am a business-man. True, the sight of an old windjammer has the power to touch something deep inside me as it did Prolss. But he – like me – sublimated the thought into a concept as new as rocket travel. I'm telling you that the great golden age of sail is dead. Dead. The sailing ship was killed by four factors: it needed large, skilled crews – and crews cost money; it had limited manoeuvrability, especially in congested ports where tugs were necessary – and tugs cost money; the sailer's speed was low; the windjammer had small hatches, which were difficult and costly to load, especially with the clutter and tangle of rigging. *Jetwind*'s design disposes of each of these problems.'

'Even a good business-man has been known to buy a pup,' I remarked.

Thomsen kept his cool at my lack of acceptance, as he must have done a thousand times before, trying to convince critical audiences.

'Before the 1973 world fuel crisis the sailing ship as a commercial proposition was a non-starter. It was that crisis which put it back in business. For half a century cheap fuel – coal and oil – put paid to the windjammer. It simply could not compete. It was slow, expensive, and passage times were anyone's guess. Since 1973 each successive fuel crisis has made the sailing ship more commercially viable. The actual break-even point arrived when bunker fuel touched fifteen dollars a barrel.'

'Today that price sounds like happy times.'

'Would you believe it?' Thomsen said. 'The fate of the windjammer hinges on a fluctuation of a mere two dollars a barrel.'

'You're over-simplifying,' I replied. 'As fuel prices rise, so do your overhead construction costs. The same applies to the windjammer as to motor ships – maybe even more for a sailing ship which is a one-off piece of construction.'

'That is a good point,' Thomsen conceded. 'I found it in practice during the eighteen months of *Jetwind*'s building. Everything cost more than the original tenders. Nevertheless, the major factor in putting sailing ships back on the high seas is the cost of fuel. Wind is for free. No matter how long or how short the voyage, wind costs not one cent.'

Don said, 'The papers say *Jetwind* can do twenty-five knots in a full gale.'

Thomsen threw away his half-smoked Perilly impatiently. 'You don't want to believe everything the media say,' he put in. 'They always get it wrong, dress up the facts for sensation. *Jetwind* won't – can't – attain twenty-five knots. But she is capable of twenty-two.'

'No sailing ship *has* a speed,' I interrupted. 'A speed potential, yes, but a speed, no.'

Thomsen eyed me penetratingly. 'You must have thought a lot about these questions before you undertook the record attempt in *Albatros*.'

'At that stage the record also was only a potential,' I grinned.

He laughed with me. '*Touché*. Unpredictable schedules killed the old-time windjammer. In this day and age things are different. Now you can keep your sailer moving because you know in advance where the wind is, and where next it's likely to blow best. One no longer has to rely on the old sixth sense the clipper skippers were said to have. The weather, the wind, is forecast for anywhere in the world, any time. The sailer can be directed literally hour by hour by satellite and other met. data to where the best winds are, what areas of calm to avoid, and so on. Weather routing is now a science. You look sceptical, Rainier.'

'You don't want to go overboard about it,' I answered. 'Weather routing has a place – within limits. It's not the be-all and end-all, I assure you. The final decision remains the captain's.'

'True,' Thomsen answered. 'Yachts – racing yachts in particular – are comparable to the famous pace-making clippers – *Cutty Sark*, *Thermopylae*, and the rest. What interests me as a ship-owner is not a vessel which is capable – your speed potential, Rainier – of limited bursts of speed like the *Cutty Sark*. It is *average* service speed.'

Don said, 'You make it all sound very down to earth.'

'That is the name of the game,' Thomsen replied. 'That is why I built *Jetwind*. I have put every voyage time of the *Cutty Sark* during her prime twenty years through the computer. Today she would be a non-starter in competition with powered ships, even with the price of bunker fuel being what it is. At her best in the Australian trade,

Cutty Sark averaged only six point five knots. What interests me far more than the lovely clippers are the great iron square-riggers which went out from Germany to Chile for nitrates at the turn of the century. That was when the day of the windjammer was, in fact, done. There was a famous Captain Hilgendorf who *averaged* seven and a half knots in regular voyages for twenty years between Hamburg and Chile. That is the sort of consistent speed which interests me as a ship-owner.'

'Then what do you expect from *Jetwind*?' I asked.

'To compete with powered vessels, she has to have a service speed of between ten and twelve knots on any voyage,' he replied. 'But make no mistake about her speed – potential speed, I should say. She can achieve twenty-two knots in a Force Nine gale. On any point of sailing she is at least sixty per cent faster than the great old-timers like the legendary German nitrate five-master *Preussen*. She is a flier, born and bred. That rig of hers develops no less than forty thousand horse-power in a Force Nine gale – about two-thirds of the thrust of a World War II light cruiser's turbines. Shaped alongside well-proven four-masted barques, *Jetwind* develops up to one hundred and eleven per cent more driving thrust. To evaluate *Jetwind's* design, we carried out hundreds of simulated crossings of the Atlantic, in both directions. We found she would average from ten to twelve knots eastward from America to Europe, and eight to nine knots in the opposite direction.'

'What about calms, doldrums? Not even Weather Routing can stop the wind from not blowing.'

'In a flat calm, *Jetwind* has three small auxiliary diesels of five hundred horse-power each. They will drive her at eight knots and can also be used to power the hydraulic mechanisms for the masts and sails and to supply electricity to the ship. She also has powered bow and stern thrusters for manoeuvring in port. *Jetwind* can spin on a dime, using them in conjunction with her own sails.'

Don asked, 'Doesn't the screw act as a drag when she is under sail?'

'No,' answered Thomsen. 'It has a variable pitch and is

housed in a nacelle which is retractable when not in use. It is as different a concept from the old auxiliary as her sails are from a clipper's.'

I said, '*Jetwind* sounds magnificent – as a computer print-out. Things that work in a wind-tunnel don't necessarily work in a Southern Ocean gale.'

Chapter 4

As an answer, Thomsen threw down a photograph in front of me. It was an aerial shot of *Jetwind* leaving harbour, taken from above her port bow. It was an exciting, novel sight, as beautiful in its own right as any classic clipper. There were six towering masts with gleaming light alloy yards. White dacron sails were snuggled to each other to form an unbroken quintuple aerofoil the full height of each mast with hardly any space showing between them. She had a lean hull painted dark green with a gold stripe. There was not a crew man to be seen.

'Does that look like a paper ship?' Thomsen's voice was abrasive.

'I've never seen a rig like that,' I said. 'I wonder, though, how she steers without jibs or staysails . . .'

'You don't seem able to get the image of old sailing ships out of your mind,' he snapped back. 'Can't you see, man, she is *new*, new as tomorrow? You're saying what a thousand sceptics said when I originally planned *Jetwind*. Every ship-owner I approached for financial backing said, "It's all very nice, but . . ." Hell, man, don't you feel what *Jetwind* represents? The new age of sail!' He went on, his voice rising. 'I've backed this hunch of mine to the tune of twenty million dollars. I tell you this, Rainier, if *Jetwind* is a success I intend to build a fleet of *Jetwinds*. Five more. I'll show the doubters! Five more – that means I need financial backers – and backers have to be convinced.'

Why, I asked myself, had Thomsen flown to Knysna to meet me? It wasn't as if I could offer him backing. My total assets were a few sea-damp clothes in *Albatros*'s locker.

'What happened to *Jetwind*'s attempt on the Montevideo-Cape record?' I asked. 'I last heard of her in Montevideo as *Albatros* staged down the South American coast for the Horn. Radio news has been out since I cleared the Falklands.'

The muscles round Thomsen's mouth went taut. 'Get me another drink, will you, Don? I need it. So you haven't heard about *Jetwind*, Rainier?'

'No.'

'Then let me clear the decks, so to speak, before I answer your question. I built *Jetwind* as a commercial proposition. I built her in the firm belief that she can compete on near equal terms with steam or motor ships. Her maiden voyage was planned to be a shop-window promotion. I selected a route on which one can be pretty sure of the wind – Montevideo to Cape Town. Just right for bulk cargoes – wheat, maize, ore, coal. It is also short enough to hold the public's interest – three thousand, six hundred and twenty nautical miles. It used to take old-time windjammers twenty days. I gave orders that *Jetwind* was to do it in thirteen. An average of almost twelve knots.

'*Jetwind* made the run from the Channel to the Equator in fifteen days – as good a time as any accomplished under sail. She made another good run from the Line to the River Plate – as she bloody well should have done, with the wind and the currents all in her favour down the South American coast.

'I had a first-rate skipper in Mortensen. If any skipper was capable of demonstrating *Jetwind*'s mettle, it was him. I'd given him strict orders not to open her up until he got on the Montevideo-Cape leg. The ship was also in the process of shaking down, although she had only minor teething troubles – nothing to worry about. Mortensen said she handled sweetly, a real thoroughbred. He was happy with her.'

'Was?' I asked.

33

Thomsen could not control his agitation. 'Mortensen is dead. Everything has gone wrong since.'

'What happened?'

Thomsen lit another Perilly, but threw it away before he had taken more than one deep gulp of smoke.

'*Jetwind*'s attempt on the record caught the public imagination – the media's likewise. Every pressman, radio commentator, TV camera eye, was upon her. I had arranged a grandstand finish here in Cape Town. In anticipation of it, I flew out a dozen of the world's top ship-owners to meet the herald of the new age of sail. And now, here they are – waiting! One of them, Sir James Hathaway, is travelling with the ship. He is a sail enthusiast. If he backs me, the others will follow like sheep. Sir James wanted to see for himself how *Jetwind* handled at sea. Now . . . !'

'I guess ship-owners are more conservative even than sailors when it comes to accepting innovations,' I said. 'I know how I felt when I was first confronted with the Venetian Rig.'

'Mortensen got away to a flying start from Montevideo . . .' Thomsen went on.

'I saw it on TV,' said Don. 'She looked splendid coming out of the River Plate.'

'Looked!' exploded Thomsen. 'She could have looked any way she liked, so long as she had performed!'

'What happened then?' I asked.

'Mortensen was killed, that's what! He chose his wind carefully for the start and the expected ongoing weather for the Cape. *Jetwind* took off like a bomb. In three days she logged a thousand miles. Then he was killed.'

'How?'

'I couldn't – haven't – got any details from anyone about how it actually happened. *Jetwind* has one of the finest communications systems afloat. With Mortensen, all I had to do was to pick up a phone anywhere and I could speak to him. All I can make out is that Mortensen was killed in some kind of an accident involving the sail furling gear.'

'But from what you've told us, any competent officer should have been able to press the right tit and sail her.'

He spun round and glared at me, and I saw how really touchy he was.

'I wasn't trying to be funny,' I added. 'You obviously had good back-up men under Mortensen. What was to prevent them taking over and bringing the ship on to the Cape?'

He replied in a kind of snarl. 'I hand-picked every goddam one of them. Including the first officer, Anton Grohman.'

'Grohman? His name rings a bell.'

'He made the headlines during the last round the world yacht race. One of the boats was sinking off Brazil. He was nearby, and rescued the crew in his schooner.'

'Now I remember. From what I recall, Grohman did a terrific job.'

'He did. Then,' Thomsen added grimly. 'I met him in Germany while *Jetwind* was being built. He wanted a job. He had all the qualifications, and excellent references. I'd already hired Mortensen as captain but I had no doubts about Grohman's abilities. Until . . .' He threw back the last of his drink.

'Until when?' I asked.

'Until Grohman reported Mortensen's death, and I instructed him to take command of *Jetwind* and carry on to the Cape. The next thing I heard was that *Jetwind* was heading for the Falklands.'

'You must be joking!'

'Captain Rainier, I wish to heaven I was!'

'Any sailor worth his salt would know that such a diversion was plain mad.' I found myself sharing Thomsen's anger. 'The Falklands!' I repeated in disbelief. 'If *Jetwind* was a thousand miles off the South American coast on course for the Cape, Grohman must have swung clean into the teeth of the prevailing winds and currents to head for the Falklands. He must have been crazy!'

Thomsen said bitterly, 'That's what Grohman did.'

'I would have given any skipper who did that the chop – pronto,' I said.

Thomsen went on. 'The day Mortensen was killed *Jetwind* was running with a fresh southwesterly abeam – one of her best points of sailing. She was logging a steady sixteen knots in a rising sea. Weather Routing reported a big low astern of her, with the promise of a big blow – enough wind to take Grohman fast to Gough, which is halfway to the Cape. I know what conditions were because I spoke to Mortensen a few hours before his death. The prospect of a sustained storm thrilled Mortensen; he was piling on sail. He hoped to achieve *Jetwind*'s theoretical maximum of twenty-two knots before it was over. Then . . .'

Thomsen collided with a table as he strode unseeingly about the room. What he went on to say made his face leaner, tougher, and he himself taller than he really was.

'Grohman put the ship about, and *beat into the gale for days*. The Falklands! Of all places, why? That is where *Jetwind* is now. In Port Stanley. That's why I reacted the way I did when you told me you'd been close to Port Stanley when you cut through the Jasons in *Albatros*.'

'Who was the next man in line after Grohman?'

'Tideman. John Tideman. Royal Navy Adventure Training School. Sailed round the Horn three times. *He* would know how to handle a fast ship!'

'Why didn't you appoint Tideman?'

'I told you, after Mortensen's death, I could not communicate with *Jetwind*, or I would have. Besides, I didn't know – wasn't told – that *Jetwind* had altered course. The communications system seemed to go haywire.'

'The radio, you mean?'

'No, I know the radio was working, because I checked back with Weather Routing. The ship was still acknowledging weather advice. But all I got were some cryptic telex messages when he was finally approaching the Falklands. Something about formalities surrounding Mortensen's death . . . a lot of crap! But that isn't the end of

36

the story. Once Grohman reached Port Stanley, the authorities held *Jetwind*.'

'You mean arrested?'

'Held is all I know. Investigations. Inquest into Mortensen's death. I tried phoning for clarification. If you want to blow a gasket, just try phoning Port Stanley.'

'It's absurd,' I replied. 'The British authorities in Port Stanley . . .'

'It was not only the British who stalled,' he retorted. 'It was the Argentinians. They also put their damned dago fingers in my *Jetwind* operation.'

'But the Falklands are British,' Don said.

'Argentina doesn't give a damn,' Thomsen snapped back. 'They have claimed the islands for generations. They even have their own name for them – the Malvinas. I wish I knew what got into that fool Grohman to put his nose into that thorny nest of international politics. All he needed to do was to carry on to Cape Town.'

'When did all this happen?' I asked.

'A week ago. *A week!* A week ago *Jetwind* anchored in Port Stanley! She was originally due in Cape Town five days ago and now she's harbour-bound while a dozen of the world's top shipping tycoons snigger in derision!'

'What does Sir James Hathaway say about this Falklands business? He's on the spot.'

'He is *in* a spot,' Thomsen retorted. 'He is being held in a kind of protective custody aboard *Jetwind*. The Argentinian authorities have refused to allow him to return via the mainland – a matter of bureaucratic red tape involving his travel permit. He must be chewing the rudder pintles off *Jetwind*. Every extra day he is ship-bound in Port Stanley, my chances of obtaining his financial backing diminish.'

'What about the other ship-owners?'

'Polite, but increasingly sceptical about *Jetwind*. They bring up the old cliché, something always happens to a sailing ship. Something did. Twenty million dollars' worth of floating computerized gadgetry is tied up in an obscure port. But I'm not beaten yet,' he said in a steely voice.

I said tersely, 'You didn't come here to cry on my shoulder.'

'*Jetwind* is still viable. I've decided to send the ship-owner party off on a cruise to Gough Island.'

'To Gough? What the hell for? It's only halfway from South America to the Cape.'

'That's why! I'll show 'em still!' he went on. 'Gough is fifteen hundred and fifty nautical miles from the Cape. It's two thousand, one hundred and fifty miles from the Falklands. *Jetwind* can cover that distance in a week if she's thrashed to the limit. My party will be travelling aboard the South African research ship *Agulhas* due to relieve the weather station on Gough. I'm planning to have *Jetwind* intercept the *Agulhas*, and give a demonstration of her – in full flight, so to speak. That'll get 'em! They'll buy my project yet, if they can see her like that! I'll convince Hathaway, too! Given the right skipper she can do it.'

Don obviously knew all about the *Jetwind* drama. He made a great fuss over Thomsen's empty glass. He was clearly deeply concerned over the whole affair. Turning to face Thomsen, he said, 'Axel, I think the time has come to tell our friend here the purpose of our meeting.'

'Right,' said Thomsen in an authoritative manner. 'Let me come to the point, Rainier. I need a sailor, a man with guts, a man who's not afraid to take chances and pick up a challenge.' He came close to me with his fists clenched as if he meant to hit me. And flinging a fist in my direction, he said, 'I need YOU!'

Chapter 5

My state of exhaustion suddenly gave way to full alertness. Thomsen's offer triggered off in my mind's eye, like a slow-motion repeat TV run, some of the hazards I had survived in *Albatros* in the Southern Ocean. Beneath me again was a green and white monster wave down whose side *Albatros* had pitchpoled, out of control, with seventy-five knots of wind flattening its crest and searing the ocean's surface raw white, like an irradiated cancer exfoliating. Another mental picture followed: an ice-blue ocean in the vicinity of Gough and on every side a convoy of huge tabular icebergs stretching to the horizon, rearing and plunging like mobile casemates. Strangest of all, however, had been the swirling, steamy mist surrounding the bergs. It lent the scene an unreal, mystical quality, the quality of a dream. A final image was the dreaded Cape Horn itself – it had unveiled itself for an unprecedented half-hour of calm at the outset of *Albatros*'s voyage. I had lived out these sights – alone.

'The answer is no,' I said.

Thomsen had been leaning towards me in that peculiar aggressive attitude; now at my refusal he drew back.

'Don,' he said calmly. 'Would you go and get my brief-case from the car?'

Sheila appeared at the door at that moment; Don had sense enough to sweep her away with him.

Thomsen eyed me. I saw him for what he was – tough, prepared to fight for what he wanted. His fancy diamond pin and dolphin lighter weren't part of the real man.

'So you're going to chicken out?' he said contemptuously.

'I haven't chickened in,' I retorted. 'Now look here, Mr Thomsen, I've been twenty-six days alone at sea across the wildest ocean in the world. I'm dead on my feet. I need a rest.'

'Don't give me that stuff, Rainier. Sure, you've done a great job with *Albatros*. Now there's an even greater job awaiting you with *Jetwind*.'

Don and Sheila reappeared. Don dumped Thomsen's brief-case and they beat a hurried retreat when they heard the drift of our discussion.

'*Jetwind* has lost so much time that it's hopeless . . .' I began.

Thomsen did not seem to be listening. He pulled a plan from his brief-case and threw it in front of me.

'Look! *Jetwind!* There has never been a ship like this before! One hundred and twenty-five metres long, twenty-one in the beam, nine deep. Look at her proportions! Six masts! Neither you nor anyone else has ever seen masts like those! Stream-lined, aerodynamic, hydraulically trimmed – perfect. High tensile steel for the lower, light alloy for the upper sections. The masts are designed to offer minimum wind resistance. She's beautiful, she's fast – by all that's holy, man, can't you *feel* what this ship is?'

I could, and I did. But my appreciation was at a distance, the distance of a drawing-board plan. I had not experienced the real thing.

'I thought her yards would be wider,' I remarked.

I was aware of Thomsen's keen scrutiny of me as my interest grew. 'They have been criticized by comparison with those of the famous clippers. They are as deep as the fastest, but not as wide. Still, that counts for nothing. As I've said, those old fliers are dead. What matters here is the shape of the aerofoil – that has been evolved by means of the wind-tunnel.'

I studied the plan further. 'I see she's got accommodation for passengers.'

'Aye, for twelve, in the stern. Well out of your way on the bridge.'

'What do you mean, "out of *my* way"? I said No, didn't I?'

'I was just generalizing.'

Noting the design closely, I continued, 'I don't care for all the clutter of bridge structure so far for'ard – the position of it seems to be thought out in terms of a steamship. The captain of a sailing ship must be able to *see* his sails in front. I would have sited the bridge much further aft, abaft the mainmast.'

'*Jetwind*'s bridge is not so much a bridge in the accepted sense as a control centre,' replied Thomsen. An imperceptible change had crept into his voice. His former aggressiveness had disappeared. Perhaps he was playing his fish far more skilfully than I gave him credit for.

'Data is fed into the controls and consoles in the wheelhouse from sensors, computers, and all the rest of the electronic gadgetry located in various parts of the ship and masts,' he explained. 'Sailing *Jetwind* is not an operation like in an old windjammer where the skipper relied on his senses and experience. His nerve-ends in *Jetwind* are electronic. They are twice as quick and ten times more accurate than human intuition.'

'I'd back my own senses against electronic sensors when it comes to a Southern Ocean squall,' I replied. 'They come at you suddenly from any point of the compass. They jump about like a hipped-up bird in a disco.'

'It would be very difficult to catch *Jetwind* aback,' Thomsen countered. 'Her entire sailplan can be furled in twenty seconds flat. It would take some squall to do better.'

'Did Mortensen establish that at sea – or is it just another wind-tunnel print-out?'

'Wind-tunnel.'

'How much free-board will *Jetwind* have when she's fully laden?' I asked.

'What do you have in mind? Anything to do with the bridge?'

'Yes and no.'

'Free-board will be almost four metres.'

'That's precious little when it comes to beating close-hauled in the Roaring Forties,' I answered. 'She'll be taking it green over her rails, especially if she's being hard pushed. That means a hell of a lot of sea will be coming over her lee rail – it's going to be worst at the spot where the bridge is located. That's exactly where she'll put her rail under. Any man on that long uncluttered deck will stand a pretty fair chance of being swept overboard. If the bridge were further aft, it would serve as a break-water.'

The exchange of technicalities was establishing a closer link between us. I found myself being carried away.

Thomsen laughed. 'I can't get you away from thinking in old-fashioned terms, Rainier. You're visualizing a deckful of men pulley-hauling at a spider's web of ropes. *Jetwind* doesn't have any men on deck in a blow. The crew mans stations either on the bridge or below-decks. Forget the word windjammer. That's what the old-timers really were – jammers into the wind. *Jetwind* is different.'

'In a wind-tunnel.'

'You keep saying that, and it underlines my point. That is why I built *Jetwind*. To *prove* the space-age rig by trial at sea.'

'You talk as though there were only one revolutionary rig – yours, *Jetwind*'s. What about the Venetian Rig?'

'I know, I know,' he answered broodingly. 'It was a major decision I faced. In fact there are two splendid space-age sail systems which are exactly opposite. Both are based on sound observation and scientific theory. You can't fault either. There is the contrast between a highly efficient wind flow in conditions of flow stability . . .'

'Rarefied aerodynamics are beyond me,' I interrupted.

'They should not be and must not be,' he replied impatiently. 'The new age of sail is a young person's world. Everyone – men and women – involved in *Jetwind* is *young*. The scientists, the aerodynamicists, the engineers, are all young. You, Rainier, are young. Wake up and go along with it.'

'Right now I feel about a hundred,' I replied. 'I'm clapped out, as I said, dead on my feet. All this is aircraft talk . . .'

'Pull yourself together,' went on Thomsen in the same tone. 'Aerodynamics, flow, stability – yes, but aircraft, no. I grant you that when *Jetwind* is beating upwind, her sails are experiencing flow which is in some ways similar to air flow across an aircraft wing. Running downward is another story. The comparison is much closer to a parachute than a wing. You know the type of special multi-slotted ribbon parachute used to slow down jet fighters on landing? That's where the similarity comes in.'

'All this balancing of pros and cons must have given you ulcers – especially at the price of twenty million dollars.'

'The final and twenty-million dollar question was, how much efficiency could be sacrificed to improve efficiency? The aerofoil rig finally beat the Venetian Rig by a short head.'

'Then hard luck stepped in and messed it all up.'

'Hard luck, hell!' he snapped. 'It was a sonofabitch named Grohman. I can still make it. But I need your help, Rainier. You are my man. I am offering you the captaincy of *Jetwind* – here and now.'

'I couldn't do justice to the job in my present state.'

'Rubbish! You're a sailor. The old China clipper skippers went without sleep for *three months* racing home! Three months, with only a cat-nap now and then in a deck-chair lashed to the weather rail! And you've been without proper sleep for only twenty-six days! It's less than a ten-hour flight from Cape Town to Buenos Aires. You can sleep all the way, recharge your batteries. You'll be as right as rain after that. You can have a further night's sleep on the journey to the Falklands. That's more than enough for a sailor like you!'

Still I stalled. 'Fair enough. However, I've never even set eyes on your space-age marvel. By your own admission, *Jetwind* is a highly complex machine, all push-buttons and computers. I'm a practical sailor. I haven't a clue how to operate her. I'll probably dismast her first time out.'

As I temporized, my eye fell upon Thomsen's photograph of *Jetwind*. The towering aerofoil sails and stream-lined masts had a stylized beauty all of their own. I remembered a similar strange exultation when I had first seen the Venetian Rig's reefing lines streaming contrary to the wind's direction – it had been a kind of mystic revelation of man's complete conquest of the wind.

Thomsen waited for the kill now he saw he had me hesitating.

'There'll be a lot of delays,' I added lamely. 'Air tickets to arrange, clearances, connections, and so on . . .'

'Your seat is booked on the Aerolineas Argentinas Boeing leaving Cape Town for Buenos Aires tomorrow. From Buenos Aires you will fly to Comodoro Rivadavia in the south and onwards to the Falklands. You will have my full written authority to act as you think fit – fire anyone, hire anyone, bribe anyone. Only, *for Pete's sake get going*!'

Fatigue, they say, gives an extra dimension to perception. It was not only the challenge which influenced my decision. *Jetwind* would, I told myself, give me the vehicle to prove whether the awesome thing I had sighted among the wild waters of the Southern Ocean was real, or the substance of shadows, a lone sailor's hallucination.

'I'll do it,' I said.

Chapter 6

Dinner began with champagne and ended with a telephone call.

Whether or not Sheila had anticipated that there would be something to celebrate as a result of Thomsen's meeting with me, I am not sure, but certainly the meal was a treat I might have dreamed about when chewing ship's biscuits and raisins in *Albatros*'s cockpit. Thomsen made handsome amends to Sheila for his earlier unsociableness towards her, blaming it on his anxiety to sign me up for

Jetwind. I was reminded of my earlier impression of people being drawn to him like filings to a magnet. Certainly Sheila warmed under his charisma. We drank to *Jetwind*'s success; in our euphoria we toasted the new golden age of sail.

Suddenly Thomsen put down his glass and eyed me.

'Peter,' he said. 'You've overlooked a most important aspect – pay.'

'Frankly, I never thought of it.'

'I believe money is important. What do you expect to be paid?'

'I've no idea. I don't know what the job's worth.'

'There is no real yardstick for this. It's a one-off job – special.'

'Short-term, too – you want me at Gough in a week, then another week or so after that to Cape Town.'

He shed his affability like a shirt. 'Don't think that if you reach Gough on schedule you can coast home to the Cape. The last leg is shorter. Your service speed is to be twelve knots – that means under a week from Gough.'

'The shorter the time, the shorter my pay, it seems.'

'On the contrary, the quicker you make it, the more I pay.'

'What do you suggest?'

'I will pay you five thousand dollars a day to flog the hide off *Jetwind*. For every day under a week you reach Gough, there'll be a bonus of ten thousand dollars. For every day less than a week you take from Gough to Cape Town, you earn another five thousand dollars.'

'Either you're very reckless or very desperate.'

'I have already gambled twenty million on *Jetwind*. I'm staking everything on you to put the project back into orbit. It's as simple as that. What are a few thousand dollars more?'

We drank to it. Looking back on the occasion, I am inclined to think it was tension rather than alcohol which made Thomsen loquacious. He talked volubly all through the meal about the velocities, angles and forces acting on a sailing ship; the equilibrium of those forces; the aerodynamic performance of *Jetwind*'s rig and the hydro-dynamic performance of her hull. He dilated on side forces and thrust components; the damping effect of the sea-way motions of a sailing ship compared to power. He even got to sketching rough graphs and jotting down constellations of algebraic symbols. It was all too esoterically technical for me; Don looked owlish; Sheila smiled a fixed hostess smile.

As Thomsen brought his dissertation to an end, he began a barrage of phone calls to London, New York, Buenos Aires, Cape Town. He seemed to be issuing orders in every direction concerning *Jetwind*. Finally, he became flushed and angry at not being able to raise Port Stanley.

All I craved was sleep. I said my farewells. Don motored me to the jetty where I had moored *Albatros*'s dinghy. He and Sheila had tried to persuade me to stay overnight with them. Finally Thomsen accepted the guest room which had been prepared for me. He and Don were to call for me early and Thomsen and I would fly to Cape Town.

I rowed out to *Albatros*. As I reached the yacht, my hackles rose. One does not spend a month alone in a boat, listening to every creak of its structure, without being able to sense a change on board. In a flash I knew I was not alone.

The intruder was hidden by the cockpit overhang on the starboard side, which housed *Albatros*'s rather elementary instrument panel.

I took a heavy pin from the rail and vaulted inboard.

The man spun round and faced the improvised weapon.

'If you've any ideas of souvenir hunting, forget it!' I rapped out. 'Get below! I mean to have a look at you!'

The first thing I was aware of was the American accent. 'These instruments are Rube Goldberg stuff. What about critical sailing angles, optimum course, speed made good?'

'What's that to you?'

'I would have expected that sort of thing, after this boat's track record.'

'Half of those instruments don't work any more. They drank too much Southern Ocean.'

46

My eyes were adapting to the darkness. My visitor was shorter than me, but square and stocky. His dark hair, cut unfashionably short, was brushed back from the temples, his chin was as square as his powerful shoulders, and heavy brows completed the impression of determination and strength. He wore a dark, tight-fitting sweat-shirt and sneakers.

He seemed quite unconcerned about the fact that he was a trespasser. 'I don't understand the downwind performance of the Venetian Rig . . .' he began.

'You don't have to, until we've sorted out why you're on board my boat. Below! That door's not locked. Switch on the left.'

'Okay,' he replied. 'My question will keep till later.'

He did as I said. The cabin had a welcome, familiar deep-sea smell.

My captive looked round. 'The guy who designed this must have been either a pinch-gut or a monk.'

He didn't look like a petty thief to me. I liked his easy laugh, as if he knew in advance that he would be exculpated. Humour ran from his mouth up into his brown eyes.

He held out his hand. 'I'm Paul Brockton. Boy, I thought the America Cup Twelves were pretty stark below, but this!' He indicated the cell-like spartan scantlings. 'I thought you would have taken up a crash-pad ashore rather than sleep here any more.'

I said, although now I wasn't convinced of my accusation, 'Is that why you took the opportunity to sneak aboard my boat?'

He smiled and shook his head. 'I've been waiting for you for about half an hour. If I'd wanted, I could have cased the whole boat and got the hell out again, and you'd never have been the wiser.'

Somehow, I believed him. He faced me with a half smile and a slight lift of his left eyebrow. He reached into his shirt pocket and pulled out a pack of Paul Reveres. I noted the ripple of powerful muscle under the close-hugging fabric.

'Listen, Brockton,' I said. 'I'll give you the benefit of the doubt. I've had people on my neck all day; I'm dead beat. I want some sleep, and I intend to get it. What do you want? Say it quickly.'

'I want your story and that of *Albatros*.'

'You a newspaper-man?'

'No. American yachting journal – the *Deep Sea Sailer*. I'm looking for an exclusive.'

'You reporters all are. There's nothing new left to be told. *Albatros*'s record is on the board now. That's all there is to it, even for the experts who may read *Deep Sea Sailer*.'

'There's always something new if you know the right questions to ask.'

'I don't intend to answer any questions, however clever. Nor do I intend to be interviewed. When I came aboard I intended to make myself a cup of coffee before turning in. You can stay and share it, if you wish.'

'I'll do more than that. I'll make it, if you'll tell me where things are.'

He got the gas going and I sat on a locker seat.

'You didn't come from America to write up *Albatros*,' I said. 'What's behind your visit, Brockton?'

He fiddled wtih cups and sugar. 'The big story was, of course, *Jetwind*. I flew out to cover her arrival in Cape Town. The record attempt has aborted, as you may have heard. So logically *Albatros* was the next best.'

'I heard about *Jetwind* – tonight.'

He was very acute and tried to milk the line. 'Why . . tonight?'

'I had dinner with *Jetwind*'s owner, Axel Thomsen.'

'I noticed him around during the day. I wondered what he was doing in Knysna. Pity. *Jetwind* had the makings of a winner.'

'She's faster than those America Cup Twelves you mentioned.'

'Who says?'

'Thomsen. On paper she is, at any rate. Wind-tunnel tests proved it.'

'Is that a fact? I was aboard *Courageous* and *Independence* when they worked out off Marblehead back in 76. They were engaged in a trial horse contest one against the other in preparation for the Cup. If you want to see every goddam thing optimized and then re-optimized, take a look inside an America Cup Twelve.'

'None of them could do twenty-two knots in a Force Nine gale – especially in the Southern Ocean. *Jetwind* can.'

Brockton contemplated me. 'I've sailed with skippers like Ted Turner of *Courageous* and Lowell North of *Enterprise* and if ever there are guys who can extract the last hundredth of a knot out of a hull, it's an America Cup skipper. They are refined, highly sophisticated machines, those Twelves.'

'And therefore unsuited to the Southern Ocean.'

'Could be.'

'With a gale on her quarter or beam, *Jetwind* is probably the fastest sail-powered hull ever to figure on the high seas.'

'By contrast, a Twelve is relatively slow downwind,' he answered. 'You have to tack 'em at critical angles for best performance.' Brockton screwed up his eyes. 'You seem pretty sold on *Jetwind*, Peter. You wouldn't think you'd just proved that the Venetian Rig is the fastest rig afloat.'

'*Albatros* is a yacht, *Jetwind* is a ship,' I answered. 'That's the difference – Paul,' I added, taking him up on his use of first names. Perhaps I wanted to psych myself into believing in *Jetwind* because deep down I was not sure of her true capabilities.

Brockton whipped the milk off the stove to prevent it from boiling over.

'If you look in the for'ard locker, there's a bottle of Navy rum,' I said. 'It helps the coffee.'

He found the bottle, unscrewed the cap and sniffed. 'Boy, that sure is nanny-goat sweat.'

We laughed about it. Brockton had an easy man-to-man way.

'Keeps the icebergs down south at a respectable distance,' I remarked.

He brought the steaming mugs and put them in front of us on the swivel table.

'From what I hear, "down south" are the operative words for *Albatros* – you kept much further south than is customary.'

'Customary? What is customary any more, Paul? What some old windjammer did, or what modern techniques dictate?'

I noted that I was echoing Thomsen. Perhaps *Jetwind* made one think like that.

'You sure stuck your neck out in a little craft like this – what was your track?' he asked.

I got up and pulled a metal object from a locker. I handed it to Brockton. 'First, take a look at that. Life harness hook from *Albatros*'s cockpit. See how it's straightened out? A wave did that.'

He weighed the heavy hook in his hand and shook his head. 'And you?'

'When the hook gave up, I went overboard. The next wave scooped me up and deposited me neatly back in the cockpit.'

'Congratulations to your guardian angel.'

'That's what happens – down south,' I replied.

'Sometimes, maybe.' He brought me back to the subject of *Albatros*'s track. 'Show me where this happened.'

As I got out my track chart, I wondered further about Brockton. If this was eliciting information, the extraction process was certainly painless.

He pored over the chart for some minutes before he asked, 'What made you choose such an unusual course? It disregards the Great Circle route between Cape Horn and the Cape.'

'Wind,' I answered. 'I had to have wind, plenty of it, all the time. Plus a current that would add speed to *Albatros*. I went north about the Falklands on a favourable slant, cut through the Jasons to use the tide-rips . . .'

'Jeez! The Jasons!'

'That's the second time I've heard that exclamation tonight. Thomsen said the same thing.'

'It takes a sailor to know what it means. And you also disregarded the biggest hazard of all – ice?'

'Ice isn't so hazardous if you keep a sharp look-out.'

'One man can't keep a sharp look-out for twenty-six days on end. You had to sleep sometimes.'

'Sometimes,' I echoed.

'You'd never have made it in winter-time.'

'It's still summer down there. The bergs drift continually in the general direction of Gough. The warmer the seas, the smaller they grow.'

He pointed again at the chart. He was close to me; he was sweating. Even Navy rum doesn't act that quick. I froze when I saw the place he indicated. It was about 600 seamiles southwest of Gough.

'What took you here?'

He was watching me closely. 'Wind,' I answered curtly. 'I went where the best winds blew.'

'Did you choose this course yourself, or was it Weather Routed?'

I resented his probing.

'I sail by what I feel,' I replied offhandedly. 'Not by what some boffin halfway across the world tells me what the weather should be where I am.'

'Are these exact day-to-day fixes marked on the chart?'

'No. They were by guess and by God.' The relaxed air had gone out of our talk. 'At the point you're interested in I hadn't had a proper sight for a week.'

'Ah!' The remark might have meant something. He followed it with a large gulp of rum-laced coffee.

His next query was phrased carefully. 'The area where my magazine considers a story may lie is in your inner reaction to such a long voyage alone. A study in depth, so to say, of the mind of the lone sailor.'

Did Brockton know – or suspect – anything of my secret that he should have pinpointed the place where it had happened? How could he, I asked myself. There had been no witnesses, not one for a thousand miles. I told myself I was becoming unnecessarily sensitive. Nevertheless, I decided to fob Brockton off.

'Listen, Paul,' I said. 'As far as I'm concerned there isn't a story in lone sailor soul-searching. If you're looking for a hard news story, the *Jetwind* record attempt is on again. I am her new captain. Thomsen offered me the job tonight. Tomorrow I fly to Buenos Aires from Cape Town, and then on to the Falklands.'

My earlier inner questionings about Brockton were revived by his over-kill reaction to my news. He gave me an all-American grin and pump-handled me. 'Boy, what a scoop! This'll lick the ass off the other reporters sitting back in Cape Town playing crap games to pass the time of day!'

'I thought you wrote for the *Deep Sea Sailer*.'

'Not only,' he replied. 'A small outfit like that couldn't afford to fly me out to the Cape.'

He seemed to take a sudden hold on himself, as if aware of his over-reaction, and went on in his previous manner to which I had been attracted. 'Peter, I'm glad for your sake. If any man can make it, you will. Nevertheless, to reach Gough from the Falklands in a week is one hell of a tall order. But you're the man to put the *Jetwind* project back in orbit. I'd like to be able to tell the world about it as it takes place.'

'What do you mean?'

'Take me along in *Jetwind*. From what I hear she's got plenty of spare passenger accommodation. A day-by-day write-up of her progress will put the public back on Thomsen's side. You're still riding the crest because of *Albatros*'s run. The two go together, news-wise.' He slipped the question – it was only later that I remembered it. 'I guess you'll be taking the same route as in *Albatros*?'

I must have nodded agreement, but primarily I was considering whether *Jetwind* could afford a supernumerary aboard like a reporter.

I sensed his tenseness and attributed it to anxiety regarding my decision.

'Right – you can come, if you can wangle a seat aboard the plane tomorrow night. If you can't, it's off. I won't wait.'

He laughed and said enthusiastically, 'I'm damn sure you won't, Peter. You'll get that flier moving the moment you step aboard.'

'I hope so.'

'Meaning?'

'This is off the record,' I said, and I gave a brief outline of Captain Mortensen's death, the so-called arrest of the ship, and Grohman's discussions on the mainland.

Brockton stood abstracted until I reminded him, 'You've got a lot of hard talking to do on the phone tonight, Paul, if you're to tag along with me – first, for a connection to Cape Town in the morning and, more important, on Aerolineas Argentinas tomorrow night.'

'Nothing is going to stop me being aboard those planes tomorrow – nothing,' he asserted. 'I'll be sitting waiting here on the jetty first thing with my bags.'

He started to leave, then came back and said, with such undisguised sincerity and warmth that I was glad I had decided to take him on, 'Peter, you've given me a big, big break. Bigger than you can guess. Maybe I'll be able to tell you about it some day. It's more than I ever expected when I came aboard tonight. Remember that, will you?'

Chapter 7

I dreamed that *Jetwind* was tearing out of control towards a monster iceberg. Her masts were without sails: a great wind was hurling her along by thrust on the stream-lined yards alone. Inside the bridge a computer was flashing and chattering insanely, 'wind-tunnel negative, wind-tunnel negative'. Then the dial would clear itself and begin all over again in a kind of frenetic repeat print-out. The monster berg, steaming and ill-defined, filled the entire horizon – it had the evil menace of a nightmare. I heard the pitch of the gale change; *Jetwind* accelerated; I awoke in a sweat.

The air-brakes of the Boeing 747 of Aerolineas Argentinas were on; it was their sound that had penetrated my eight-hour sleep across the South Atlantic from Cape Town to Buenos Aires. Now, to find myself descending towards the great estuary of the River Plate in broad sunlight – we had taken off from Cape Town after midnight, in a blustery southeaster – had in itself the quality of a waking dream. Beyond the plane's window on my right I spotted the luxury resort of Ciudad de Punta del Este where I had tied up in *Albatros* when staging south to Cape Horn: the lighthouse with its tall, round, white masonry tower was unmistakable. The sight of it again, with sleep still fogging my senses, made me wonder whether the intervening six weeks' events had indeed taken place – *Albatros*, the record, *Jetwind*.

However, it was all real enough on landing. So was the obstructionism of Argentinian officialdom once they learned that Brockton and I were bound for the Falklands. Brockton had been as good as his promise in securing a seat – next to me – on the full aircraft. I think it owed much to his command of Spanish. His fluency was certainly the key factor in smoothing the way for me to obtain a travel permit called a 'white card' which all British subjects entering the Falklands by air via the southern Argentinian town of Comodoro Rivadavia are required to carry. Despite the fact that the Falklands are British, the Argentinian authorities insist that they are rightfully Argentinian territory, and the 'white cards' are a way of asserting this claim by bureaucratic harassment of British travellers.

At the mention of the Falklands, officials started the 'work to rule' routine on Brockton and me which left us well behind the other passengers. Further, the name *Jetwind* and the fact that I was her skipper turned obstructionism into thinly concealed hostility. I was still suffering from sleep dosage withdrawal symptoms – either I needed more, or none at all. It was only Brockton's patience and his Spanish which saved me from exploding.

After innumerable questions and much note-taking, our 'white cards' were finally issued. We made our connecting plane by a whisker.

Late that afternoon, after a wearisome flight southwards, when I finally came out of my heart-of-darkness sleeping jag we arrived at the oil-field town of Comodoro Rivadavia, jumping-off point for the final leg, next day, to Port Stanley.

Later Brockton and I were drinking a glass of wine in the creeper-covered patio of the Spanish colonial Austral Hotel, which contrasted nostalgically with the upstart modernism of the town itself, centre of one of Argentina's most important oil-fields. The town's streets had a superfluity of raw concrete walls, most of which seemed to be graffiti-ed with the same slogan in big red letters – 'Las Malvinas son nuestras'.

I was relaxed, warm and comfortable in the secluded twilight. The *vino rosado* was good, if a trifle sweet for my palate. I liked having Brockton around; our acquaintance was turning to friendship, especially after the 'white card' unpleasantness. I was gratified that my first impressions of the man had proved correct.

Robbie Lund, proprietor of the Austral, came to our table. He was an amiable, big-boned Scot whose grandfather, in common with hundreds of others of Hebridean descent, had settled southern Patagonia towards the turn of the last century. Originally they had been 'kelpers' in the Falklands and later were responsible for the famous Patagonian wool boom.

'So you're the new skipper of *Jetwind*?' he asked.

'Yes. It surprises me how many people in Argentina seem to know about the ship.'

'You wouldn't know why, would you?'

'No. A record attempt of that nature doesn't seem to be the sort of thing to create much popular feeling.'

Two kids appeared suddenly, and Lund said something to them in Spanish, indicating the entrance bell. They shot off excitedly.

Lund excused himself for the interruption, and continued the conversation.

'And you wouldn't know either, Mr Brockton, in spite of the fact that you speak Spanish so well?'

'I guess not, except that everyone's hackles seemed to rise when *Jetwind* was mentioned.'

Lund chose his words. '*Jetwind* has kind of split public opinion down the middle in Argentina.' He dropped his voice. 'A hotelier has to be careful. Split, left and right.'

Something of the *bien aise* went out of the evening. 'You mean, politically left and right?'

'Aye, I do.'

'Who dragged politics into a neutral subject like a record-breaking attempt?'

'You may well ask, Captain Rainier. You see, *Jetwind* is tied up in the Falklands.'

'Don't I know it!'

'The ship has become a kind of symbol, if I may put it that way.'

'A symbol of what?'

Lund glanced about uneasily, then replied. 'Hasn't your friend translated the slogans on the walls of the town? They've shot up like mushrooms ever since *Jetwind* was known to be in Port Stanley.'

Brockton repeated the Spanish. '"Las Malvinas son nuestras" – the Malvinas are ours. As good nationalists, they don't tolerate the name Falklands. The question of ownership of the Falklands has been a point of friction for generations. Now the whole controversy has flared up again – because *Jetwind* was forced to make for Port Stanley.'

'Forced? Who says forced?' I asked. 'The ship was *en route* from Montevideo to the Cape when her captain was killed in an accident. Her first mate, Anton Grohman, turned and like a frightened rabbit made for Port Stanley.'

Lund sat down and stared. 'That isn't the story that has been circulated in Argentina.'

'Now I see,' I replied. 'Grohman is an Argentinian. The Falklands are a delicate political issue, and Grohman thought it would make good political capital.'

Brockton blew in the mouth of the wine bottle as if underscoring my remark. It emitted an odd, menacing, horn-like sound.

'Whose side is he really on, Mr Lund?' he asked.

Lund replied thoughtfully. 'Captain Grohman stopped over here a few days back on his way from the Falklands . . .'

'Grohman isn't *Jetwind*'s captain any longer,' I corrected him. 'He was temporarily in charge after Mortensen's death.'

Lund contemplated me shrewdly. 'It was a clever thing to call himself captain in the papers – politically, I mean. A storm is being stirred up round *Jetwind*.'

'A political captain makes a half-assed sailing captain,' said Brockton.

'If Grohman is not aboard *Jetwind* when I arrive tomorrow, I sail without him,' I said. 'The more I hear of him, his intrigues and his political involvements, the less I like him.'

'I wouldn't say Grohman isn't a good sailor,' answered Lund. 'But he's a true-blue Argentinian – half-Spanish, half-Scots. In addition, there's wild, dangerous blood in him, probably Indian. The mixture could produce strange characteristics.'

'Thanks for the tip,' I replied. 'But I think I know how to handle him.'

Lund flashed a grin at Brockton. 'I reckon you would.'

The two youngsters suddenly appeared carrying a bell. Lund gave them some coins and handed the bell to me.

'This ship's bell comes from the wreck of an old barque which has lain beached in the Straits of Magellan for donkey's years. Her name was the *Ambassador*; the man who built her also happened to be named Lund. No relation that I know of. I salvaged her bell a long time ago, just for the hell of it. Now I'd like you to have it for *Jetwind*. I said *Jetwind* has divided public opinion. Down here in the south we're mostly of Scots and British descent – we're on your side, Captain Rainier. The bell's sort of to wish you good luck. You manage to get that ship out of Port Stanley and you'll have every mother's son in these parts doing a Highland Fling for you.'

'I'll manage all right,' I said. 'Who's going to stop me?'

Lund was looking over my shoulder. He made a quick silencing gesture and stood up. I pivoted round. A man was striding on to the patio. He was carrying a silver-handled riding crop, a *rebenque* the Argentinians call it, as I learned later. The whiteness of his officer's cap accentuated his swarthiness and dark, over-large, penetrating eyes. Deep lines from nostril to chin might have been tooled into his lean cheeks by riding the pampas or standing sea watch. He was young – about my age. But his ancient Indian blood had made the handsome Spaniard in him prematurely mature.

'Señor Grohman,' said Lund. 'May I introduce Captain Peter Rainier, who, I believe, is taking over command of *Jetwind*?'

Brockton and I were sitting next to one another – Lund's half-turned introductory gesture included us both.

Grohman stopped short and slapped his leg with the whip.

'Which of you is Rainier?'

I remained still and regarded the angry face. I said emphatically, '*Mister* Grohman, let's get this straight. I am Captain Rainier – understand?'

I heard Brockton gasp; Robbie Lund moved out of the line of possible cross-fire.

'On whose authority are you taking over?'

I kept my cool despite his provocative air and tapping whip.

'Just pick up the nearest phone and call Axel Thomsen in Cape Town. I have his number right here. I was with him only last night. He'll be more than delighted to establish contact with the man who blew *Jetwind*'s chances. He's been trying to get hold of you ever since you inexplicably put into Port Stanley.'

That stopped his tap-tapping and his hectoring air.

I added, 'If you want on-the-spot proof, I have a letter of appointment signed by Axel Thomsen. However, I don't have to parade my credentials to you or anyone else. I am captain of *Jetwind*, and I stay that way.'

Grohman shifted his ground at my tone. He indicated Brockton. 'Who's this man?'

'I could be anyone.' There was a strange note in Brockton's voice which I was to recall later. For the moment, though, I was fully preoccupied with Grohman. 'But I happen to be an American newspaper-man.'

'Sit down, Grohman,' I continued. 'We have a lot to talk about.'

Lund seemed quite anxious to leave the battle-field, and moved away.

Grohman threw the ornate whip on the table like a gauntlet of defiance and sat down.

'First,' I said to him, 'get this absolutely clear. Mr Thomsen didn't specifically ask me to fire you but he gave me blanket authority to do what I wished in the best interests of *Jetwind*. I'll beach you here and now if you don't behave more like a ship's officer than a Mafia strongarm boy. I don't like that whip. Get rid of it before anything else.'

Our eyes locked. They seemed to stay that way for minutes. Watch out for that Indian blood, a bell rang at the back of my brain, or he'll come at you with a knife.

But he didn't, although I was ready to hit him – hard. Instead, he pulled in his breath like a deep sigh as if he'd reached some inner decision which hurt him but which was expedient. He thrust the whip out of sight under the table.

His truculence had not wholly disappeared, however. He said, 'If this man's a reporter, I don't want him listening to a private conversation.'

Brockton half-rose. 'Hold it, Paul.' I told Grohman, 'He stays.' I indicated the bottle. 'Paul,' I added. 'See if you can find us some Scotch. I can't stand more of that sweet stuff.'

Grohman seemed willing to take me up on any issue, even Argentinian wine. 'It is the best wine we have ..'

'That may be, but it still doesn't make me like it. It's sweet and jammy. Ask Robbie Lund for Scotch.'

'It'll be a pleasure,' grinned Brockton.

'Now then, Grohman,' I said when he had gone. 'For the moment we'll skip the motivation – or lack of it – which landed you in Port Stanley. Once there, however, your duty was to stick with the ship, not to flip-flap round South America where no one could contact you. What in hell's name made you leave?'

His lean body started to surge forward in anger; it cost him an effort to hold himself in check. There was a kind of suppressed fire about the man. I thought he could be dangerous with a little provocation. Nevertheless, I had no intention of soft-soaping him.

He chose his words. 'I had an obligation to inform the Argentinian authorities.'

'Are you crazy? An obligation to inform foreign authorities about *Jetwind*'s activities in a British port! What the devil has *Jetwind* got to do with Argentina? Your authorities were difficult enough about granting my "white card" when they heard I was *Jetwind*'s new skipper.'

'That police officer will lose his job for granting it.'

That jolted me. 'How would you know? It only happened this morning.'

The slightest sneer tugged at the left-hand corner of his mouth. 'I have friends.'

'It seems so, Grohman. They seem more important than sticking to your job. What is behind all this coming and going?'

My tone needled him into replying just as Paul arrived with the Scotch. Grohman stuck to the wine. He banged down his glass angrily.

'I was doing what was right. You do not understand – or you do not even want to understand – how delicate the political situation is over the question of the Falklands.'

'There's enough about it written over every wall in town,' I observed.

'Las Malvinas son nuestras!' he echoed heatedly. 'Who first sighted the Falklands a century before the British ever came near – a Spaniard, Americo Vespucci, in 1502 . . .'

Brockton said over his glass, 'Vespucci wasn't a Spaniard. He was a Florentine.'

The derision in my snort was like throwing petrol on a fire to Grohman. Now and then he stumbled to find an English word as his speech free-wheeled angrily.

'Maybe, maybe, but he sailed for Spain, Vespucci did. It was also he who discovered the Tierra San Martin long before the British or Americans, nearly three centuries later . . .'

'Tierra San Martin?' I asked. 'Where now would that be?'

'He means what the rest of the world calls the Antarctic Peninsula,' Brockton filled in ironically. 'All nations agreed to standardize the name in the sixties. Except Argentina.'

I was glad to have Paul to support me in this verbal duel. He seemed to be particularly well informed for a newspaper-man.

'For a hundred and fifty years we have been wronged,' Grohman went on, knocking over the wine bottle with a vehement gesture of his left hand. 'The Malvinas originally belonged to Spain. They were stolen by the British! After the Spanish colonies in the New World had revolted against Spain, the Malvinas passed legally to the new United Provinces of La Plata and we tried to occupy them – legally . . .'

Brockton again came to my assistance. 'You are over-simplifying, friend. The whole story is much more complicated than that and although I don't hold with British colonial methods, in this case they were right.'

Brockton's cool assessment seemed merely to provoke Grohman further. 'It is not only the Falklands that the British stole! All the groups of islands on the southern flank of what you call the Drake Passage were stolen from Argentina by Britain. Who rightly owns what you Americans call Graham Land, or the South Shetlands, or the South Orkneys? We registered our claims in the properly recognized international way during World War II when we left a formal document buried in a metal cylinder asserting our rights to the whole sector between

61

twenty-five and sixty-eight degrees west and southwards of latitude sixty south . . .'

Brockton said roughly, 'Argentina waited until they thought they could catch Britain with her pants down because of the war. If I remember right, however, the British had sense enough to send a warship and remove all signs of Argentinian occupancy and the emblems they planted.'

'It was typical of British aggression . . .' Grohman began.

'Listen,' I interrupted. 'I didn't come here to hear a lot of historical crap about who owns what. All I know is that the Falklands are British, that my ship is held up there, and that I mean to get her out. Falklands, Malvinas – whatever.'

'You must understand, that is *why Jetwind* is detained!' Grohman retorted. 'In 1966 a group of Argentinian patriots staged a token invasion by air of the Falklands to reaffirm our claims to the islands. Argentina does not recognize British sovereignty – the Malvinas are ours! That is why I went to the mainland! I reported to the proper authorities the death of Captain Mortensen. *Jetwind* must remain in Port Stanley pending clarification of the circumstances of Captain Mortensen's death. That is why, when he was killed, I made for Port Stanley. It is an Argentinian matter.'

'Go and tell that to the Royal Navy,' I retorted.

My attitude towards *Jetwind*'s first officer was clear: he had committed a severe dereliction of duty towards his ship's owner, and I had yet to discover what lay behind his smoke-screen of politico-historical claptrap. I was not prepared to accept his explanation at face value. Yet Brockton surprised me. He was deadly serious towards Grohman and seemed to weigh judicially every word he said, despite the fact that he himself seemed better armed with fact than the Argentinian.

Grohman turned contemptuous. 'The Royal Navy! Do you remember 1976? Do you remember your so-called research ship, the *Shackleton*, snooping about in our waters with depth-charges and electronic gear aboard? The

Argentinian destroyer *Almirante Storni* opened fire on it for illegal activities. The *Shackleton* turned and ran for Port Stanley . . .'

'That appears to be a common occurrence in these parts,' I remarked.

'The British warship was probing our naval secrets!' rapped out Grohman. 'We opened fire legitimately when it refused to surrender . . .'

Once again Brockton came to my rescue. 'The *Shackleton* was simply an oceanographic research ship measuring the extent of continental drift off the Horn,' he said briskly. 'Your so-called depth-charges were seismic charges for use in sonic underwater observations. The *Almirante Storni* demanded that she submit to arrest – on the high seas. The British captain quite rightly sought shelter in the nearest British port – Port Stanley. His ship holed up there until the storm blew over. It was all part of Argentina's continuing campaign of harassment over the Falklands.'

Grohman looked as if he could have knifed Brockton. 'We have proclaimed a two-hundred-mile territorial limit round the Malvinas,' he said. 'Therefore the British warship was inside Argentinian territorial waters.'

I drained my drink and got up. 'I am not prepared to listen to any more of this nonsense,' I said. 'Tomorrow I fly to Port Stanley. Are you accompanying me, Grohman, or are you staying here?'

'I am coming.'

'Good. We'll be on the same plane. I intend taking *Jetwind* to sea as soon as possible.'

Grohman gave an unamused smile. 'You call my reasons nonsense. You will see tomorrow they are not.'

'Say what you mean, man!'

Brockton had also risen to his feet, apparently more concerned than I was at Grohman's air of truculent triumph.

'An Argentinian warship – the same *Almirante Storni* – is at this moment on her way to Port Stanley to detain *Jetwind.*'

Chapter 8

I disbelieved him – until next day.

Our plane was over the ocean, about an hour out from Comodoro Rivadavia, heading for the Falklands. The scheduled flight time was about two and a half hours. The obsolescent F–27 Argentina Air Force plane was grinding its way southeastwards; the mainland was out of sight behind. The day was clear and bright but the far horizon was a purplish line – the menace of Southern Ocean weather, the unsleeping threat of Cape Horn. It looked a good day down on the surface. Only occasionally did I spot a white crest. It was a rare in-between day when the wind was making up its mind from which quarter to rip in next – northwest or west.

I had just been handed a thin, stale sandwich and a cardboard cup of synthetic fruit juice by a cabin dogsbody who sported an Air Force uniform and a rash of acne. He, like the rest of the four-man crew, treated Brockton and myself like patients with a highly infectious disease. Brockton had the window-seat next to me. Suddenly his stocky frame stiffened and his square jaw went rigid like a bull mastiff confronting the bull.

He dropped his voice below the level of the other passengers' hearing. 'Grohman wasn't conning you, Peter. Look out there.'

I was slow to pick up the ship's profile against the mirror of water.

'That's her – the *Almirante Storni*.' Brockton's voice was full of concern.

I craned forward to see; out of the corner of my eye I noted one of the flying crew slide back the curtain into the cabin and beckon Grohman into the cockpit. Grohman was sitting with a group of four fellow-countrymen. At take-off I had wondered what their business might be in Stanley.

'How can you tell at this distance?' I asked Brockton in surprise.

He scraped at his jaw with his knuckles, as if the quality of his shave worried him.

'Ex-United States Fletcher class,' he replied. 'You can identify 'em anywhere by that high mast for'ard with the heavy stay on the port side. It supports the radar gear.'

When the destroyer rose on a wave, I made out her distinguishing feature.

'Gives the ship a lopsided appearance,' I said. 'How do you know though that she's the *Almirante Storni*?'

'The U.S. turned over some Fletchers to Argentina in the fifties,' he said. 'They were a pretty successful class. They did a great job during the war, odd mast or not.'

'You're sure she's the *Almirante Storni*?'

'Sure.'

The previous evening I had dismissed Grohman's statement about the warship's mission to detain *Jetwind* as patriotic claptrap; now the evidence on the sea below was irrefutable.

I said in an undertone, 'She's square on course for the Falklands.'

'Yeah. I reckon she'll be off Stanley during the night. A Fletcher's best cruising speed is about fifteen knots. I guess that's what she's doing now. She's got no problems with either the sea or the weather.'

'You seem to know a hell of a lot about the Fletcher class, Paul.'

He appeared hardly to hear my comment, he was concentrating so hard on the warship. It was coming quickly into fuller view now. 'Served in 'em.' His jaw was set hard, and his eyes were screwed up against the sea glare. Or against something else.

He swung away from his tight scrutiny of the warship. 'What do you intend to do about it, Peter?'

That was the question which had been avalanching

through my mind from the moment Paul had confirmed the ship's identity. Until then I had been inclined to take all Grohman had said about the Falklands-Argentina situation as emotional Latin posturing and sabre-rattling. That warship heading determinedly towards the Falklands, however, gave a different dimension to the problem. The fact that Grohman knew in advance that the destroyer was on its way added a sinister dimension to him as well.

As if to underscore my suspicions, the pitch of the plane's engines changed.

'We're going low,' muttered Brockton. 'What happens now?'

The F–27 was losing height. All the passengers – about fifteen of them – were at the windows. Grohman's group of Argentinians were laughing. One of them turned and threw a strange look at me.

The F–27 made a low run over the warship from astern. The entire crew seemed to be on deck gesticulating. A signal lamp on the bridge sparked small lightnings as we swept overhead. I counted the armament – four big guns and six smaller ones, and banks of quadruple torpedo-tubes. Even a warship wouldn't fancy being at the receiving end of such hardware; *Jetwind* had only the wind for armour.

Then the plane banked, and this time came in from over the warship's port bow, the side on which the stay braced the high radar mast just abaft the bridge.

The crude, almost lash-up look of it, acted as a catalyst to my brain.

Jetwind's escape plan fell, ready-made, into my mind.

I threw myself across Brockton to get the best sight of the radar mast before the plane passed over. I had to photograph every detail of it in my mind! *Jetwind*'s life – and mine – would depend on it.

Brockton looked astonished at my urgency. I whispered, 'What equipment is mounted on that mast? Quick!'

'Search and tactical radar, fire-control for the guns . . .'

'Any other back-up radar?'

'No. It's all concentrated there – her entire brain centre.'

'Any other search gear – visual?' I demanded.

'No. Everything's electronic.'

On the plane's next pass I spotted officers grouped on the bridge. The F–27 roared over so low you'd think she had been doing a victory roll. Perhaps she was – in advance.

I drew back from the window, my mind racing – calculating angles, times, distances, the height of *Jetwind*'s lower yards. She might be able to pull it off – if. I tried to recall exact bearings for the narrow exit from Port Stanley seawards. I could not. I had consulted the chart only superficially. The critical element would be wind, lots of it, from the right quarter. A Cape Horn blow would suit me best, whereas today's conditions would be useless. However, I reminded myself that such a day was usually the precursor to bad weather.

The F–27 left the warship and settled on her previous course for Port Stanley. I checked my watch. It was 9.30. We were due at Stanley at 11. That allowed me only half a day of daylight, a long twilight, and some of the night to organize *Jetwind*'s break-out. Any one of half a dozen imponderables could wreck the plan now formulating in my mind. For instance, where was *Jetwind* moored in relation to the narrow entrance which locks the port of Stanley proper from a larger outer harbour known as Port William? Port William, in turn, led to the high seas. Had I the expertise to manoeuvre such a radically new type of ship as *Jetwind* if she were, say, moored to a quayside or jetty? That was the biggest gamble of all! The Stanley exit faced north-south, and if the wind were dead in *Jetwind*'s teeth, I could never make it. The wind would have to be either from the northwest or southwest or, best of all, from the west.

These thoughts scraped along my nerve edges. I wanted to hurry, hurry, see what the situation was in Stanley! I felt as if I wanted to get out and push the lumbering F–27 along. And in our wake was the *Almirante Storni* – steadily lessening the distance to Port Stanley.

That raised another critical question for my plan. 'Paul,'

I asked, 'are you sure that the warship will reach the approaches to Stanley during the night?'

He gave me a searching look at the abrupt tone of my question. 'That's as I read it, Peter.'

'What's to stop her making port and tying up?'

'Nothing – except the crew is Argentinian. I believe the entrance is tricky in darkness. Otherwise, she's got all the technical equipment to cope.'

'Do you know Stanley yourself?'

'No. You're the big enchilada in these waters.'

Probably the biggest question shadowing my plan was – would the Argentinian warship choose to negotiate Stanley's narrow, dangerous entrance on her arrival or hold back until daylight?

'What's your guess?'

For an answer, Brockton nodded towards the group of Argentinians whom Grohman had just rejoined from the cockpit.

He said softly, 'Don't look so damn worried – they're not.'

There seemed to be a holiday air about the party. Again, I speculated who they could be. They all looked tough and sunburned.

It was as much frustration at not having to hand the data I needed to work out my break-out plan as the colossal uncertainties surrounding it which ate like acid into me for the remainder of the flight. Its interminable slowness was relieved later only by the sight of the Jason Islands below; beyond, southeastwards, loomed the mass of the two main islands of the Falklands group itself and their scatter of several hundred satellite isles. There was no indication westward – the gale quarter – of my wind of salvation.

Paul and I had not spoken again; now, as if sensing my need to scrutinize and assess, he silently swapped seats with me.

Suddenly we were over Stanley.

I was taken aback by the beauty of two things. First, the harbour itself, snugged between low hills, about seven and a half kilometres long and one and a half kilometres at its widest point: beyond, through a small gap between two low headlands – not more than 300 metres wide – a broad waterway opened up between serrated coves leading to the high seas. The rare sunny day painted the inner harbour bright cobalt; the low hills on every side were exquisite pastel shades of grey, green and purple, pocked frequently with scrubby brown patches of a low-growing plant.

I had no eyes for nature's beauty. It was the loveliness of the man-made thing riding at anchor offshore which commanded all my attention.

Jetwind! I fell in love with her at first sight.

Her long, lean hull was dark green against the cobalt water; her six masts were taller than the spire of the cathedral standing at the head of the main jetty and dominating the brightly coloured iron roofs – blue, red, lime-green, yellow – which sloped down to the water-front. The sheen on *Jetwind*'s steel and light alloy masts and yards gave her a purposeful, up-and-go look.

The pilot circled over the harbour, no doubt thinking he was treating his passengers. My mind, until now seething with frustration at want of information, clicked like an activated electronic calculator. Unwittingly, within a few minutes, I was supplied with vital tactical information. *Jetwind* was moored about one and a half kilometres from the entrance gap, rightly named The Narrows. The two high points flanking the entrance were high enough to block *Jetwind* from the warship's sight as she approached from seaward.

From my vantage-point I could plot the entire break-out – *Jetwind* and the *Almirante Storni* out of one another's sight on either side of The Narrows by virtue of the intervening range of hills, except for the very tip of *Jetwind*'s masts. This was too small a target for the destroyer's radar to constitute a major danger. It meant, however, that from the mast-head the destroyer would be visible to *Jetwind* while she remained invisible herself until she entered The Narrows proper. Keeping *Jetwind* out of view until the last possible moment would require split-second timing and manoeuvring.

The plane then circled the outer harbour – Port William – before turning to approach the airfield on the western side of the town near the water's edge.

It banked for the landing. It was from this direction that the wind must come; I was relieved to note that there were no high hills to blanket its passage towards *Jetwind*. We made a bouncy touch-down and taxied to the airport building whose new yellow paint was beginning to peel from the onslaught of innumerable gales. The plane's arrival seemed to be the event of the week – a bevy of Land Rovers lined the fence with adults and children gaping as the passengers filed into the terminal.

My first urgent task was to get aboard *Jetwind*, take a quick look around, and then talk to the authorities. I chafed at the delay when a lackadaisical but amiable customs officer wanted to know the background of Robbie Lund's bell. The Spaniards, someone had mentioned, had first named the Falklands after Our Lady of Solitude – that was how it appeared to me, unhurried, utterly remote. The bell seemed to interest the official far more than Brockton's hard-fabric, business-man's black brief-case which he had kept at his feet during the flight; the official cursorily checked it without examining the contents.

Brockton and I lagged behind the rest of the passengers and his Argentinian foursome were quickly cleared and disappeared. Brockton and I had few exchanges since our arrival. I had enough to think about without making polite conversation. Paul seemed to realize it. I liked the man for his silences as much as for his words. It appeared to me, however, that when we finally reached the immigration desk he subtly jockeyed himself to be first in line.

He handed over his passport. His bulk barred me from seeing the document. The official was about to frank it, then stopped.

'Just a moment, sir.'

He disappeared into an inner office. He was away about five minutes and came back looking slightly flustered.

'Will you come this way please, Mr Brockton?'

Paul went. I stood around for about ten minutes, becoming more and more impatient. Through the windows I saw the passengers being loaded into a closed Land Rover for transport to the town. I noted, too, that the sky had become slightly hazier.

Finally, the official emerged.

'What's the problem?' I asked.

He avoided my eyes. 'No problem. We don't get many Americans in this part of the world, that's all.'

I surrendered my own passport. The official examined the selection of *Albatros* port clearances, and then with added interest, that of South Africa.

'What is the purpose of your visit to Stanley, sir?'

I could just make out *Jetwind* from where I stood. I gestured.

'*Jetwind* – I'm her new skipper.'

He looked surprised. 'But – Mr Grohman is the captain. I've just checked him through.'

In my eagerness to be up and away, my fury needed all my control to keep it from exploding.

'I assure you he is not. *I* am.'

The man clammed up at my tone. 'Sorry, sir. I cannot discuss anything outside a passenger's own personal affairs. Will you wait a moment?'

Same formula, same delay, same inscrutable politeness as for Brockton.

'What is wrong?' I demanded.

'There is nothing wrong,' he replied blandly. 'Not yet.'

Paul's ten minutes' delay was stretched to twenty in my case. The empty airport building felt as if Our Lady of Solitude had moved in.

Finally, I was asked into the Senior Immigration Officer's sanctum. (In the Falklands, the pecking order among colonial officials is as rigid as diplomatic protocol.)

He played the cards close to his chest. 'You say you are the new captain of *Jetwind*, Mr Rainier?'

'You'd think it was a crime, considering the reaction it has brought both here and on the mainland.'

'So?' He was urbane. 'You had no problems with your "white card"?'

'A little more than you're giving me.'

He remained unruffled. 'I could make things impossible, you realize.'

'Why should you?'

I had not been asked to sit down. The SIO regarded me through a swirl of cigarette smoke.

'I don't think you understand what an . . . ah, embarrassment . . . your ship has been, and continued to be, to the authorities here, Captain.'

'If Grohman had carried on to the Cape, none of this would have arisen.'

'It is our duty to cope with the situation as it has arisen. I wonder if I may make a suggestion to you, Captain Rainier?'

'I'm listening.'

'Let me telephone Mr Ronald Dawson, who is Chief Magistrate. Perhaps we could arrange for you to meet in the course of the next few days.'

I saw the double play, diplomatic heel-dragging. A few days, more delays – what were they all playing at?

'I shall be delighted. As soon as possible. Today, after lunch.'

He appeared nonplussed at my hurry. 'There is always plenty of time in the Falklands, Captain Rainier. You will learn that, I hope, to your advantage.'

Everything inside me was crying out against this verbal fencing. I kept my cool, however.

'With or without immigration clearance?'

He acted surprised. 'We have nothing against you, Captain. You are a British subject. You have a British passport. But *Jetwind* is a delicate political problem, I trust you realize. We want to guide you in making the correct decisions. In addition, of course, there is a legal aspect concerning the late Captain Mortensen.'

'What is that?'

'I would be exceeding my functions if I discussed Mr Dawson's duties with you,' he returned. He picked up the phone. 'Ronald? I have with me Captain Rainier, the new skipper of *Jetwind* . . .'

I heard an exclamation at the other end of the line. My man laughed a little uneasily. 'No, of course not. There is no reason not to. He wants to see you – he has suggested this afternoon after lunch but I have told him . . .'

There was an interrupting crackle. 'No, of course I didn't realize you would like it that way. Today, at two? Good. I'll inform Captain Rainier.'

His suavity was a trifle bent when he spoke to me. 'Mr Dawson agrees that the sooner you and he meet, the better.'

He got up stiffly and handed me my passport with the air of a diplomat handing an enemy-to-be an *aide-memoire*.

'Good luck, Captain Rainier. And, if I may give you a little off-the-record advice, don't attempt anything rash with that ship. You may get hurt.'

'I'll remember that.'

I joined Paul, who was waiting outside the airport building by a battered Land Rover truck which had been assigned to take us into town.

There was the faintest stir of wind from the west.

Chapter 9

'Welcome aboard, sir.'

John Tideman's smile and *Jetwind*'s big digital bridge clock illuminated simultaneously. It was one o'clock – two hours since I had landed. The time reminded me forcibly that I had wasted those hours navigating official channels silted with latent obstructionism. Finally, even the short boat journey from the public jetty to *Jetwind*'s mooring had assumed the length of a voyage.

Tideman might have said, welcome to wonderland. The sight of *Jetwind*'s bridge, bisected by the gleaming steel pillar of No. 2 mast, overrode my chafing fret against time. I had never seen a bridge like it – a miracle of consoles, instruments, panels, dials, lights and switches. Inwardly I felt a pang of dismay. If I were to bulldoze through my escape plan that night, I had somehow to get the hang of the ship's complicated technology within the next few hours.

Brockton, who had accompanied me from the shore, said, 'I thought I'd seen everything in sophisticated instrumentation aboard America Cup Twelves – but this licks everything!'

I liked Tideman immediately for his modesty. He was about my own age, I guessed. He had long hair and a Viking beard fringing a lean jaw. I visualized his place rather at the wheel of a deep-sea racing yacht in oilskins and goggles against a Southern Ocean blow than in the custom-cut dark green uniform and white cap which were regulation rig for *Jetwind*'s officers. He wore it with a certain insouciance.

'It looks like a space-age scenario, but basically it's relatively simple,' said Tideman. 'You don't want to let it overawe you. I was, at first.'

'I wouldn't even know where to start,' Brockton replied.

Tideman looked inquiringly at Brockton. He obviously did not understand Paul's position aboard. I explained briefly. Then I said, 'Give me a run-down on the main controls as quickly as you can. I want to know what I'm doing, soonest.'

'We're sailing soon, sir?' he asked eagerly.

I did not reply and he went on more formally. 'I don't want to intrude on Mr Grohman's position as first officer, sir. Perhaps I'd better call him. He came aboard about an hour ago. I am sure he's not aware that you're here.'

I had noted the white decks, the way the light alloy yards had been burnished, and the general shipshape condition and Bristol-fashion of *Jetwind*. And it was Tideman who had been in command for the days Grohman had been away messing about on the mainland.

'You've kept the ship in pretty good nick,' I answered. 'You do the explaining.'

He looked pleased and said, 'She's ready for sea.' I warmed to him further when he said, without flattery, 'First, my congratulations on your record in *Albatros*, sir. I know what it implies.'

No mention of his own three trips round the Horn, no attempt to sell his own abilities. Yet his seamanship was apparent in *Jetwind*'s splendid condition. Had he allowed the crew to become demoralized after their let-down from Grohman's back-tracking on the record, it would have been reflected in the state of the ship. In a remote port like Stanley, with no diversions, that meant not an iron fist but a combination of respect and discipline.

Tideman led Brockton and me to three walk-around consoles grouped about the big stainless steel wheel; the centre one was in the standard navigation position.

'This is the actual nerve-centre,' Tideman explained. He indicated six levers, all in the 'off' position. 'These operate the hydraulic mechanisms for the six masts – you can swing 'em or trim 'em to any angle or any way you like, either in tandem or individually. Like this – look behind you, sir.'

He eased over a lever and the high tensile steel mast structure started to swivel. There was no noise, no sense of power. Yet the thing weighed a score of tons and was fifty-two metres high.

'That's Tuesday in action,' Tideman said. 'We can do the same for Monday, Wednesday, Thursday and Friday.'

'Monday, Tuesday, Wednesday?' I echoed.

Tideman laughed. 'The names of the weekdays are just a gimmick, but it makes the masts more personal than merely Number One, Number Two and so on. I got the idea from the old *Great Britain* – her six masts were known by the days of the week.'

I had been aboard the *Great Britain* in a Bristol dry-dock during her restoration after one of the world's great salvage feats in 1970 when she was towed from the Falklands to Britain after lying as a hulk in Stanley for over eighty years. However, Tideman's information about the names of her masts was new to me.

Nevertheless, it was again Brockton who surprised me by the extent of his knowledge about this remote part of the world. He gestured beyond The Narrows.

'The inlet where the *Great Britain* lay beached isn't far beyond the gap – Sparrow Cove, it's called. We'll see it on our way out.'

I pulled the discussion back to the present. 'Show me how the yards operate,' I told Tideman.

'All yards on every mast can be moved in unison or individually,' he went on. 'Personally I like 'em best trimmed in a slight spiral on the weather side. My view is that it gives better results. Mr Grohman disagrees.'

'Go on telling me what you think,' I said.

He glanced at me keenly. 'You can set the yard trim either manually to the angle you decide, or you can hand over to the computer, which will do the job for you. Or you can – ' he indicated another switch ' – work on manual override while the computer is in use, just the same way as you drive a car on automatic. You really can't go wrong.'

The enclosed, air-conditioned bridge felt like a glasshouse to me. 'I have to *feel* the wind,' I told Tideman. 'All this remote control and mollycoddling . . .' I gestured at the big windows, several of which were strip-heated to remain clear in freezing weather.

'I had the same feeling at first,' agreed Tideman. 'It isn't what we Cape Horners are accustomed to. It is surprising, though, how soon one adapts to it.' He indicated another bank of push-buttons.

'These are to set or to shorten sail. The operation can be carried out on each mast separately, from mainsail to royal, or synchronized, as with the other controls.'

I remembered a remark of Thomsen's. 'It took twenty seconds to furl everything, I was told. It doesn't seem possible.'

'Say thirty seconds at the outside, not much more,' he replied. 'It's faster than the fastest crack yachting crew can achieve. The operation is so quick that it's almost impossible to catch the ship aback.'

Tideman moved on to a closer, smaller console. He was slightly disdainful. 'These are bridge commands to the diesels which operate the hydraulics, the screw and supply power to the ship – she consumes a lot.'

The escape plan was uppermost in my mind. 'So no preliminary warming of the diesels is necessary then?'

'No.

'Driving the auxiliary engine to power the ship in times of calm is really their secondary purpose,' he went on. 'The propeller nacelle complete can be raised into the hull when she's wind-driven. This is the switch. It's stowed that way now. Otherwise, it's mainly a question of pitch control over the screw.'

'Has power been used much?'

'Captain Mortensen disliked the auxiliary as much as I do,' he answered. 'If you're sailing a sailer, sail it, he said. However, these two powered gadgets here are pretty useful – there's a six-ton White-Gill thruster in the bows and a Pleuger four point seven-ton thruster at the stern. Using them, you can make *Jetwind* spin on a sixpence.'

'How long does it take to get *Jetwind* under way?'

'It depends where she's lying, of course. At an open mooring like this one, a few minutes.'

'A few minutes!'

That was better than the best I had hoped for in regard to my break-out plan.

'Yes. Figuratively speaking, the ship's speed of manoeuvre took me aback to start with. One doesn't have to take man-power into consideration. Everything is machine-driven. The officer on duty alone operates the sail plan from this central situation.' He added, with deliberate intention behind his words,

'I'd like the opportunity to show you.'

'Not yet. Anyway, you couldn't with the wind as it is.'

Tideman, however, seemed to want to press the point '*Jetwind* is lying ideally at this moment. There's a slight run of water coming in through The Narrows – maybe half a knot. Her head is pointing right for the exit. We could be up and away in minutes, as I said.'

How long, I asked myself, would *Jetwind* take to cover approximately one and a half kilometres to The Narrows? What speed would she have worked up to in that distance? Would it be sufficient – have enough power, in other words – to carry out my design against the *Almirante Storni*? If the wind failed me when the time came, I could make a criminal fool of myself and the ship.

'Depending on the wind, as I said,' I replied.

'Aye – depending on the wind,' he echoed. 'But you know yourself, sir, that we're close enough to the gale pattern of the Horn for the weather to break from one of three directions only – the northwest, the west or the southwest.'

In other words, from the quarter which suited *Jetwind*'s sailing qualities best.

'What do you make of the prospects at present?' I asked.

Tideman hid his real opinion behind a smoke-screen of technicalities.

'*Jetwind* was being Weather Routed from Bracknell via Portishead radio when we left Montevideo for the Cape,' he answered. 'Once we became harbour-bound in Stanley, the service was discontinued.' He indicated a Japan Radio Co. facsimile weather chart recorder mounted forward on the bridge. 'Metbrack was supplying us with interpretation of satellite pictures of the weather ahead and astern of the ship. That's also come to an end. Consequently, I don't know what's now working up from the direction of the Horn.'

'Where *did* you learn all your expertise?' I asked, a trifle ironically.

'The Royal Navy has several highly specialized technical and communication courses.'

'Fine,' I replied. 'But when you were skippering yachts round the Horn you didn't have all this scientific crap at your disposal. You and your weather instinct had to be one jump ahead of the next squall or you wouldn't be here today. That's the sort of opinion I value.'

'Sorry,' he apologized self-consciously. 'But the same applies to you – as it did in *Albatros*.'

I began to like Tideman in the same way as I had Brockton. He gestured landwards. Sapper's Hill backed Stanley and a long defile, called Moody Valley, entered the port on its western side.

'From that haze, I'd say we were in for a blow. I reckon further that it's blowing like the clappers at this moment over Drake Passage and the Horn.'

'When do you think it could start here?'

'Any time. Weather works up very suddenly. A matter of hours.'

I had tentatively set midnight as the break-out deadline. I might even have to wait until dawn – my actions would be governed by the *Almirante Storni*'s. With the logistics of my escape plan in mind, I switched suddenly from weather to what must have seemed an irrelevant subject to Tideman.

'All the lower yard-arms on all six masts are hinged, aren't they?'

'Yes, for loading. They're swung up out of the way of dockside cranes.'

I wasn't considering loading. The genius who had thought up *Jetwind*'s hinged yards never dreamed of the purpose to which I intended to put them.

'Demonstrate,' I ordered.

He fingered a switch. With uncanny silence again, the big streamlined yard above us folded flush against the mast in a matter of seconds.

Tideman followed me with interest.

'On a time check, I reckon I would need just over one minute to furl all sail and stow the lower yards in place afterwards,' I said.

'Correct,' he answered. 'I don't follow, though. In dock the sails would be furled already.'

'In dock, yes.'

'There would be no purpose in the operation while the ship was travelling under sail.'

Except to knock out the *Almirante Storni*.

The test of lifting the lower yards completed the tactical plan in my mind. It would require steel nerves and razor-

79

edged timing – and, above all, good wind. I must have lapsed into an abstracted silence because Brockton began to talk to Tideman about America Cup trials.

'The America Cup triallists use a computer which gives a read-out on the downwind leg for optimum speed made good,' he was saying. 'The computer's memory has been previously programmed with the best speed for each wind speed . . .'

'No computer ever sails a ship,' interrupted Tideman. 'The final decision is a man's, and that man is the skipper.'

'Agreed,' replied Brockton. 'Yet data the computer supplies contributes critically to the ship's performance by working out the optimum speed made good. In other words, the best course that will take the boat to the next waypoint, plus the best sailing angle, plus the best trim of each set of sails . . .'

In reply, Tideman activated the read-out dials on the last of the three big control consoles.

'This is *Jetwind*'s own special box of tricks,' he said. 'There are sensors on every mast from mast-head to keel logging wind direction, wind speed and apparent wind angles. There are other sensors in the hull recording the ship's speed, drift, rudder angle, heel. All this information is fed into a micro-processor inside the console and here are the answers – ' more dials came alive ' – apparent wind angle, true wind angle; true wind speed; ship's speed; speed made good to windward.'

'It looks goddam good,' Brockton said in admiration.

'The ordinary sort of compass isn't sharp enough for the degree of sensitivity these readings require,' Tideman went on. '*Jetwind* has a special electronic dual-axis flux-gate compass which is linked to the autopilot.'

Listening to their technical conversation, another link in my break-out strategy formed in my mind: I would use Brockton and his expertise.

I said, 'In the face of all this, I reckon sailing by the feel of the wind on your neck or cheek is out.'

'I've done both,' answered Tideman. 'You'll find very soon that *Jetwind*'s is the more challenging way of sailing.

You're dealing –' he indicated the banks of the dials ' – with real data. You can't bluff yourself. If the computer says the ship is sailing at only eighty per cent of what she is capable of, that's it. You have to accept it. Trying becomes much harder.'

'We found that with the Twelves,' Brockton added. 'All data is subjected to interpretation – the better the skipper, the better the interpretation. That goes for the skipper likewise, when it comes to the final decisions.'

'Even the electronic experts recognize that the human element is the final judge,' said Tideman. 'We've got a couple of small mobile hand-held terminals which operate in the crow's nest. The idea behind them is to have manual input – that is, what the look-out himself is spotting – to supplement what the electronics are recording. The skipper can use this information in conjunction with the computer or by itself. The method is especially valuable when you're conning the ship in confined waters where there are frequent and rapid changes of course. We found it worked splendidly when we brought *Jetwind* into Montevideo through the mass of shoals and shallows of the River Plate estuary.'

Confirmed waters; shallows; frequent and rapid changes of course – it added up to the Port Stanley Narrows.

'What about navigation?' I asked. 'Apparently *Jetwind* has everything that opens and shuts.'

'Come here, I'll show you,' said Tideman. He led Brockton and me to an office abaft the bridge. On the way he paused at a bulkhead clustered with switches and read-out lights.

'Control for the ship's fire-alarms, automatic extinguishers and cross-flooding controls,' he explained. 'There are five doors throughout the accommodation as well as watertight bulkheads. All emergency doors are held open magnetically until they are released from here. It's a super-safety system and it's backed up by monitors in case of ice damage to the hull.'

The navigation room itself was like a space-shot control centre. Focal instrument was a JRC satellite navigator which, Tideman explained, could plot *Jetwind*'s position to within half a kilometre. The instrument, he added, was automatic and gave highly accurate and continuous position fixes while the ship was under way. There was also a Nippon Electric deep-sea echo sounder, a weather chart repeater from a bridge master instrument, repeat read-outs of the mast-head anenometers, relative wind speed and direction recorders.

In the adjoining radio room we surprised a fair-haired young man who seemed to be engaged in some esoteric ritual with a hand-held electric radio and direction finder held over a chart. Tideman introduced him as Arno, a Swede. Arno's enthusiasm for the equipment was unbounded – it had been installed by Marconi – and he rattled off names like Apollo main and reserve receivers, Sentinal crystal unit, two Conqueror main transmitters, Seacall selective receiver, Siemens teleprinter with world-wide range. There was, of course, radar in addition, an exact twin of the Decca set on the bridge.

I surveyed the instrumented room; I realized what was bugging me, as it had done on the bridge and in the navigation office. All these superb instruments were dead. Not one of them was functioning because *Jetwind* herself was not alive. She was fast asleep in a god-forsaken port at the backside-end of the world. They needed a Prince Charming to light up their sophisticated faces.

Not a Prince Charming, I corrected myself. The kiss of a Force Nine gale and a free-wheeling sea.

That kiss I meant to give *Jetwind*.

Tonight.

Chapter 10

Back on the bridge with Tideman – we had left Brockton involved in technical conversation with Arno – I said, 'You've demonstrated push-pull levers and toggle switches until my mind boggles. What I really want to see now is the power plant – the sails.'

He consulted a bank of dials before answering. 'It would be too risky while at anchor to set even a royal to demonstrate for you. You've no idea how powerful even *Jetwind*'s small sails are, given a light breeze only.'

'I'm not asking you to set any sails. I want to go aloft and see for myself,' I added. 'I would also like to inspect the place where Captain Mortensen met his accident.'

For the first time since our introduction I felt a shadow of reserve on Tideman's part.

He nodded at the mast towering through the roof of the bridge. 'Up there, in Tuesday – Number Two mast. Tops'l yard service bay.'

'Let's go.'

He seemed unwilling to take me aloft. He said, 'You can't see much while the sails are furled. Is there any particular point you'd like explained?'

'The whole works. Everything is new to me.'

'I think the best person to do that is the sail-maker. The aerodynamics are above my head.'

'Fine,' I replied. 'I'm in a hurry. I have to go ashore soon. Give him a call.'

Tideman picked up an intercom phone and said to me, 'Not him, sir – her.'

'Her? What do you mean?'

'*Jetwind*'s Number One sail-maker is a woman – Kay Fenton.'

'A woman?'

83

He held the phone poised. 'Why not? Mr Thomsen discovered her when she was taking a sail and mast course at the Stahlform yard in Germany – the world's master mast-makers. He enlisted her as a junior member of the Schiffbau Institut's design team. She's been intimately concerned with the wind-tunnel testing of *Jetwind*.'

I looked at him questioningly. 'So have you, from the sound of it. I thought you'd joined the ship after she'd been built.'

'No,' he replied. 'I was involved at the design stage as well.'

'I didn't know the Royal Navy was as keen as all that on the lost art of sail.'

I felt somehow that I had trodden on thin ice. He replied impersonally. 'We have the Navy Adventure School for sail trainees. I sailed yachts belonging to the School round the world.'

'You mean, skippered?'

'That's right. They gave me the experience in sail necessary for *Jetwind*.'

Something still eluded me about Tideman. 'As second officer,' I added.

He answered me a trifle defensively. 'Captain Mortensen was a very fine sailor. He'd graduated in square-riggers and knew deepwatermen. My background did not include them. Also, he was from the Aaland Isles. You know what that implies.' Holding the telephone still, he asked, 'Shall I call Kay?'

'Yes. Tell her to come quickly.'

He dialled 'S' on the intercom and said to me while the instrument rang, '*Jetwind*'s phones are automatic – all the main control-points have code-rings, "S" for sail-maker, "O" for bridge – officer of the deck, "E" for engine room – and so on.'

We waited. 'I'll bet Kay is stretched out full-length on the deck stitching a sail,' he said. 'You must visit the sail-room – it's big enough to house a whole sail spread out. Kay's favourite habit is to lie down and work at them.'

The phone came alive. I heard a burst of background music and Tideman said, 'Kay! Switch that damn thing down, will you? The skipper wants you . . .' There was a pause and he eyed me. 'No, the *new* skipper, Captain Rainier. Yes, he's on the bridge now. At the double, please.'

'You will have common ground with Kay – she's another Cape Horner,' Tideman said.

'Was she one of the all-women crew yachts in the last Round the World?'

'No. She was sail-maker in *Peripatetic II*. There was one other girl aboard, the navigator. I reckon it must have been the Round the Worlder which threw Kay's marriage. Marriage and the deep sea don't go together.'

'She's divorced, then?'

'Aye. The guy was a starchy up-and-coming young London stockbroker, I heard. Couldn't stand the absence, and the adulation Kay got over the race. *Peripatetic* finally finished sixth, which was no mean feat.'

'Is that all that broke it up?'

'Kay's not that sort. Aboard *Jetwind* we sort of regard her as the Old Lady of the Sea.'

'Meaning?'

'Well, she's twenty-six, and that's a ripe old age amongst this crew. Their average age is twenty. They even look upon me as the Ancient Mariner – I'm twenty-seven.'

'Same as me.'

'Jack, our other sail-maker, is really our Old Man of the Sea – he's thirty.' He grinned. 'He's a wonderful practical sail-maker but he hasn't Kay's flair for the theory. I myself don't understand half the maths she talks when she gets on to sail aerodynamics.'

'Are there any more Cape Horners aboard?'

'Aye. Four of my own lads from the Adventure School. Then there's Pierre Roussouw, who sailed with Tabarly. And the bo'sun, Jim Yell. As you probably realize, a bo'sun in this sort of ship has a very special position. There are only two officers, apart from the captain – Grohman and myself. Yell is a sort of sergeant-major – not that this crew needs chasing. But they're fretting, and the sooner we get to sea, the better.'

Tideman's remarks about the chain of command made me wonder again where Grohman was. Protocol required that he should have been on the bridge to greet me in the first place. Nevertheless, I had resisted a temptation to summon him. I wanted to find out about things without him around. It seemed to me, however, that he was cocking a snook at me by his continued absence.

I said, brusque with inner tension, 'I hope they get their wish. There is an Argentinian destroyer on her way here to detain *Jetwind*.'

Tideman stared at me in disbelief and then exclaimed, '*Detain!*'

'That is my information. She will arrive tonight or tomorrow.'

I was saved from further explanation by Kay Fenton's arrival. I had been unprepared, in the light of Tideman's 'Old Lady of the Sea' description, for the person who came quickly through the bridge door. She was tallish, with a mod style hair-cut which made her blonde hair lighter than it really was where it had been sun-bleached above her ears. The long legs of her black velvet corduroy pants were dotted with scraps of dacron sail thread. Her slim breasts were free under a green woollen shirt. The Pacific seemed to have left something of its blue in her wide eyes, and Cape Horn something of its greyness. The damped-down turbulence at the back of them was her own.

She held out her hand to me. As I gripped it we both laughed. She had forgotten to remove her sail-maker's leather palm.

'I'm not really as horny-handed as all that,' she said. I welcomed the way she repeated the handshake after removing the palm. I also liked the low modulation of her voice. Like her eyes, it seemed to have a background of sadness.

She by-passed a whole ocean of social conventions by getting down to the subject which, basically, interested both of us.

'You made the correlation between the theoretical performance of the Venetian Rig and its practical one look a bit battered, Captain Rainier,' she said. 'We tested your rig at the Schiffbau Institut. If we had had *Albatros*'s actual performance figures then, we could well have plumped for a Venetian Rig for *Jetwind*.'

Tideman added, 'It takes a sailor to achieve *Albatros*'s results, Kay.'

Then she asked me with the same eager air as Tideman had shown previously, 'Now that you're here, will we be sailing soon?'

I dodged the question. 'Mr Tideman has given me a rundown on *Jetwind*'s controls. Now I want to see the sails themselves – the real power house. I would also like to see the exact place where Captain Mortensen met with his accident.'

She flashed a glance at Tideman. 'John?'

His voice lacked any inflexion. 'I considered you'd be the best person aboard to explain the merits of the sails.'

'Let's make it as quick as we can,' I said. 'I have to see the chief magistrate shortly after lunch.'

She gave Tideman another inquiring look and then said, a little uncertainly, it appeared to me, 'Let's go.'

After operating one of a bank of switches on a nearby console, she led me down a ladder to a central well immediately abaft and under the wheel-house itself. The mast ran through it. Access to its interior was via a steel door which slotted into the curvature of the mast. Kay explained that this servicing door was held shut magnetically until released by the bridge control she had manipulated.

She put on the lights. I was surprised at the diameter of the mast inside. There was room for two people abreast, although it narrowed higher up. A steel ladder was clamped to the wall and a trunk of intertwined copper tubes, which combined were thicker than my leg, sprouted skywards out of sight above. These were the hydraulic pipes to control the yards. They were linked in twin, each pair with dials and valves. It looked more like a plumber's paradise regained than a ship's mast.

'Come!'

Kay started up the ladder. Her sneakers made no sound on the rungs. Within seconds she had outpaced me. Up and up we went, Kay drawing ahead at every step. Finally, out of breath, I reached her, perched in a compartment on what looked like a tiny steeple-jack's seat. This compartment was the juncture point of topsail yard and mainmast. Higher, the diameter of the interior narrowed to become the top-gallant mast, and the material changed from high tensile steel to light alloy. The top-sail yard-arm itself was largely hidden from view except via slits through which the sail rolled in and out along stainless steel runners.

Kay followed my inquiring scrutiny of the gleaming mechanisms and valves.

'These hydraulics are basically the same as are used to operate the rudders of large ships – suitably adapted, of course.'

I said, getting back my breath, 'I heard you're called the Old Lady of the Sea. If old ladies go up ladders like that, give me the advanced generation any day.'

She laughed with a mixture of humour and reserve. 'The guys all think I'm crazy. I have an exercise routine. I run up this ladder to the crow's nest every morning before breakfast.'

'What's that in aid of?'

'All day I sit at a sewing-machine stitching sails or at a desk doing maths. Put simply, the bottom doesn't benefit by it.'

I gestured at the servicing compartment. Its most unusual feature was a pair of what looked like gigantic vertical roller-blinds, about nine metres tall, tightly wound with sail.

'I suppose I'll get used to it,' I said, 'but at the moment it all seems like black magic to me. Strangest is having *hollow* masts.'

'They're correctly termed unstayed rotatable profiled masts,' she answered seriously. 'They've been custom-made by aircraft manufacturers.' She added with a touch of anxiety, 'You're going to try and make time, aren't you? *Sail* her?'

'My brief is to reach Gough Island within a week. I intend to.'

She considered my statement for a moment, then answered, 'You'll need all the luck.'

'Isn't it a tradition that any sailor who has sighted Cape Horn will have good luck for the rest of his – or her – career?'

Her face became expressionless. 'It didn't bring me luck.'

'Meaning?'

She shrugged and was silent. Then she resumed in a different tone altogether. 'It's also a legend that anyone rounding Cape Horn has the right to have a pig tattooed on the calf of the right leg.'

Her amusement had an infectious quality, contrasting with her serious, sombre air of a moment before.

'*I* did.' She reached down and pulled up the leg of her corduroy pants. 'There. It's mainly gone now. It wasn't a real tattoo, only a kind of self-eradicating transfer.' Her mood changed mercurially. 'Louis thought it was disgusting. How could a lady go out to a party in London with a pig tattoo showing through her stocking?'

'Louis?'

'Husband. Ex. I did it for a laugh. Strangely, it was one of the things he battened on for the divorce.'

'I expect it was only a symptom.'

The colour now in her cheeks had nothing to do with the effort of climbing the ladder. 'Why shouldn't I? Old grandfather Fenton – I remember him still – had his whole forearm tattooed . . .'

'Is that where your sailoring genes come from?'

'He wasn't a sailor – he was a prospector,' she replied. 'Believe it or not, he went and lived on Gough Island between the wars prospecting for diamonds! Those were the days when a ship might have called once in a year – or never.'

'I never knew Gough was anything but a weather station.'

'Grandfather's expedition was long before it was

89

inhabited. Maybe I'm a throw-back to the old man Perhaps it's his same spirit of adventure which brings me here, or made me sail round the world. Anyway, it'll be interesting to see Gough.'

Her remark brought me back to the hard realities facing. *Jetwind*.

I replied a little offhandedly, 'I don't intend to stop. If you do see Gough, it would only be a glimpse. From there I'll be high-tailing to the Cape like a bat out of hell.'

Again she asked eagerly, 'Then we're sailing – soon?'

'I didn't say so. But the race against time, the week, starts tomorrow.'

I sensed that by being non-committal I had lost her. She said distantly, 'John said you wanted to know about the sails?'

I felt I needed her on my side for what lay ahead. 'Listen, Kay,' I said. 'I intend to wring every knot, every half knot, out of this ship every mile of the way – and it's a long way. I'm a rule-of-thumb sailor, you're the specialist. I want you at my elbow to give advice when I hell-drive *Jetwind*. Automatics aren't the answer as far as I'm concerned. It's the human flair which counts in my scheme of things.'

Her response was to draw up her knees to her chin, squatting on the tiny circle of steel. It made her look more sixteen than twenty-six. I looked down at her, gripping an overhead cat-walk which gave access to the yard and rollers.

'Then you've got to appreciate how different *Jetwind* is from any ship that has gone before,' she said. 'First, I don't like the term sails. I prefer aerofoils.'

'Sails mean – sails, to me.'

'I'll stick to sails, then. Take a scientific look at the shape of the sails of an old racing China clipper and you'll see the resemblance to an aircraft wing – a slender trapezoid or triangle with a curvature parallel to the longitudinal axis. Therefore those ships were fast . . .'

'Stick to one-syllable words and I'll follow you.'

'Those early clipper sails were efficient aerodynamically.

90

However, as soon as ships became bigger, the sails had to be split in order to be handled physically by their crews. That destroyed their aerodynamics. Later windjammers looked super but aerodynamically speaking they were a nightmare – hopelessly inefficient. And as for that spider's web of rigging!' She gave a shudder. 'It does awful things to one when you see them under test in a wind-tunnel.'

'They worked, Kay. They also put some of man's most beautiful creations on the face of the ocean.'

'You're wrong!' she retorted vehemently. 'It's *Jetwind* that's beautiful, more beautiful than the best of them! Don't you appreciate the beauty of this sail plan – an unbroken aerofoil from deck to truck? Not individual sails slopping about on their own but a single entity with all the grace and power of proved mathematics behind it! As for *Jetwind*'s masts – there's never been anything seen before on the high seas like the Prolss mast!

'You have to regard them and the sails as one propulsive unit. We found by tests the optimum speed for a quite definite trim of the sails. We also had to determine the optimum curvature of the yards, by comparison with the sail force curves.'

'It's the end result that concerns me.'

Kay seemed to have more data stored in her mind than a computer memory bank. But however fascinating all this theory was, my first problem was a practical one, the logistics of *Jetwind*'s break-out. I cut in on her rarefied theorizing. 'Kay, what's *Jetwind*'s best point of sailing?'

She answered without hesitation. 'With the wind on the beam or slightly abaft the beam?'

'Best strength?'

'Gale. Force nine.'

'Reefed down?'

'Naturally.'

'Relative course angle?'

'One hundred and thirty-five degrees.'

'Speed?'

'Twenty-two knots.'

I said, 'On paper.'

She burst out passionately. 'If anyone can get that out of her, *you're* the man to do it! You thrashed *Albatros* across the face of the ocean as no man has ever thrashed a ship. We heard it on the radio.'

I added, 'I intend to flog *Jetwind* until she makes Gough in a week or she falls apart at the seams.'

Provided you first manage to break out, a voice nagged at the back of my mind.

Kay's voice vibrated still. 'At her maximum, the aerofoil sail-plan delivers forty thousand horse-power. You've only got to have the nerve and the guts to use it!'

Twenty-two knots, under ideal conditions. The *Almirante Storni* could bullet along at thirty-five at full bore, depending on the state of the sea. She must never get the chance to use her speed advantage. That was my scheme.

Linked to my plan was the need to deploy all *Jetwind*'s power rapidly. How fast could she accelerate from anchor to the ten knots I considered the minimum required? Could she work up to that speed in the mere kilometre and a half which separated her from where she lay now to The Narrows?

'Did you ever carry out any flying start tests in your wind-tunnel?' I asked.

'I don't follow you.'

'Say, for example, I wanted to accelerate *Jetwind* from a moored position to the maximum she could achieve under the wind conditions then prevailing, how would I set about it?'

'What wind velocity are we talking about?'

That was the kicker. At its worst, I must assume that the wind would be blowing only a moderate breeze of about sixteen knots by the early hours of the following morning. Anything above that would be a bonus in *Jetwind*'s favour.

'Say, Force Three to Four.'

'And the sea?'

'If she was moored, it would be calm.'

Her eyes became abstracted, and she murmured something to herself about side and thrust forces and angles of wind inflow.

Then she asked incisively, 'She would naturally be carrying all sail?'

'You bet.'

'I make it eleven knots, at her best point of sailing.'

Eleven! I had hoped only for ten. If the wind were stronger than Force Three or Four, I'd have thrust in hand for my purpose.

Yet Kay still had not answered my question – how *soon* could I draw on that amount of *Jetwind*'s speed? I couldn't be more specific without revealing my plan. I had no intention of doing so – to anyone.

'As for acceleration?'

'It's not the sort of thing we tested for.'

I changed the subject. 'Kay, what's this curious waxy smell in here – like furniture polish? Is it the hydraulic fluid?'

She indicated one of the giant 'rolling-pins'.

'Dacron doesn't smell.'

'It's not the sails themselves but what's on them,' she explained. 'To protect them against infra-red and ultra-violet ray sun damage, they have a special kind of plastic coating. You can imagine what a suit of sails like this costs. Mr Thomsen asked the Schiffbau Institut to find some substance to protect the sails so a new flexible plastic was specially developed.'

I looked about me. 'This is where Captain Mortensen was killed, isn't it?'

The animation went from her face. 'Right here in this bay. He's supposed to have been trapped between those two rollers.'

'Supposed?'

'I can't understand how such a thing could have happened,' she said vehemently. 'First, the sail was supposed to have been jammed on its yard-arm runners. How? At the Schiffbau Institut we carried out thousands of preliminary reefing and sail-setting tests under every simulated condition of wind. Mr Grohman brought Captain Mortensen here to demonstrate a fault to him . . .'

My mind leapt ahead to my coming interview with the chief magistrate.

'You don't believe the account of the tragedy?'

'I didn't say that. All I do say is that, I can't understand how it could have happened. The ship was making time in a rising sea and gale and we were all thrilled with the way she was performing. Then this!' She jumped off her perch and came close to me. She indicated a switch on the mast wall. 'Apart from the bridge consoles, there's a fail-safe control right here. All Mr Grohman had to do was to press this button and the rollers would have stopped. And . . .' she indicated levers on the rollers themselves ' . . . here are hand cranks as another emergency measure. They operate the travelling runners manually in case of power failure. There was no power fault! *What happened?*'

'That's what Mr Thomsen keeps asking. Why did Grohman make for the Falklands when he could have carried on to the Cape?'

'God, oh God!' she exclaimed savagely. 'It was awful. *Jetwind* was like a funeral ship. *He* abandoned the record attempt and headed into the gale. Day after day! Forcing *Jetwind* to go that way! Into that same god-awful gale which would have blown us all the way to the Cape!'

'I wish Mr Thomsen could hear you now,' I said. And I gave her the gist of Thomsen's plans to try and recoup *Jetwind*'s prestige.

She plucked at a loose thread at the bottom of the sail roller. Her big eyes were full of controlled fury.

'Fine, fine!' she exclaimed. 'But when are we sailing? Every time I ask you when, you dodge the question! What sort of jinx is bugging *Jetwind*?'

I lit a cigarette after offering her one, which she refused. I had decided to treat her as an ally; as an ally, she had to know what was in my mind.

'There is no jinx, Kay, but there's something equally serious,' I said. Then I outlined Grohman's remarks that

94

Jetwind would be detained, the imminent arrival of the *Almirante Storni*, the bureaucratic stalling port, and finally my forthcoming interview with the chief magistrate in half an hour or so.

When I had finished, she remained silent. Then she burst out, 'What has *Jetwind* to do with some obscure squabble between Argentina and Britain over the Falklands? She's a ship, not a pawn in a petty political game! She's *my* ship!'

'Mine too, Kay.'

'You're not going to let them do it, are you, skipper? Keep her boxed up here to rot! Why don't you up-anchor now – right now – and get the hell out of here before the destroyer can catch us . . .'

'The *Almirante Storni* is capable of thirty-five knots,' I answered. 'She'd come after *Jetwind* if I did. She'd catch us before we'd gone a hundred miles.'

'What do you mean to *do* about it?' she demanded.

'I'll plan my strategy after I've seen the chief magistrate. Meanwhile, what I've told you is between the two of us.'

'Of course,' she said. 'There's something important I failed to mention, though – there's an important fail-safe system built into the masts for the ultimate emergency.'

'The ultimate emergency?' I echoed.

She gestured upwards. 'Yes. In the unlikely event of *Jetwind* being knocked down on her beam-ends by a squall, self-destructing explosive ring charges are built into the junction of the top and top-gallant masts. The charges are designed to blast away the top-gallant masts, either individually or together, to enable the ship to right herself again.'

'That seems very drastic to me.'

'The masts can't be cut away because there's no rigging,' she went on. 'The charges operate on the same principle as the ejector seat of an aircraft.'

'Who fires the charges and from where?'

'You'll see the "chicken button" as it's called on the

main bridge bulkhead. It's painted scarlet, and to get at it one has first to break a glass – like a fire-alarm.'

'Things would have to be pretty far gone before one resorted to such extreme measures,' I said. 'Now – a final question: how does one get out on the yard itself from here?'

'There's this exit hatchway. It's held shut magnetically, like the ship's watertight bulkheads. Here's the switch. First, though, I have to obtain permission from the officer of the deck.'

She dialled 'O' on a red-painted phone on a mast bracket. I wondered why Grohman hadn't used the instrument at the time of Captain Mortensen's accident. The sail rollers could have been halted via the bridge controls.

Kay said, 'John? I'm opening the main tops'l yard-arm for the skipper to take a look-see – okay?'

The door slid open and we ducked through. The yard itself was wide enough for Kay to stand on. She balanced, without retorting to the safety grab-handles.

The vantage-point gave me a magnificent view of both ship and anchorage. The Narrows entrance seemed perilously close. Between Navy Point and Engineer Point, its twin land flanks, the grey-green water was coming in from the deep ocean beyond the outer anchorage. The sea had lost its brilliant cobalt of the morning. Neither headland was high; none of the hillocks running east and west of them was as high as *Jetwind*'s maintruck. Therefore a lookout in the crow's nest could see clean across the intervening land to what the *Almirante Storni* was up to.

Then I turned round, and looked astern. Stanley town with its brightly coloured tin roofs still reflected the sunlight which was now becoming increasingly hazy.

Next my eyes went deck-wards to admire *Jetwind*'s long, lean hull. I stopped short. Two of *Jetwind*'s big lifeboats were being swung out from the stern. There was a group of men at each. A third boat was already heading towards the main harbour jetty.

'What goes on down there?' I demanded.

Kay shook her head.

I ducked back through the hatchway, picked up the phone and dialled. Tideman answered.

'Who gave orders for the boats to be put out?'

I had half anticipated his answer. 'Mr Grohman, sir.'

'What are they supposed to be doing?'

I wasn't sure that I had heard his reply correctly. 'A picnic! Did you say a picnic?'

'Aye, aye, sir. A picnic – rather an outing, for the crew. Through The Narrows to Cape Pembroke on the open sea.'

'Recall those boats – at once, d'you hear? From now on, no boat or man is to leave this ship without my express permission – understand?'

Chapter 11

I banged down the phone. Kay was standing by uncertainly.

'I'm going down to sort this out,' I snapped. 'Thanks for the conducted tour. I have the picture now.'

I started down the ladder. Before I had gone a rung or two, she called 'Skipper!'

'Yes?'

'I'll be invoking Cape Horn good luck for your interview this afternoon.'

I was halfway out of the service bay, my head and shoulders still showing. I had a worm's eye view of Kay from the level of her ankles. From that angle she seemed all long legs and big eyes. There was something in those eyes that I needed, the way things were crowding me. Our eyes locked for a long moment.

I said, before I had consciously decided to involve her in the break-out, 'Kay, I'm holding a skull session in my cabin tonight. Tideman and Brockton will be there. I would like you, too.'

She was very acute. 'Do they know?'

'Not yet.'

Her expressive eyes became very thoughtful. 'After you know the results of your interview with the magistrate?'

'With or without, it makes no difference.'

'You're going to take the risk?'

'Yes. That's why I want the three of you. I need your help and know-how!'

'Apart from your own.' She leaned down impetuously and touched my forehead with the tips of her fingers. 'You'll have to take the rap – you know that.'

'I know that, Kay.'

She went on looking at me, then added, 'I'll troll for a blow tonight, Peter.'

'You do that, Kay.'

She waited, as if she expected me to say more. I was tongue-tied by all the cross currents. I said, 'Tentatively, ten tonight in my cabin with the others?'

She nodded. I hurried down the ladder to the bridge.

Grohman was already there. His slick *Jetwind* uniform offset his aquiline Spanish features. I felt by comparison rather like a bum-boat skipper in the black cold-weather rig I had hastily bought in Cape Town. Tideman pretended to be consulting a switch panel; Brockton was in a neutral corner near the radio office door.

Grohman tried to defuse the situation, for he must have been aware of my orders.

'Lunch has been waiting, sir, if you'd care to come. I'm sure you would also like to meet other members of the crew.'

I decided to play it cool and not precipitate a crisis. 'You mean, those that haven't gone off on a picnic,' I retorted sarcastically. 'Lunch is off. There's to be no picnic. This isn't a bloody Sunday school party.'

Grohman remained unruffled, a trifle supercilious. 'I understand you have already cancelled my orders about the boats.'

'Picnic!' I exploded. 'What does a **fit** young crew like *Jetwind*'s want with a picnic, for crying out loud!'

I suspected why Grohman kept his control under my unequivocal stand. He was playing from strength – the strength of the destroyer's approach.

'I felt that the morale of the crew was being affected by being cooped up in port,' he replied evenly. 'They needed a diversion. I arranged an outing in the ship's boats to Cape Pembroke – there's a fine beach there where they can swim and camp overnight . . .'

Overnight! I saw his game. Half *Jetwind*'s crew would be absent next day when the *Almirante Storni* made port. It was a subtle method of immobilizing the ship. Not even automated *Jetwind* could sail with only half her crew.

I cut his explanation short. 'As of now, the entire crew goes on regular sea watch. Four hours on, four hours off, plus the usual dog-watches. All shore-leave is cancelled. Is that clear?'

Fortuitously, Grohman had given me the opportunity to put the crew on full alert without raising suspicions of a break-out. It was a secrecy problem which had solved itself. Another – unsolved – was how to get a synoptic weather forecast from Weather Routing without revealing that I was preparing to put to sea. I urgently needed to know what was happening to the weather in the 400 sector of ocean between Cape Horn and the Falklands.

'But,' Grohman was protesting, 'the Ladies Circle has arranged a special movie show at the Upland Goose for those staying behind tonight and we shouldn't disappoint them . . .'

'The Ladies Circle can and bloody well will be disappointed,' I answered. 'What is the Upland Goose, anyhow?'

'It's the one and only local pub,' Tideman interjected.

'Forget it,' I snapped. 'Put 'em to work. Sailoring, not cinemas, is what a crew needs. That's what they signed on for.'

'Circumstances have changed since then,' commented Grohman. His temper was beginning to rise.

'Thanks to you,' I retaliated. 'I intend to have my crew

sharp and seamanlike, in port as well as on the high seas.'

Grohman bit his lip; Tideman said in his best officer-of-the-watch tone, 'What are your orders about the boat that is already ashore, sir?'

'What is it supposed to be doing?'

'Collecting supplies for the picnic. Beer, barbecue mutton, and so on.'

'I'm going ashore myself in a few minutes,' I replied. 'I want a small boat – I'll give the men at the jetty orders myself.'

'There's only one supermarket in the town,' Grohman said. 'The loss of that amount of trade will cause ill-feeling if you suddenly cancel it.'

'You're very considerate about other people's feelings, Mr Grohman.'

He rode the rebuke. 'This is a small place. You don't understand the situation.'

'It is not by my choice that *Jetwind* is holed up here,' I retorted. 'Remember that. This ship's place is on the high seas, not stagnating in this god-forsaken little port. A crew's a crew, and for me they work like a crew. Or else. Remember that, too. Further, you'll take the deck – now,' I told Grohman. I had done a quick mental calculation of watch-times so that Tideman would be on duty with me for the break-out. 'Get my boat alongside. I'll be back in an hour.

'Any questions?' I added rhetorically.

There weren't any, of course, after that, but Paul, who had stood outside the blast area, intercepted me as I left the wheel-house with Tideman. 'Any objection if I go on casing the air waves with young Arno, Peter?'

I wanted to say, I'd give anything for a weather intercept. Instead I replied, 'Okay, Paul. I want a word with you when I come aboard again.'

Tideman and I set off down the deck. As we passed No. 4 mast, 'Thursday', where the engine room was situated, Tideman said in a casual tone, quite different to his attitude on the bridge; 'Do you also want the diesels to go on sea or harbour duty?'

Did he suspect that I had something in mind for the night?

'Full sea watch,' I replied.

At the stern, men were securing the two boats I had recalled. They fell silent as we approached but there didn't seem to be any anger or resentment directed at me.

The small outboard was bobbing under the counter. I was just about to swing myself down a rope, when a tall, elderly man dressed in a fancy dude yachting outfit erupted from the companion-way. I knew at once it had to be Sir James Hathaway whose presence on board I had completely forgotten.

'You the new skipper?' he barked. 'Damn well hope you can do better than that dago who got us into this god-forsaken hole! Wait until Axel gets to know about this. Confined to the ship. Disgraceful! British territory, too. What the devil goes on here? Not even allowed to communicate with the outside world. And what, may I ask, do you propose to do about it, young man? Never thought much of sailing ships. Always trouble of one kind or another . . .'

He'd have gone on ranting had I not matched decibels with him.

'Sir James,' I shouted, 'Sir James, just a minute please. Just a minute. Yes, I'm the new skipper. I've just arrived here. My name is Peter Rainier and I'm just off to discuss matters with Mr Dawson, the chief magistrate. I have instruction from Mr Thomsen, who appointed me not two days ago, to get this ship out of this hole, as you call it, and I intend to do it. Now, I have an appointment to keep, and if you'll forgive me, I must go.'

And without paying further attention to him, I slid down into the waiting outboard, kick-started the motor, and accelerated across the calm waters to the main jetty.

I tied up as a party of men, laughing and joking, came down the hill with their arms full of parcels. I stopped one of them with cartons of beer under each arm. He looked as big as the cathedral spire in the background. I guessed he was one of Tideman's sailor-paratroopers.

'I'm the new skipper,' I told the men. 'I'm sorry, lads, but the party's off. All that stuff will have to go back. I'll sign any receipts for the supermarket's benefit. Then get yourselves back aboard.'

The big man hugged the cartons. He asked with the same eagerness as Tideman and Kay had questioned me, 'We're sailing, are we, sir?'

'Today?' demanded another.

I knew a good crew when I saw one. These were the sort of men who wouldn't baulk at putting the gaskets on a sail in the wild icy bedlam of a Southern Ocean gale at midnight.

I evaded a direct reply. 'I'm hurrying to an appointment uptown. I'll let you know.'

'No picnic either?' asked another. He looked more like a machineman than a seaman.

'You can go by yourself if you like,' I jollied him. 'But I won't guarantee I'll stop the ship and pick you up at Cape Pembroke as we pass by.'

That raised a laugh. I left the men arguing a little ruefully about lugging the stores back up the hill.

As I turned from the jetty past a row of so-English, red brick, bow-windowed houses with green, red and light blue roofs to walk the half mile or so to the magistrate's office, the machineman's voice reached me faintly. 'That new skipper's a bit of a bastard but I think I could go along with him.'

It was more than I could say of Mr Ronald Dawson.

The chief magistrate's office, situated at the western end of the harbour between the Secretariat and the Town Hall, overlooked what was known as the Government jetty. His office was dominated by a framed print of Keith Griffin's fine painting of the S.S. *Great Britain* on her maiden voyage. There was also a contrasting blow-up photograph of the famous vessel lying derelict in Sparrow Cove – just beyond The Narrows – before her historic salvage and restoration in 1970. An old ship's mercury barometer, nearly a metre long, all glass and brass, completed the nautical air of the office. The rest of the atmosphere was provided by Dawson's supercilious attitude.

His one concession to my being a fellow human being was his perfunctory handshake. Boxers in the ring do it more kindly when they are about to batter one another.

His eyes ranged over my workaday sailor's rig. 'My information is that you are to replace Mr Grohman as captain of *Jetwind*.'

'My information is that Grohman was never appointed to command the ship.'

'So?'

'I had it from the owner himself.'

Dawson had a way of drawing in the left-hand corner of his sandy moustache with his lower canine tooth after he had spoken, as if sharpening his next words.

I said, without mincing words, 'Grohman wasn't able to handle the situation after Captain Mortensen's death. He blew the record attempt – and his own chances.'

The canine tooth gnawed. 'That is only a matter of opinion.'

I shrugged. 'I didn't come here to discuss the merits or impropriety of my first officer's actions.'

'They enter very much into it, Captain Rainier. You may bluster and denigrate him, but you fail to recognize the peculiar and particular circumstances prevailing in this part of the world. There are some who consider him to have acted quite correctly.'

'If you're going to throw the Argentina-Falklands political situation at me, you're wasting your time. It has nothing to do with *Jetwind*.'

'On the contrary, *Jetwind* has everything to do with it. That is why I have summoned you here this afternoon. Mr Grohman has a full understanding of the delicacy of the situation. It appears you don't.'

'Is that why he turned and scudded for port a thousand miles from any country's territorial waters?'

'You make your opinion of Mr Grohman very clear, Captain.'

'Because I fail to understand how a long-standing and

nebulous territorial dispute can be used to justify what I regard as poor judgement and lack of command ability, to put it mildly.'

He said pointedly, 'Captain Rainier, the entire legal jurisdiction of the Falklands Dependencies is under my sole control. That being so, I would rule that Mr Grohman acted correctly since he had a murder on his hands.'

'Murder?'

'I cannot, of course, anticipate the outcome of the inquest on Captain Mortensen, but there is *prima facie* evidence of unnatural death.'

'Of course it was unnatural. I believe he was suffocated by being caught in the roller-furling mechanism of the sails.'

'We shall of course hear expert evidence on that,' he replied judicially. 'The true cause of death might have escaped an ordinary medical man, but in this case I was fortunate in that Sir William Hall-Denton was my guest.'

He eyed me to note what effect the name-dropping had on me. My silence expressed my knowledge of Sir William Hall-Denton.

'Sir William is a leading London pathologist,' he explained. 'A good friend and a passionate philatelic expert. You know, of course, of the Falklands' place in the realm of philately.'

I didn't. I was more interested in Captain Mortensen's death.

'Sir William interested himself in the case when the body was brought in. He established that death, in fact, was caused *prior* to the apparent suffocation in the sail roller. There was a small bruise at the base of the neck which pointed to the fact that he was probably dead by the time he was enveloped by the sail. He had most likely been struck by a blunt instrument.'

I said, marking time while I digested this news, 'Where is Captain Mortensen's body now?'

Mr Dawson indicated a building beyond the Secretariat. 'There. In the hospital mortuary.'

'So Grohman must either have known or suspected.'

Dawson lifted one shoulder. 'It is not for me as presiding officer of the inquest to prejudge any witness.'

Dawson's news had thrown me. A question ripped through my mind – had I misjudged Grohman as a treacherous bastard when he had, in fact, had justification with a murder on his hands? Who had murdered Mortensen, and why? Then I got a grip on my racing thoughts. I reminded myself that Grohman had been far from any authority on the high seas. He, as captain, was the sole judge of the situation. There had been no reason to sacrifice the record. If he had suspected foul play, he could have proceeded, body and all, to the Cape.

'Well?' Mr Dawson's word gambit was that of a grand-master who is sure of his kill.

I said, more confidently than I felt, 'At sea, the ship's master has complete authority. If it took a top-flight London specialist to pinpoint the cause of death, Grohman himself could not have realized it.'

'He might have had reason to suspect.'

'Suspect someone? In that case the captain has the right of arrest. Did he detain or question anyone? Has he aired his suspicions to you?'

The grand-master saw his game slipping away.

He said stiffly, 'He would have been exceeding his duties to voice a mere opinion.'

I felt I had regained firmer ground. 'Grohman is an Argentinian, who was temporarily captain of a ship registered in Falmouth . . .'

'The Falklands was the nearest British port,' interrupted Dawson.

'You're talking legalistically,' I retaliated. 'The situation isn't as simple as that.'

Superficially it might have been simple, had I not seen and heard the violent reaction on the mainland over *Jetwind* or encountered the obstructionism of the Argentinian officials. Nor could I forget Grohman's air of triumph when I had provoked him into telling me that the *Almirante Storni* was on her way to detain *Jetwind*. You don't send a warship to hold a ship for a case of suspected murder.

Dawson tried to short-circuit the interview. 'I am glad, Captain Rainier, that you agree the matter is not simple and that you have come round to my way of thinking.'

'On the contrary, I have not,' I answered. 'Grohman knew well enough that by bringing the ship here he would raise a political hornets' nest. In fact, that may well have been his purpose.'

Mr Dawson was clearly taken aback by this suggestion. 'You must not forget that Argentina claims territorial waters of two hundred sea-miles offshore and has filed claims with the United Nations to these islands and all others for a considerable sector of the Cape Horn area . . .'

'I've heard the claims,' I interrupted. 'They're absurd.'

'Argentina regards the Falklands as Argentinian territory,' he continued. 'You have to accept that fact when you live in this part of the world. Therefore, Grohman brought the ship to what he regards as an Argentinian port.'

'Where, then, does *your* legal jurisdiction as a British official come in? It means nothing, from Grohman's point of view.'

I had Dawson nailed, and he knew it. He slid out from under my attack. 'The position of the Falklands is an explosive issue, and Mr Grohman is an Argentinian. I am happy to be able to tell you that tomorrow we are expecting an Argentinian warship for a courtesy visit. She is the *Almirante Storni* and Captain Julian Irizar and I will have consultations over Captain Mortensen's death.'

'What the devil has it to do with the Argentinian Navy?'

He displayed long-suffering patience. 'I have been attempting to convey to you that we have here a knife-edge situation which requires consultation and good neighbourliness in order to continue our *modus vivendi*.'

I suppressed my intended retort. If I played my fish right I could find out the *Almirante Storni*'s time of arrival.

I said casually, 'We spotted the warship from our plane on the way over. When is she due in?'

'We have made special provision for her to tie up tomorrow morning early,' he answered. 'She should reach the outer harbour of Port William about ten tonight. She'll anchor there and come in later when it's light enough. The Narrows are tricky in darkness and there is no official pilot in Stanley.'

'I'd like to be up to see her come in,' I said, hoping I was keeping the inference out of my voice. 'What time will she come through?'

'The Narrows have an odd characteristic,' he said more readily, apparently glad to ditch the subject of Argentina-Falklands relations. 'The sky is generally clearest over the entrance at about two in the morning, even when weather is working up. Port Stanley is far enough south to be able to see landmarks quite clearly at that time. When daylight comes, the cloud cover usually closes in. My guess is that the destroyer will negotiate The Narrows in the early hours. Captain Irizar knows the port well – he's been here before.' He eyed me speculatively. 'I hope – in the interests of good neighbourliness – that you will show Captain Irizar round your ship. *Jetwind* is quite a talking point.'

'I shall be delighted to show Captain Irizar my ship at close quarters,' I replied.

How close, only dawn and The Narrows would show.

What Dawson had now revealed about the *Almirante Storni*'s intended movements had sewn up all but the final link of my plan. The weather and the wind. I wanted to sick up at the rest of Dawson's pontifical papering-over of the legalistic and diplomatic niceties. What was the true reason behind Grohman's decision to bring *Jetwind* to the Falklands? Beneath all his shadow-boxing there was, I was convinced, some powerful secret motive. I also meant to find that out – once I had put a safe distance between *Jetwind* and the Argentinian warship. I also had no illusions about the furore that would follow *Jetwind*'s break-out.

Perhaps Dawson took my silence for second thoughts; he decided to exhibit a flabby iron fist.

'You realize, don't you, Captain, that *Jetwind* is required to stay in port until after this business of the inquest has been cleared up?'

'Required? By whom?'

'The law.'

'You've just said the place is so small it doesn't even have a harbour pilot.'

'I would have thought you would be perceptive enough to see through the presence of the *Almirante Storni*, Captain.'

'You mean, you would tolerate the services of a foreign warship to detain *Jetwind*?'

'I spoke of good neighbourliness,' he replied blandly. I wondered whether the left-hand wisp of his moustache would survive if our conversation went on for much longer. 'In this remote part of the world, there might be services required – and rendered – in the interest of that good neighbourliness when there was no suitable . . . ah, instrument, ready to one's own hand.'

'I get the message,' I said bluntly.

Dawson rose to terminate the interview on what he obviously considered a winning note.

'Then I hope Stanley will have *Jetwind*'s company for a while longer and you will forget about such things as record-breaking in the greater interests of the region.' He forced a hand as limp as a wet sail upon me in token of his triumph. 'I shall pass on your invitation to Captain Irizar tomorrow.'

I thought of the night ahead. 'Maybe I'll even see him myself.'

I hurried through Dawson's door into the clean air, cleaner than I had left it an hour before.

It was keen – the first knife-edge gust from the Drake Passage.

Chapter 12

By two bells in the middle watch – nine o'clock that night –
the wind was blowing fresh from the east across the
anchorage. *Jetwind* lay with her head to it. She tugged at
her anchor cable as if eager to get going. I was in the crow's
nest at the summit of No. 2 mast, directly overhead of the
bridge, the mast I had visited with Kay. From my vantage-
point, fifty-two metres above the deck, I could see the
occasional surge from a white horse. The wind was
building up; there was a lot more punch still to come.
There couldn't be enough, for my business with the
Almirante Storni.

I moved round to probe beyond The Narrows into the
waters of Port William's outer anchorage. Where was the
Almirante Storni? Any moment the warship should
become visible. A cloud, fringed yellow along its edge by a
track of reflected shore light, whipped at zero feet across
the quartet of low hills separating us from the outer
anchorage. These hills terminated at Navy Point, The
Narrows' Western head-land. The cloud moved so fast
that in no more than a couple of seconds it seemed to have
blanketed the 300-metre passage, blacked out the navigation light on the opposite side at Engineer Point, and
obscured a trio of further low hills on the eastern side of
the entrance gap. Then the cloud blacked out the crow's
nest itself. The wipers were ineffectual against the thick
vapour.

I cursed the cloud. A visual sighting was the only way for
me to spot the destroyer and give me the edge, since my
eyrie was a few metres higher than the highest of the
intervening hills. The warship's radar might indeed pick
up the tops of *Jetwind*'s masts but that would not be
significant in a port with other ships about.

I put out the overhead light to extinguish any reflection from the crow's nest windows and peered into the darkness. If the destroyer came to anchor, she would – presumably – display normal anchor lights. Was the destroyer already in Port William? Was Captain Irizar playing possum with a blacked-out ship? I dismissed the idea. Captain Irizar had no reason to suspect anything on *Jetwind*'s part. I was staking everything on the *Almirante Storni* navigating The Narrows in the small hours, based on Dawson's opinion that that would be the best time because of the local cloud peculiarity. If, on the other hand, Captain Irizar decided to anchor further out at sea, my break-out would abort because from that angle of approach he would spot *Jetwind*, and I was basing my entire plan on remaining invisible.

I had to get out tonight, and I had to prevent the Almirante Storni *from pursuing me!*

My nerves were too wrought-up to wait another hour for my council of war. I decided to summon the team now.

I picked up the phone, dialled Kay's cabin. 'Will you come to my quarters right away?'

'Is there anything wrong? You said ten o'clock.'

'I know. Nothing's wrong – yet.'

'I'll be right there.'

Brockton was not in his cabin but in the radio office with Arno. I decided to collect Tideman from the bridge *en route* to the meeting.

I found the bridge with its lighted consoles and static dial lights like a stage waiting for the players to enter.

'Everything okay?' I asked Tideman.

'Aye – just checking the hydraulics. All three diesels are operating.'

'I've put the time of our meeting forward – it's now.'

He gave me a searching glance – perhaps I was showing more tension than I was aware of.

He said to the helmsman – one of his own sailor-paratroopers, 'I'll be in the captain's cabin. Call me if anything crops up.'

'Aye, aye, sir.'

My cabin, reached via the chartroom and navigation office, was beneath the starboard wing of the bridge. Kay and Brockton were waiting. The place was warm compared to the chill of the decks; wooden panelling made it additionally snug. It was quiet, too: no creak or murmur of the ship's fabric penetrated the rubber buffer strips on the doors and sound insulation behind the panelling. The accommodation was luxurious, if I'd had time to enjoy it.

I locked the door and waved the three of them into comfortable seats while I leaned against my big desk. Kay had shed her working rig in favour of navy slacks and pale mauve blouse under a jersey-knit waistcoat whose cut emphasized the line of her breasts, making her look twice as feminine.

'I'm not going to beat about the bush,' I started off. 'I intend taking the ship out tonight.'

For a moment there was startled silence. Kay jumped up and hugged me spontaneously, and Brockton pump-handled my hand.

'I always knew you were a one-way guy, Peter!' he exclaimed delightedly.

However, my words seemed to produce most effect upon Tideman. He was looking directly at me when I made my announcement. There was a split-second fire burst behind his eyes; his face went taut like an instant face-lift.

'Now?' he jerked out. 'Now? I can be under way in ten minutes . . .'

I laughed and shook my head. Kay was still close enough for me to detect a trace of perfume.

She said enthusiastically, 'I thought *I* was keen to go, John! Ten minutes!'

Tideman seemed oblivious of her, and said to me, 'What's our course to the Cape? *What's our course!*'

Brockton's momentary euphoria also vanished. He repeated Tideman's question. 'Yes – the course, Peter?'

'You're all rather jumping the gun,' I said. 'First, I need your help, each one of you. I want to discuss the logistics of the break-out . . .'

'Break-out?' repeated Tideman. 'That's a strong word.'

'And I mean it,' I answered. 'Listen . . .' I outlined my interview with Dawson and his veiled threat to enlist the *Almirante Storni* against *Jetwind*. When I came to Captain Mortensen's suspected murder, Kay looked very grave.

'I felt all along that there was something about that so-called accident. It was impossible, as far as the furling mechanism was concerned,' she said.

'Murder only adds to our problems,' I pointed out. 'It strengthens Dawson's hand, in fact. It could, in fact, give him some justification for calling upon the *Almirante Storni* for assistance.'

'Which means that the destroyer would pursue *Jetwind* once Captain Irizar discovers the bird has flown,' added Brockton.

Until then Tideman had been the perfect officer, highly efficient, deferential, somewhat Navy-formal. Now the mettle of the man who on three occasions had bull-whipped racing yachts through the wildest seas in the world broke through.

He rose impatiently. 'What the devil have we been waiting for – we've lost hours! The wind's been good since this afternoon! We could have been away on the high seas by now!'

'I was tempted also,' I replied. 'But there's another consideration . . .' And I explained to Kay and Tideman, with the help of Brockton, about Grohman's angry exchange with me at Comodoro Rivadavia and its disturbing political under-currents.

'Dawson is playing along in the interest of what he terms a *modus vivendi* between the Falklands and Argentina,' I added. 'I don't know how Grohman fits in. However, I believe he's playing some deep game of his own.'

'Then why did you allow for four Argentinians to join our crew as extra hands? They can only complicate the issue,' said Tideman.

'What did you say?' I asked incredulously.

'We didn't need any extra hands,' Tideman added.

'You must be joking,' I said. '*I* certainly brought no one with me from the mainland.'

'Say, remember those guys with Grohman in the plane, Peter?' asked Brockton.

I felt the same surge of alarm as when I learned about Grohman's proposed picnic. It was another sinister straw in the wind.

Kay added, 'There wasn't room in the foc'sle for them with the rest of our crew. Grohman has housed them in the passenger accommodation.'

I faced their stares and said tersely, 'You have my word that I brought no crew with me.' Then I asked Tideman, 'Are the men sailors?'

'Aye. Good ones, too, from what I could make out. They speak only Spanish.'

'Maybe they're crew from Grohman's old schooner and he took them on when he thought he was going to be the skipper,' I said. 'It's too late now to send them ashore, damn it, without giving the game away. Besides, there'd be too many formalities. Apart from you three, no one knows we're sailing tonight. I want to keep it that way.'

'We're wasting our time with all this talk,' Tideman said. 'Why don't we get the sail on *Jetwind* now?'

'Sorry, John. Until the *Almirante Storni* actually puts her nose into The Narrows, *Jetwind* does not budge.'

'Why?' He looked at me as if I were mad.

'What's behind the stalling?' asked Brockton.

I looked at each in turn as I explained. 'I summoned you here tonight because I felt I knew you well enough to trust you in an extreme situation. Equally, I hope you will trust me. I'm saying this because I realize that there are questions in your minds whose answers you will have to take on trust.'

'Such as?' asked Tideman.

'I have taken a major decision for which I alone can assume the responsibility. It is a captain's decision. I will tell you what I intend to do once the *Almirante Storni* shows up in The Narrows. I alone will have to take the rap for the consequences. I do not wish to implicate you. The matter is too serious. If you don't know in advance you cannot be held responsible after the event.'

'Who by?' asked Kay.

'International opinion for one,' I answered. '*Jetwind* versus the Falklands is a powder keg ready to explode. Dawson is trying to keep the lid on by appeasing Argentina. What I intend to do tonight will trigger the explosion. It's too late now for any of you three not to sail with the ship. However, you're free to withdraw from assisting me if you feel you cannot cooperate on the basis of being only half informed.'

'I'm with you – naturally.' Kay's voice was tense.

'The sooner we sail, the happier I'll be,' repeated Tideman.

Brockton said unhesitatingly, 'I go, whatever.'

I warmed to him. But a second later, I found myself questioning his intentions when he struck what I felt was a false note. 'Oh boy, what a story!'

'There'll be no story yet,' I retorted. 'No use of the ship's communications either.'

'Okay, okay,' he said. 'Forget it!'

'Now listen, Paul. There's no sign yet of the warship – I've just come from the crow's nest. That's to be your spot. I want you there for the next couple of hours. Report the moment you sight the *Almirante Storni*. My guess is that she'll anchor in the main fairway just outside The Narrows. Then, the moment she up-anchors after that, I have to know. I have a hunch that she'll do so when the sky clears in the early hours, as I'm told it does in these parts.'

'You can count on me all the way,' replied Brockton.

'Fine,' I said. 'That's not all. You're an America Cup expert. You've watched those craft wring every knot out of a situation . . .'

'Correction,' he smiled. 'Every hundredth of a knot. Timing is as hairline as that.'

'Our own position is going to change like lightning,' I went on. 'Once this ship enters The Narrows, I want human, as well as mathematical, appraisal of the way things develop. So you'll use a portable analogue computer and give me – every thirty seconds, or every second, if necessary – manual feed-in. I'll make any further decisions on the basis of what you supply. You'll be one of the most vital elements in the entire break-out operation, Paul.'

'I'll do it – and not just for the hell of it, Peter.'

Tideman added, 'I don't know what's on your mind, Peter, but remember you have precious little room in which to manoeuvre in The Narrows – it's only three hundred metres wide.'

'That's where I need you, too, Kay. None of us has any idea at this stage what the wind speed will be, say at two o'clock or whenever the destroyer makes her entry. There's one hell of a lot of unknown quantities at this moment. But I must have at least ten knots speed when we enter The Narrows.'

Kay's eyes became abstracted as they always seemed to when she was busy with a calculation. 'It's a hell of a short take-off distance from anchor. Our harbour course is roughly a dog-leg, right? The first is the longer part, which will bring us to the southern entrance to The Narrows. Then, an almost right-angle change of direction to take us through – right?'

'*Jetwind* keeps out of sight behind the intervening hills until the last moment before The Narrows,' I added. 'Our mast-head, where Paul will be stationed, is a fraction higher than the hills. So I'll keep the royals stowed until the last possible moment so there's no chance of detection. Once I set them, it will be too late – the race will be on.'

'Too late?' queried Tideman, voicing the question which was clearly in all their minds. 'Too late for what?'

'Sorry. That's the part of my plan you must take on blind trust. If it fails, it's the end of *Jetwind*. And of me.'

Chapter 13

There was a deathly silence, which I broke.

'There's something else. I'm not inviting any opinions about it. I want Number Two anchor cock-billed from the end of the fore-yard from a couple of metres of chain.'

Tideman repeated the order as if to reassure himself he was hearing right. Kay and Brockton stared in incredulous silence.

'That's correct,' I said. 'John, that task is priority once you leave this cabin.'

'The crew is keen to get to sea but I'm afraid this business of the anchor will appear like a rank-pulling exercise to them,' he said. 'It seems, if I may say so, utterly purposeless, especially following on your cancellation of the picnic. The old-timers had a name for it – chipping the anchor cable.'

'I hope to change their minds before the night is out. Meanwhile, my order stands. Do it, will you, John?'

'Of course. I wasn't speaking for myself. But haven't you forgotten Grohman? All this activity must give him an idea that something is up.'

'I certainly haven't forgotten him. Take a look at the way I've arranged the watches. He's off duty during the vital early hours.'

'Once you give the order to make sail Grohman – and everyone else in the ship – will know.'

'By that time it will be too late for him to do anything, if indeed he is contemplating anything.'

'He knows this ship, Peter, and he's a good sailor,' Tideman went on. 'One touch of the wrong button could upset everything.'

'We must consider Grohman to be hostile because we don't know what's behind his political motivations,' I replied. 'I can't take any chances. But, like it or not, we're stuck with Grohman till we reach the Cape.'

Tideman went on, 'Make no mistake, I'm one hundred per cent behind the idea of getting to sea and your scheme to elude the *Almirante Storni* – whatever it may be. I don't want to sound as if I'm throwing cold water on it, but where is it going to get us? Or *Jetwind*?'

'What are you driving at?'

'We slip past the destroyer in The Narrows. Fine. She can't turn there, it's not wide enough. All she does then is to carry on to where the inner port opens out, make a U-turn, and come after us at full speed. She'll catch us before she's halfway to the open sea. Into the bargain, you will have deliberately provoked counter-action. I'd say it would be much better to slip away to sea at this very moment.'

All three eyed me expectantly. I was greatly tempted to take them into my confidence. But the implications were too great. I repeated to myself what I had said to myself before, I alone would have to take the consequences.

'I asked you earlier to take me on trust. That is still what I say.'

Kay came tactfully to the rescue. 'You're going to make one man aboard this ship very happy – Sir James Hathaway.'

I laughed ruefully. 'When I talked to him earlier on I was surprised he didn't rip the panelling off the bulkheads.'

Kay steered Tideman away from something else he seemed about to say.

'Was he still acting up and hopping mad?'

'Let's say he'd rather go to sea in a sieve than set foot in a sailing ship again, let alone buy one.'

'He was keen enough while Captain Mortensen put her through her paces,' added Tideman. 'But of course once Grohman took over it was a different matter.'

'Everything always comes back to Grohman,' Brockton concluded.

I shrugged, checked my watch, and straightened up. 'Paul, up you go to your perch in the crow's nest. Report to me on the intercom the moment you spot lights in the main fairway. Bearing, distance, position. If you have any doubts . . .'

'I guess I know a Fletcher class lights as well as anyone afloat.'

'She may be rigged up differently than when she was U.S. Navy,' I replied. 'I reckon her spot will be near Ordnance Point, in the main fairway, as I've just said.'

'Why there?' asked Tideman. 'There's plenty of room elsewhere.'

'Because at almost any other place one or both the beacon lights at Navy Point or Engineer Point are obscured. They are essential for her entry. In the fairway sector I'm talking about, a ship can sight both lights at the same time. I consider the *Almirante Storni* will anchor there to get an exact fix of her position. Later, when it's light enough to see both headlands, she'll navigate The Narrows proper.'

I hoped I wasn't talking myself into a tailor-made plan which made no allowance for contingencies.

I swamped my doubts with more orders. 'Kay, I want you to keep busy at your sums. I want optimum readings and sail settings at intervals of every half an hour from now until we sail – and after too. Clear?'

'Won't it seem odd if I'm seen on the bridge working out calculations to no apparent purpose?' she replied.

'Use this cabin,' I said. 'Everything you need is here.'

'Where is Grohman now?' asked Brockton. He seemed to attach more importance to the Argentinian than the rest of us.

'Probably in his cabin – he's off watch now,' I replied.

I rounded off the briefing. 'John, I'll take the bridge while you get on with rigging that anchor to the yard.'

He laughed. 'Slave-driving a crew in the middle of the night in a cold wind – a bucko mate from the past, that's John Tideman!'

His mood was infectious now that the die was cast. We all laughed with him, which broke up the party and the tension.

The stress returned in the next hour, however, and mounted feverishly while I waited on the bridge for a sighting report from Brockton. The wheel-house was quiet, over-bright from the strip lighting. The banks of dials gazed back unwinkingly at me. All except the anenometer read-out, which continued to log the wind's rising strength: twenty-one knots, then twenty-two, suddenly twenty-five. I resisted the temptation, as the minutes dragged, to check on Brockton. He knew his job, I told myself. I rejected the further temptation to pace up and down the bridge, Hornblower-like. The helmsman had nothing to do but watch me. He lounged, eyes half-shut, on his high stool by the wheel.

Three bells – 9.30.

Nothing from Brockton.

Kay came in. I was glad to see her. I kept her longer than the abstruse technicalities required. When she had gone I found it harder than ever to sit out the long wait. I even found myself sweating slightly. The only distraction was the sound of Tideman's anchor gang at work.

Four bells – 10.00. Half watch.

To pass the time, I decided to familiarize myself further with the instrument consoles. First the main cabinet.

The intercom buzzed making me jolt.

I stopped in my tracks. At that moment Kay entered through a rear door. She, too, stopped. Our eyes met.

Paul's voice vibrated. 'Warship navigation lights in the main fairway channel. Three white, forward steaming light lower than sidelights. And – ' his Navy formality cracked somewhat ' – I don't know why in hell she's showing it but it helps us – she's displaying an amber quick-flashing light about two metres above her after steaming light.'

My throat was tight. 'Is she coming in, Paul? What's her position?'

'Exactly where you predicted – in the fairway beyond The Narrows. Hey, wait!'

'What is it, man?'

'She's mounted a white all-round light amidships – the

steaming lights are out – gee whizz, she's anchored! Peter, she's stopped!'

'You're sure?'

'Sure as hell. Come up and see for yourself.'

'I will. Keep your eyes skinned, Paul! Report the slightest movement or change. Wait – black out the crow's nest. The mast-head will be visible from the destroyer.'

'I did so as soon as I spotted her, skipper. I'm sitting alone in the dark. It's getting goddam cold.'

'I'll send you something hot.'

'I'll have to piss over the yard-arm.'

'Hold it till a rain squall comes. No one will know the difference.'

Kay fetched a vacuum flask of coffee for me to take to Brockton. On the ascent up the mast ladder, the cold increased step by step. If the wind kept mounting, the rain would turn to sleet by morning.

I joined Brockton and took a long look at the destroyer through the night glasses. Captain Irizar might have been wanting to make quite sure we identified his vessel. A bright light amidships – usually carried only by moored submarines – and an amber flashing light silhouetted the warship's main distinguishing feature: that heavy mast with its clutter of radar and firing gear, supported by the clumsy stay. All this was clearly visible since the destroyer had swung head to wind, like *Jetwind*, and her port side was parallel with us. Between the two ships rose a range of low hills.

As I concentrated on the destroyer I made an assessment of how she would have to negotiate The Narrows. In order to comply with the rules of navigation, the destroyer would have to keep over on the Navy Point side. As I planned the escape, we would then race through on the opposite flank, or Engineer Point. That would leave the warship's stayed mast exposed to *Jetwind*. Exposed and vulnerable.

A recurring low cloud squall jetted across my vision, blotting out the *Almirante Storni* and everything else.

'Paul,' I said, 'if Dawson is right, I reckon these squalls

will come with fewer intervals between them as the night progresses.'

'Should he be wrong?'

'I'm staking everything on his being right. He's lived in Port Stanley for years. The cloud clearance has to do with the wind heating itself as it pours down the hills. It dissipates the cloud temporarily until the point is reached when the overall temperature becomes too low for the phenomenon to be effective.'

Brockton asked very quietly, 'You're sure of what you plan to do when the *Almirante Storni* up-anchors, Peter? The consequences could be hell for a lot of people and things.'

'That's why I want to take all the responsibility on myself, Paul.'

'Okay, you're the boss. I for one wouldn't mind sharing it. Nor would John – or Kay.'

'Thanks,' I replied. 'But I prefer to work it out alone. Anyway, now we know where the destroyer has anchored there's no point in my hanging around here. Let me know the situation as soon as the squall has passed.'

'Will do.'

The four hours that followed were as nerve-wracking as a depth-charge hunt when a sub lies doggo and silent on the bottom of the sea, not daring to breathe.

Eight bells – midnight. Change watch. My watch.

Tideman remained on duty with me. His anchor job was completed. The massive piece of metal dangling from the fore-yard gave *Jetwind* a lop-sided appearance. Jim Yell, bo'sun-quartermaster and top of Tideman's Adventure School team, took over the wheel. I would need the best and coolest helmsman for the job ahead.

The wind remained in the west quarter. It was intensifying and becoming colder all the time. By one o'clock it was gusting over thirty knots, a near-gale. That gave all the wind I needed. The sky was clear of cloud. The waves picked up size. *Jetwind* snubbed her anchor chain, heaved short on my orders to the last few fathoms for a tearaway start. The cards were all on the table.

With that strange camaraderie which crisis and the small hours seems to engender, Kay and I drew closer. Her calculations needed only minute onward adjustments. We checked them a score of times until we knew them by heart. On several occasions when I could stand the silence on the bridge no longer, I went to her in my cabin. We talked about her passage of Cape Horn in the Round the World race, my run in *Albatros*, of what a man thinks alone, alone on a wide, wide sea – and what a woman thinks.

Four bells, 2.00. Half watch.

The intercom screeched. Paul's voice was excited.

'Get on the bitch-box, and rouse out those sleeping sons of bitches below! The *Almirante Storni* is on her way!'

Chapter 14

◆

'Hands to make sail!'

I found myself shouting over the ship's public address system – Paul's bitch-box – as if I were roaring orders on an open deck in a gale.

'All hands! All hands! At the double!'

Jim Yell leapt to the wheel as if a shot of adrenalin had picked him up bodily from his lounging-stool. Tideman moved swiftly to station at the big central walkaround console.

'Break out the anchor!' I ordered.

He spoke into a voice-tube. 'Bridge here! Full power for all hydraulics!'

He banged down the voice-pipe and manipulated the sail and mast controls, watching expectantly for my next command.

'Back all yards on Numbers One and Two masts: Trim Numbers Three, Four, Five and Six three-zero degrees off the wind. Make all sail to the top-gallants – no royals. Stern thruster – full ahead port; bow thruster – full ahead starboard!'

The purpose of my orders was to box *Jetwind*'s head hard round to face in exactly the opposite direction to which she now lay, bow to the west wind. I would employ the backed sails to swing her bows, while the other sails, in normal position, gave her momentum forwards and sideways. Add to this ten tons of solid shove from the two thrusters and *Jetwind* would pivot on her heels like a dancer.

She came alive as Tideman's hands played the toggles and push-buttons. Kay was at my side with her calculations.

I snapped into the bitch-box mike, 'Captain here! Black out the ship. No lights to be shown. Emergency illumination only.'

Tideman's racing fingers followed my commands. Next moment the bridge was dark except for the binnacle and green-yellow glow of the console dials.

I added, 'Black out the sidelights.'

Tideman hesitated fractionally. The law of the sea required a sailing ship under way to carry red and green sidelights, but unlike a steamship no white mast-head lights. This put me legally in the wrong in relation to the *Almirante Storni*.

'Out!' I repeated.

Jetwind swung round like a racehorse being manoeuvred into its starting-box with only one idea in its head – to streak the hell down the course. The speed of the ship's pivot-turn was electrifying.

'Cut the bow and stern thrusters!' I ordered. 'What depth of water under her?' I asked Tideman.

He checked the fathomer. 'Nine-eight metres, making nine-nine.'

That meant deep enough, but *Jetwind* had a deep hull, whose grip on the water could be supplemented by two drop-keels, one in the bows and the other in the stern. These could be raised and lowered at will. Nowhere was the anchorage deep enough to use them to advantage. To allow for *Jetwind*'s natural depth I would, in any event, have to follow an irregular course to The Narrows. A slight deviation would ground the ship on the muddy, sticky harbour bottom.

'Wind angle?' I asked.

'Two-seven-zero, true.'

So far, so good.

'Steer six-zero,' I told Jim Yell at the wheel. 'Handsomely, as she comes.'

To Tideman, 'Brace all yards as she steadies.'

The ship was in the final stage of completing her turn, the great yards above swinging with it. The thrust of over 9000 square metres of aerodynamic dacron was like shove-in-the-back acceleration.

It wasn't the sudden acceleration but a commotion which directed my attention behind me. It was Grohman. He had hastily thrown on his clothes – his shirt was not yet buttoned. His previous neat, rather sinister Spanish grandee air had given way to a savage intensity reminiscent of a stooping giant condor. His head and nose were thrust forward like the Andean bird of prey; his eyes above his stubbled cheeks seemed to burn.

He came at me with his sleeves rolled roughly to the elbows, like a fencer about to lunge.

'Did I hear – *Hands to make sail*?'

It wasn't a question, it was an accusation. There was even more arrogance in it than he had displayed at Comodoro Rivadavia.

'You're not on watch,' I responded roughly. 'And I'm the captain of this ship!'

He behaved as if he hadn't heard. 'You're taking the ship out!'

'You're damn right. Straight to the Cape.'

'You can't sail without clearance!'

'Says who?'

'It's illegal! The inquest!'

My attention was on the compass needle. 'Steady as she goes,' I told Jim Yell. 'Hold her like that!'

In manoeuvring the ship, I missed the feel of the wind on

the nape of my neck; I wanted instinctively to tell Yell to keep his eye on the weather leech of the foresail in order to steer by the wind. Instead, I had to interpret a complex series of read-outs before acting. More accurate, perhaps, but much less human.

My blood was up. *Jetwind* had a wonderful racing feel – there is nothing to match a ship which responds like that, except perhaps planing full-bore down a Southern Ocean super-wave.

My attention snapped back to Grohman. I told him briefly, 'This is my responsibility.'

I saw the cords in his throat knot. Anger blazed in his eyes, then died as he said contemptuously, 'The *Almirante Storni* is waiting outside. You won't get past her.'

'She is not outside,' I replied. 'She is on her way in. You can have a closer look at her very soon – as we go by.'

For a moment he looked taken aback and then he laughed derisively.

'All this up-and-away action is very dashing – like a movie,' he sneered. 'It is also very unrealistic, Captain Rainier. The *Almirante Storni* will intercept you, now or later. It is an empty gesture.' He added with a touch of pomposity, 'I wish to publicly dissociate myself from the illegality of your escape.'

'Fine,' I retorted. 'You've said it publicly. Do you also wish to be relieved of your duties publicly?'

That shook him. For a moment I thought he was about to make a dramatic exit from the bridge in haughty Spanish style. Then a curious look crossed his face and he said, 'I will announce my decision to the captain of the *Almirante Storni*.'

'You do that,' I rejoined.

He came closer to where I stood. I ignored him and said over my shoulder to Kay, 'Stand by, will you? In a moment I'll want the optimum sail trim and rudder angles for the first mark. I'll also do a spot check with Paul right away.'

The destroyer's movements would determine any counter measures that became necessary in my plan. Only Paul could actually see what the warship was doing.

But Grohman was not finished. 'Your actions are an insult to my country's Navy,' he threw at me.

'Let Captain Irizar tell me that, not you. You are an officer under my command. Either you go along with me, or you don't. Take your choice – now.'

'I repeat my protest. You are risking the ship and its crew. I protest.'

'I'll log your protest officially. Now stand back.' I then consulted Brockton via the intercom about the destroyer's movements.

My immediate problem was to get the ship moving as fast as possible before turning head-on to face the *Almirante Storni* in The Narrows, and get *Jetwind* there to coincide with the warship's arrival. There were a series of predetermined marker points – the summits of the four hillocks which lay on the spit of land between the inner and outer anchorages. *Jetwind*'s first leg being downwind, the optimum course was less critical than what Paul could tell me about the warship's movements.

'Paul, what's new?'

'First way-point, Goldsworthy Rock, abeam. Optimum speed made good, five knots. On course. Evaluation, ninety-five per cent of optimum performance. Some slight trim needed . . .'

'Skip it,' I interrupted. 'She's running near enough on target. What's our friend up to?'

'She's burning enough lights to make her look like Coney Island,' he replied. 'That flasher amidships is the complete give-away. Any moment now, she'll be making her turn to approach the entrance – hold it, here she comes – she's coming round, round . . .'

The warship was now obviously committing herself to the northern extremity of The Narrows, manoeuvring probably by the leading beacons on the mainland in order to pick her line through the gap. From her present position she would be able to sight one light – that of Engineer Point – but the second, opposite on Navy Point, would be obscured. While that light remained obscured, we would remain invisible.

'Destroyer steadying on new course,' reported Paul. 'One-eight-five degrees.'

That was the recommended approach to the port from seawards. The move brought the *Almirante Storni* facing bow-on towards *Jetwind*'s port side.

I had a sudden fear about Grohman giving the game away. I wheeled round. He was standing near the door leading to the radio office; he seemed to have an air of controlled purpose. I fixed him with a stare while I spoke to the radio operator by phone.

'Arno! No transmissions without my express orders until the ship is clear of the land – understood?'

'Aye, aye, sir.'

'Any signals coming in?'

'Strong radar transmission, sir.'

'Relative bearing?'

He rattled off a series of figures which confirmed that *Almirante Storni* was using an instrumented as well as visual approach. Nonetheless, the destroyer was not yet fully committed to The Narrows. She was in deep water on its outer approaches. I knew she drew five and a half metres, and the depths all round her now were a comfortable ten to eleven metres. This meant that she could, if necessary, still turn safely and intercept *Jetwind*. Further towards the entrance gap, however, was where I aimed to put the cork in the bottle. Although the water was deep in the centre channel of The Narrows – over fifteen metres – it fell away on either side close to both Navy and Engineer Points to under five metres. Once in this channel, the destroyer could not turn without grounding. Another hazard was a broad fringe of kelp along this shallow line; if she did attempt a turn and tangled with the kelp her engine intakes would jam within minutes.

The kelp constituted a hazard for us as well, I reminded myself grimly, and even more so. It fringed a lee shore, the sailing ship's traditional nightmare. *Jetwind* could easily be thrust helplessly against the land by the powerful wind which was now blowing from astern but would come abeam once she made her own turn to negotiate The Narrows.

Chapter 15

Jetwind drove on and gathered speed. She had roughly a kilometre to go before making her turn into The Narrows. She was now between the first and second way-points or shore-line markers.

'Paul . . .' I started, wanting more information, but he interrupted me.

'What gives down there, Peter?' he burst out. 'Is this tub dragging lead from her ass? You're only sailing seventy-five per cent of potential! You'll never make The Narrows in time for the warship! And she's running right on schedule! At this rate she'll be through before you make your approach turn! Give her the gun, man!'

Kay saw the look on my face at Paul's news. In one stride I was at Tideman's console. Six knots, I read.

'Kay! John!' I snapped. 'Something's wrong! She should be doing eight knots by now!'

Tideman indicated the wind direction indicator. 'The wind's changing – it's veered ten degrees astern.'

'We've struck a flat spot in her sailing performance,' Kay added. 'The wind's too far aft for her to be at her best – it's almost dead astern now.'

'The after sails are blanketing those for'ard at this angle of wind,' said Tideman. 'The proper way to cope would be to tack downwind to increase her speed.'

'I can't tack in these confined waters,' I replied.

'Kay?' I hoped she might come up with some solution.

'She's doing the best she can under the circumstances,' she replied.

'Stealing the wind.'

Perhaps my acute anxiety threw the fragment of old clipper lore to the forefront of my mind. When the clippers found themselves in such a situation they reefed the sails aft to allow a flow of air to those in front. I couldn't vouch for the aerodynamics of such a tactic, but I knew it had worked. There was no time now to discuss the merits of such a method.

'Reef all sails on Number Five and Six masts aft!' I ordered Tideman.

As his fingers reached for the control switches, Kay protested. 'No, Peter, no! It won't work!'

I would know in a moment. 'Paul,' I said, 'give me a minute-by-minute speed read-out.'

It was impossible to tell simply by feel whether my desperation throw had come off.

We waited.

Then Paul's voice came through. 'Six and a half knots.'

Was it working or was it purely a momentary fluctuation of wind which had won us the extra half knot?

'Where's the destroyer, Paul?'

'Abreast Tussac Point.'

'Ah!' The cork was heading for the neck of the bottle! Where she was now, the warship could still turn for a pursuit, but within the next few hundred metres the shallows would lock her in.

'She's slowing – down to about four knots. Guess she's feeling her way.'

Then he exclaimed excitedly. 'Hey! Seven knots on the log – picking up, what's more.'

After what seemed an eternity, Paul reported again. 'Eight and a half knots nearer nine. Second way-point now abeam.'

Half a kilometre now to our turn! Then the direction of the wind would switch to abeam, *Jetwind*'s best sailing conditions. Then I would throw in the full power of the after sails as well as the royals, now reefed out of sight at her mast-heads. The time for concealment would then be over. We would be in full view of the destroyer through The Narrows entrance.

I gave Kay a knowing smile and she responded with a thumbs-up sign.

When I spoke again to Paul, my voice was hoarse with strain. 'Paul – what's happening out there?'

'Target half a kilometre, maybe a little more, north of The Narrows.'

The cork was in the bottle! The warship could no longer turn to pursue us!

The two ships converged on the narrow gap from opposite directions – the warship at four knots and *Jetwind* driving along now at over ten.

'Way-point three abeam,' reported Paul.

The final marker!

The next crucial stage was our ninety-degree turn into the mouth of The Narrows.

I waited. The silent dark bridge waited. Grohman was drawn to the vicinity of the wheel by my terse orders.

Suddenly a shore light stood out to port. Navy Point!

My heart raced as I made out beyond it a white mast-head light. Silhouetting upperworks and guns, a flashing light also swept into view. The *Almirante Storni*!

Now she could see us!

Grohman let out an oath in Spanish. 'There she is, Captain Rainier. It will be better for you to stop playing games now.'

'Set the royals! All sail! All sail!' I ordered.

'How far to our turn, Paul?'

'One hundred, maybe a hundred and fifty metres.'

'Speed?'

'Ten and a half knots – nudging eleven.'

'Stand by!' I told Jim Yell at the wheel. I felt him tense. Tideman's eyes left his instruments and he gave me a long inquiring look. What I did next was anyone's guess.

'Ready about!' I snapped.

'Turn!' It was Paul.

'Down helm!'

Jim Yell spun the spokes.

'Steer zero-zero-five!'

'Kay – quick!'

She rapid-fired our predetermined calculations; I passed them on to Tideman.

'Sail trim – thirty degrees!

'Rudder angle – thirty degrees!

'Course angle to true wind – seventy degrees!

'Angle of inflow of sail – ten degrees!'

The low loom of Engineer Point and its light – twin to Navy Point – came up out of the half light, fronted by the fatal barrier of kelp. It wasn't more than 100 metres away. We must not be pushed sideways into it.

'Drift?' I inquired peremptorily.

'Ten degrees.'

Jetwind swung at right angles towards the mouth of The Narrows. The wind switched abeam.

Then it happened.

I had not taken into account just how powerful were her aerofoils. I felt the smash of the gale and her wild lunge all at once.

Jetwind went over on her side.

The bridge canted steeply to starboard. Tideman, Kay, Grohman and myself were nearly thrown off our feet.

I grabbed a console and hung on. 'Kay, how far can she go over?'

'Nine degrees maximum!'

Tideman intoned levelly, 'Eight and a half degrees inclination!'

'Let go something, Peter!' Kay cried out. 'Half her freeboard is under! She's going clean over!'

But *Jetwind* did not. She spun round in a racing turn, shook herself upright, put her bows into one of the opensea rollers coming through The Narrows in a burst of spray, and leapt forward as if I'd thrown a throttle wide. It was a fantastic, exhilarating performance.

Jetwind straightened still further as Tideman adjusted the yards. She tore at the gap. Twelve – nearly thirteen – knots.

'All lights on!' I ordered. 'Burn all sidelights!'

Now I *wanted* the *Almirante Storni* to see *Jetwind*. It was part of my plan.

There was no doubt now that she had spotted us. The warship's silhouette elongated slightly as she turned aside a trifle to give *Jetwind* legal right of way – as little as she dared in that narrow channel.

'Paul?' I said tentatively.

'Yeah?'

'I myself am eye-balling the situation from now on.'

'Jeez!' He let out a whoop. 'Whaddayaknow!'

A warning flare fired from the destroyer bathed the choppy waters in a baleful glare. The wind caught the floating light and carried it towards *Jetwind*.

The climax, and crucial stage, of my plan was at hand.

In a minute or two the warship would be abeam Navy Point. We raced on for the next 200 metres or so to accelerate to maximum speed. We were heading – correctly, as the rule of the road required – on the side of The Narrows opposite the warship. *Jetwind* was now logging fourteen knots – soon she would make more. Under any circumstances The Narrows would be a tight fit for two ships, especially one being a sailer and travelling at *Jetwind*'s speed. The warship itself was not doing more than five knots.

I set my secret plan in motion.

'Down helm – a point and a half!' I snapped. Then, to Tideman, 'Brace up all yards two points!'

Next, 'Reef the main-courses on all masts! Up, up, up!'

'Peter! In God's name, what are you doing!' Kay exclaimed.

The checks and balances my plan required were razor-edged.

'Stow all main-yards – loading positions! Keep the fore-yard as it is!'

All lower yards were now flush with their masts as for cargo stowage, except the fore-yard from whose tip dangled the anchor.

'You're going to ram her!' gasped Tideman.

Jetwind bulleted towards the *Almirante Storni*, port side to port side – the side supporting the stay-mast supporting her electronic search gear.

The idea may have been in Grohman's mind all along;

certainly it was precipitated into action by Tideman's exclamation.

Out of the corner of my eye I saw his sudden movement. He reached for the 'chicken button' in its scarlet switchbox.

One touch of that button and the emergency explosive charges would blast away *Jetwind*'s top-gallant and royal masts. She would go wildly out of control. Then anything could happen.

Grohman's fingers tugged at the clip securing the switchbox's glass panel.

'Grohman!'

I must have yelled, moved and hit him all at once. Certainly I have no recollection of three separate movements. The blow caught him at the curve of his jaw and neck, below his right ear. He sprawled untidily in front of the helmsman.

'Keep your eyes on your course!' I said automatically. With Jim Yell such a warning was superfluous.

I regained my balance and faced round. Tideman, with iron will, kept his eyes fixed on the warship ahead. All the colour had gone from Kay's face.

Jetwind's bow now pointed obliquely at *Almirante Storni*'s. From that angle we would cut her in half just for'ard of her bridge.

I threw open *Jetwind*'s bridge window for maximum vision. The warship's siren screamed above the roar of the gale.

'Up helm half a point!'

Jetwind's knifing bow veered slightly away from its target. High above it, all of thirty metres of the fore-yard projected over both sides of the ship. I had to go in close for the yard and its killer anchor to do its job. Too close, and both ships would sink after colliding; too far, and *Jetwind*'s game would be up.

'Port, a couple of spokes!'

Tideman's choice of helmsman had been brilliant. Jim Yell was licking his dry lips, but standing up to my orders like the cool veteran he was.

Jetwind drove at the warship.

'Hold her off,' I ordered Yell. 'Just graze the destroyer's stay with the yard-arm.'

When a collision seemed inevitable, *Jetwind* straightened out at the last moment. The distance between the warship's low side and *Jetwind*'s high storm gunnels appeared to be paper thin. But *Jetwind* headed past.

I saw an officer on the other bridge screaming and brandishing his fists. All the time the warship's siren whooped like mad.

The yard-arm swept over the destroyer's side. I saw men on the bridge dive for cover as the anchor flailed at them.

They weren't my target.

The anchor struck the warship's steel deck in a shower of sparks as she rose on a wave. It ricocheted high.

I shouted my orders as it struck the stay and snagged fast.

'Starboard! Two points! Hold her off!'

There was a violent jerk. For a moment I thought the stay mast would hold, and the two ships, passing each other at a combined speed of nearly twenty knots, would be dragged together. They hung for an undecided millisecond, then the stay ripped loose. A few millions' worth of radar, radio antennae, and all the complex electronics of a modern warship were ripped out like a rotten tooth. A shower of debris scattered along the torpedo and depth-charge platform aft.

Jetwind was free.

The *Almirante Storni* fell astern, blind, helpless, emasculated.

The silence was broken by Paul's voice, stunned and hoarse with admiration. 'Now the shit will hit the fan!'

Jetwind drove clear of The Narrows, clear for Cape Pembroke and the open sea beyond, clear for Gough and the Cape.

Chapter 16

'Suspended First Officer Anton Grohman on grounds of . . .'

I stopped writing and stared at the ship's formal log. On grounds of . . . what? I looked round my cabin where the previous night we had held our council of war before *Jetwind*'s break-out. It seemed light years away instead of a mere twelve hours. The illusion of night was still present, however, because of the storm – it was dark enough to need electric light.

' . . . grounds of . . . dereliction of duty?'

Would any official inquiry consider that Grohman had failed in his duty by trying to stop his captain carrying out a crazy, outrageous action against a warship of a friendly power?

I scrapped the phrase and lit another cigarette. I wanted to get shot of the Grohman problem and return to *Jetwind*'s bridge. In the insulated confines of the cabin I could not share in the splendid exhilaration of feeling the ship tear along at eighteen knots or hear the mad music of the mounting gale. Even the motion of the ship was damped, it seemed. Even I was surprised at how steady a platform the deck presented. Her mighty sail plan – I was carrying everything to royals – was holding the ship against the bursting wave crests just as spoilers and aerofoils hold down a Grand Prix racer against a track.

We were clear of the land mass of the Falklands now. With the forty-knot gale holding abaft her starboard beam – her best point of sailing – *Jetwind* seemed determined to show exactly what she was capable of.

Blast Grohman!

I sat down and wrote quickly without pausing to weigh the words too judicially:

'. . . on grounds of endangering the safety of the ship and the lives of the crew.'

Which, I thought ironically, had been exactly what I'd done.

There was a peremptory knock at the cabin door.

'Come in!'

It was Grohman. I snapped the log book shut. I had already passed judgement on him. I scarcely wanted to hear his story.

His quick move across to my desk had something of a South American jaguar in it – lithe, muscular, sinister. I could almost imagine muscles rippling under his tight black polo-necked sweater. The collar did not reach high enough to mask the bruise and swelling on his jawbone where I had hit him.

'You're going ahead with this crazy business?' he blurted before I had time to speak.

'Listen,' I snapped. 'I don't consider I owe you any more explanations. As for an answer, take a look at *Jetwind*'s course.'

'You are still in Malvinas' territorial waters.'

'I don't know what Malvinas means,' I retorted sarcastically. 'If you mean, I'm in Falklands' territorial waters, you've under-estimated the distance *Jetwind* has travelled. We're nearly a hundred and twenty miles east-northeast of Port Stanley at this moment. That's well outside anyone's territorial waters.'

'Malvinas' territorial waters have been proclaimed as two hundred nautical miles. The same applies to all Argentinian waters.'

'Listen, Grohman,' I said. 'The sooner you forget all this crap about your country's rights, the better for your sea-going career. It's already cost you your job as first officer of *Jetwind*. You're as full of hang-ups about it as a forty-year-old virgin is about sex.'

His eyes blazed. I was reminded again of a predator. He didn't seem to take in what I was saying about his shipboard position.

'You . . . you . . . have insulted my country's Navy. You

136

have damaged one of our best ships. In Argentinian waters! You have broken international law. You have offended against my country's honour, most of all . . .'

'Cut it out!' I broke in. 'You talk like a character in a bloody Spanish soap opera. I'm on my way. Nothing you or your tin-pot Navy can do about it will stop me.'

'No?' He thrust his face at me. 'And who is the great Captain Rainier? My Navy will come after you . . .'

I gestured deckwards. 'In this weather? No destroyer could make even twelve knots the way the sea's running without breaking herself in two. You're still sailor enough to realize that. Moreover, your precious *Almirante Storni* is a dockyard job for months to come.'

'Long-range search aircraft will find you . . .'

'Nonsense, and you know it. There isn't an Orion closer than the nearest American base and that's the only plane capable of flying the distance *Jetwind* will be before anything can be done. Not even an Orion could fly safely through this weather – or what's building up.'

Mercurially, the anger seemed to drain completely out of him. What remained was more sinister than his melo-dramatics.

'You will pay for this, Captain Rainier,' he said quietly. 'You will pay for this.'

'I have suspended you, as from last night, on grounds of endangering the ship and the lives of those aboard,' I said. 'Shall I add insubordination?'

He shrugged.

'What the hell did you do it for?' I demanded. 'If you'd blasted away *Jetwind*'s top-gallant masts there in The Narrows, we'd have been into the rocks at Engineer Point before I could have done a thing.'

His silence said everything.

I went on. 'You're confined to your quarters, as of now. If you set foot outside your cabin, I'll have you locked up.'

'You, not Tideman, should have been in the Royal Navy.'

Which reminded me that Tideman had been on the bridge all night. Like myself, the feel of the great ship under our feet had banished all need for sleep and had thrown up those inner resources which only a Cape Horner can draw upon.

'That's the way it is, Grohman.' I dismissed him.

At that moment Arno, the radio operator, entered with a signal. His enthusiasm caused him to give only the most perfunctory of knocks. I still wonder how the course of events might have been otherwise precipitated had he paused long enough for me to have got rid of Grohman. Arno, of course, could not guess that Grohman had been fired.

Arno was beaming with excitement. 'Weather Routing report, as you ordered, sir. Portishead radio. They've been pretty smart about opening up their service to *Jetwind* again.'

Thomsen had laid on for *Jetwind* the skill of a special weather team at the Bracknell Meteorological Service in Britain. Its purpose was to advise and guide *Jetwind* according to data gathered from the surface, upper air, and from satellite observations on the best route to steer, wind, sea, and weather-wise. Bracknell's weather routing is the finest in the world; its communications match it.

Portishead's signal read:

TO RAINIER, JETWIND, JWXS, VIA PORTISHEAD RADIO SEVERE LOW AT 53S 58W EASTMOVING 40 KNOTS. NOW ADVISE TO FOURFOUR SOUTH THREEZERO WEST THENCE GREAT CIRCLE TO CAPE OF GOOD HOPE . . .

I snorted to myself. Bracknell was playing it safe suggesting the old conventional windjammer way to the Cape from the Horn. That wasn't the way to break records. That wasn't the way I had flogged *Albatros*. And *Albatros*'s route was exactly the one I intended to hell-drive *Jetwind* – where the great winds and the great storms were. I could do without the fancy weather satellites with their sensors to measure surface temperatures, the state of the wind and the state of the sea from hundreds of kilometres out in space. I was what the weathermen called 'ground truth' – the guy on the spot, the sailor who *knew* what was happening in his own surroundings.

I read on:

SATELLITE PICTURES INDICATE WORLD'S LARGEST ICEBERG TROLLTUNGA EITHER STRANDED OR ADRIFT IN GENERAL AREA APPROX 500 TO 800 MILES SOUTHWEST GOUGH PLUS VARIOUS LARGE ISOLATED DRIFTING BERGS. THESE CONSTITUTE MAJOR HAZARD. STRONGLY ADVISE THEREFORE AGAINST YOUR ORIGINAL PROJECTED ROUTE. METBRACK. 18/09h00.

Trolltunga! Like a film clip, a film clip merged with a dream or a nightmare, I relived what I had seen from *Albatros*'s deck. Ice – I did not know what had been ice or what had been hallucination. Rising clouds of vapour – I did not know whether it had been vapour or the shadows of a lone sailor's disordered mind. And that other thing which I had seen . . .

I heard Arno's voice as if from a long distance. 'Trolltunga, sir. I queried the word. It's a bit unusual, but the repeat spelling was the same . . .'

I looked up and saw him on the other side of the desk regarding me with a curious expression.

Grohman was standing beside him. He must have read the signal upside-down. The expression on his face wasn't curiosity. It was naked murder.

'You can't take *Jetwind* that way,' he said almost pleadingly. 'You must not . . .'

At first I attributed Grohman's expression and tone of voice to fear. Could it be that he was scared stiff? His face was white; his pallor against the blackness of his hair gave him a mortuary air. Had Grohman, in fact, turned and run after Captain Mortensen's death?

The three of us at my desk might have been a waxworks tableau. For about twenty seconds surprise, fear and contempt seared between us like a laser beam cutting into the dark places of three minds.

Then in the distance, like the end of a boxing round, there came the imperative ring of an electric bell.

'Excuse me, sir,' said Arno. 'That's my alarm. Another signal's coming in.'

He dived for the radio office.

Grohman's voice was hoarse and constricted. 'You'd be advised to take the northerly route. Bracknell recommends it. The other way . . . it's not safe . . . the signal says so . . . there's the biggest iceberg in the world . . .'

I tried to hold his eyes while I picked up the phone but he evaded mine. 'John?' I asked Tideman on the bridge. 'Come down to my cabin right away.'

I stood up and yelled, 'Grohman, pull yourself together! I'm going the way I choose, Trolltunga or no biggest bloody iceberg in the world!'

Whatever admixture of Scottish, Spanish and Indian blood ran in his veins produced a startling result. 'I warn you, do not take the Trolltunga route!' I wasn't sure any longer about my diagnosis that he was frightened.

'Get out!' I snapped. 'Keep to your quarters, if *you* want to be safe. If I find you on the bridge or in any other of the operational areas, I'll put you in irons!'

He whirled round and almost collided with Tideman coming in with Brockton.

Brockton said after Grohman had brushed past him, 'That guy looks as if he could frag you, Peter.'

'I've just axed him.'

'Make it official, for my part. Put it in the poop sheet.'

'I have already.'

Then I tossed the Metbrack signal across to Tideman. Brockton read it over his shoulder.

The reaction from both men startled me. It was as though a shot of adrenalin had passed through their veins. I could almost feel their vibrations.

'Trolltunga!' Tideman's eyes went very bright. Then, as if seeking to regain control of himself without giving away his feelings, he said casually, 'I had set the computer to our Gough position and Cape destination. Through the automatic pilot it will make the first six alterations for a

Great Circle course – all that will have to be changed, in the light of this.'

Whatever Trolltunga meant to Brockton, the news caught him off-balance. Like Tideman, his cover-up made him over-articulate.

'Trolltunga, eh? That's the biggest ice baby ever to come out of Antarctica! We located her first in the Weddell Sea from one of the old ESSA satellites way back in 1967, I guess it was. She was born big – a hundred and three kilometres by sixty. That's almost the size of the state of Delaware. And even after all these years of drifting about the Southern Ocean she's still the biggest – fifty-six by twenty-three kilometres, I think it was, the last time we measured her . . .'

I stared at him. I'd had my showdown with Grohman. He was bad news. These two were good news; on my side. However, I had finally to penetrate their cover. They had a lot of explaining to do. Ordinary yachting journalists cannot usually handle highly sophisticated electronics and discuss the dimensions and origin of the world's largest iceberg at the drop of a signal, so to speak. Nor do they ordinarily lapse into Navy jargon when their guard is down. And what was Trolltunga to Tideman? Like icebergs, five-sixths of the truth about them was concealed.

I went on matter of factly, '*Jetwind* will follow the same route as *Albatros*. Briefly, I'm taking her eastnortheast until I cross the fifty-degree south line a little short of forty west. From there on there's a one-knot current in our favour – I discovered it in *Albatros* – and we can count on a westerly or southwesterly gale almost continuously. We'll intersect the Trolltunga ice danger zone about six hundred miles southwest of Gough. After Gough it will be a straight run to the finishing tape at the Cape.'

It was as if what I had just said had erased the strain of his long stint of duty from Tideman's face. He made a great effort to be non-committal.

'How many days have we scheduled to make Gough?'

'About six and a half – as of now.'

'Good,' he said, half to himself. 'That's very good, Peter.'

Brockton said obliquely, using a similar satisfied tone as Tideman, 'By the time you got to the Trolltunga area in *Albatros* you must have been pretty short on sleep, Peter.'

I wondered what he was driving at. 'I was.'

He laughed, a kind of tell-me-all-pal laugh. 'Just the sort of time-lapse when lone sailors get tired enough to hallucinate and see their mother-in-law climbing up the mast, or even spot an imaginary aircraft flying overhead?'

He had given me the opening I was looking for.

'Sit down,' I said. 'Both of you have a lot of explaining to do.'

Chapter 17

I picked on Brockton first.

'Paul,' I said. 'I'm ready to tell you about my hallucinations. In return, you tell me who you really are.'

'What do you mean?'

'You know perfectly well what I mean. First, however, I want you both to know that I realize you're on my side. You're no yachting magazine writer, Paul. No journalist could possibly have handled all that sophisticated equipment the way you did.'

'The America Cup trials . . .' he started.

'Cut it out,' I replied impatiently. 'I don't believe it. You don't act like a reporter and you don't talk like a reporter. You haven't written or filed a single story since you boarded *Albatros*. Even in Knysna you were much more interested in my so-called hallucinations than in reportage. Now you've given yourself away again. You discuss Trolltunga like an expert. Not many have ever heard of Trolltunga except a few scientists or weather-men. But you're able to give chapter and verse about the world's biggest iceberg. Your detailed knowledge of the Southern Ocean is, to say the least, phenomenal.'

'A journalist has to know his beat.'

'Rubbish, Paul! Journalists usually have no more than a working knowledge of their subjects. As a group they lack in-depth knowledge. Not you, though.'

'So what?'

'You maintain the act fairly well normally but when the pressure mounts you give yourself away. If you want to know, you've something to do with the US Navy.'

He stood up and held out his hand. 'You win, fellah. I *am* a Navy man. Commander Paul Brockton. Glad to meet you, Peter.'

'That makes two naval men, Paul,' said Tideman.

'Thanks for coming clean, Paul,' I added. 'And now may I ask what is your function in these waters?'

'What I'm going to tell you is so classified that it could cost a man his life, if he talked.'

'You have my word.' Tideman nodded his agreement.

'Ever heard of Lajes?' he asked.

The name had a familiar ring. Before I could crystallize my thoughts, however, Tideman said, 'The American Atlantic base, on the island of Teceira in the Azores.'

'Correct.'

'Where does Lajes connect wtih *Jetwind* and the Southern Ocean? The Azores are thousands of miles away.'

'I'll come to that,' answered Brockton. 'Near the main base at Lajes is a village named Agualva. It's so small that I guess the hundred men of my command doubled its population overnight. Back at Atlantic Fleet Command HQ in Norfolk, Virginia, my men are rated officially as Naval Securities Group Activities.'

'Go on.'

'We operate what is called a high frequency direction finding facility. In plain language, we monitor the movements of Soviet vessels in the Atlantic, subs in particular. We fly regular missions using Orion T-3s way out across the Central Atlantic Ridge and drop sonar buoys. These relay the sound of ships' engines to listeners at the Agualva tracking station. We also use other methods which the Reds would give their eye-teeth to know.'

'In short, you spy on the Soviet Fleet,' I said.

He nodded, but Tideman interrupted. 'You're not telling us much that's new, Paul. All this is pretty well known. It's also known that Lajes provides staging and logistic support for the U.S. Sixth Fleet. Lajes was very much in the headlines a while back when a lease agreement with Portugal regarding the base was renewed.'

Brockton went on, 'It was also in the headlines when the Russians claimed to have discovered the site of the legendary Atlantis not so far from Lajes. You may have seen a guy called Dr Andrei Aksenov on TV announcing the news to the world. We on Lajes itself knew different. The Reds are so determined to find out about our methods that they hatched up the Atlantis story as a cover to spy on Lajes.'

'Paul – all I can say is that you are a helluva long way from base aboard *Jetwind*. That's what I am primarily interested in.'

He dropped his voice, as if fearful he might be overheard. 'Recently, I and about twenty guys from Naval Securities Group Activities set up a secret listening base on Tristan da Cunha.'

'Now we're getting closer!' I exclaimed.

'Yeah,' he replied. 'Tristan is only two hundred and thirty nautical miles from Gough Island – and *Jetwind* is on her way to Gough.'

'We'll be there in less than a week if we keep our present speed,' added Tideman.

'What made your group move to Tristan?' I asked.

'There was an impressive build-up of Red signals emanating from this area,' replied Brockton thoughtfully. 'We haven't yet been able to pinpoint the source.'

'You can't fly those big Orions from Tristan,' I said. 'No airfield can take a plane like that anywhere between the Cape and South America.'

'There is one, but it's a powerful long way away,' answered Brockton. 'On Ascension Island. There's a big airfield there which was built during the war.'

'I'd say Tristan itself is a flight of close on two thousand miles from Ascension,' remarked Tideman.

'This build-up of signals . . .' Brockton resumed.

'Naval signals?' I interrupted.

'Aye,' he said, grimly. 'Naval signals. NAVWAG has 'em all on tape . . .'

'What's NAVWAG?' I queried.

'Navy Underwater Sound Reference Laboratory. To try and track the origin of the signals, the Navy fitted an Orion with special electronic gear – everything the latest, the most top secret. We filled her up with gas until it ran out of her wing tips. Every man aboard was a specialist – twelve of them. It constituted a top secret maximum range search, acoustic intelligence. And when I say maximum range, I mean maximum range. The Orion could stay airborne for eighteen hours, maybe even a little more. I myself spoke to the pilot, Captain Bill Werner, as the plane passed over Tristan. He gave me the okay – no problems. The Orion kept going. It entered the Southern Ocean Air-Launched Acoustical Reconnaissance Zone SSI . . .'

'What in hell's that?' I demanded.

Brockton was speaking fast and became agitated. 'That's the secret zone where we suspected a Red concentration. Werner ran into bad weather but he wasn't worried. An Orion is built to stand up to that sort of thing.'

As if to emphasize what he was saying, *Jetwind* gave a sudden pitch. I heard the crash of tons of water sluice along her deck.

'Then?'

'The plane's last position was about six hundred nautical miles southsouthwest of Gough, about eight hundred and fifty from Tristan.'

Brockton paused. The only sound was *Jetwind* shrugging off the waves.

I knew what was coming.

'The Orion vanished.'

'Just like that?' Tideman asked.

Brockton held my eyes.

'No, it wasn't just like that. We happen to have a taped in-flight recording of the Orion's last moments.'

'Was there a Mayday signal?'

'No Mayday. No time for it. I guess a missile got her.'

There was a long silence. Brockton leaned towards me. It was an accusing pose.

'Missile?' I repeated.

'I'm asking you, Peter.'

'How should I know?'

He replied, choosing his words carefully, 'It's almost a month ago – doesn't that mean anything to you, Peter?'

'Should it? I was at sea in *Albatros*. I wasn't in touch with the daily news.'

'This story didn't reach the newspapers,' he said grimly. 'Never will, while Group Securities has any say.'

'Why ask me, then?'

'The time, the place, the distance – they're all right.'

'I don't follow.' But I did.

'Just before Werner went in, he had located a target with his Searchwater radar. Searchwater is newer than tomorrow's dawn. Werner went down to look. Very low, under the cloud. He made a visual sighting. He reported a yacht, moving fast, under full sail.'

Tideman was staring at me now.

'So what? Some of the yachts in the Cape-Uruguay race returned from South America via Gough.'

'It wasn't an ordinary yacht, Peter. I've studied Werner's last words until I know 'em by heart. This is what he said: "They're not ordinary sails . . . they're sails with slits in 'em . . . looks like a kinda Venetian blind the wrong way up" . . .'

The seas reverberated along *Jetwind*'s hull.

'Well, Peter? There's only one boat afloat that tallies with that description – *Albatros*.'

There was another long silence. *Jetwind*'s hull was starting to creak. I averted my eyes from Brockton's

146

accusing stare to the ship's speed repeater. The needle was nudging twenty knots.

'*Albatros?*' Brockton prompted.

I didn't reply directly. 'Did the pilot say what conditions were like?'

'Yeah, like I said, I know every word Werner said: "The whole ocean's like a vast Shivering Liz pudding made of icebergs – it's all steaming with mist and fog."'

Still I stalled. 'Shivering Liz?'

'It's a Navy phrase,' Brockton explained, still searching my face. 'Sort of gelatine pudding.'

'That's not a bad description,' I conceded. 'That's the way it was, Paul. All Shivering Liz.'

'I didn't ask about weather conditions,' he said.

'I saw the plane go in,' I answered. He gave a satisfied little sigh. 'Yet the weather and sea conditions are important to my story, Paul. It was like a dream, like the sort of hallucination you keep quizzing me about. I thought I *was* hallucinating. There *couldn't* be a plane, not there, I told myself at the time. It was thousands of miles from anywhere. There was ice all around. Mist. The sea was steaming. I couldn't distinguish what was ice and what was perhaps dream.'

'Bill Werner's Orion wasn't downed by a dream,' he retorted.

For a moment I relived that morning on the edge of sanity – that morning of the Shivering Liz ocean.

'The Orion was starting to circle – he must have spotted *Albatros*. Then a vapour trail sprang up out of the sea, from somewhere amongst the bergs. I remember how the missile's vapour trail ducked and weaved and then homed in on the plane. It hit a starboard inboard engine.'

Brockton nodded and repeated from the tape, '"Captain! Captain! There! Starboard! Coming up out of the sea!"' Hammering the point home, he asked, 'And then?'

'There was nothing.'

'Nothing? You must have seen the plane crash.'

'As I said before, I thought I was hallucinating. The

plane, the missile – everything – was swallowed up by the mist and the bergs. I saw nothing, heard nothing.'

'You must have heard the noise of the crash or the explosion of the missile.'

'I repeat, there was no sound. The gale must have blown it away.'

'You didn't search for survivors?'

'You don't put a yacht about in that kind of sea to look for a figment of your imagination.'

'*Albatros* kept going?'

'I was clear of the thick ice by afternoon. At the time I thought it was my mind which had begun to clear. Yes, I kept going – hard.'

Tideman interrupted, with a curious intonation in his question. 'Where did all this take place, Peter?'

'I don't know. I hadn't had a position sight for days because of the storm. Night and day merged. I managed to obtain a radio fix from Gough a couple of days after the incident.'

Brockton persisted. 'Why didn't you report the Orion affair?'

'To whom? How did I know whose plane it was when I didn't even know whether I'd seen one? Imagine if I had radioed a report like that. The isolation has sent him round the bend, they'd have said. Rightly, under the circumstances.'

Brockton jumped up. 'If only you had! We would have picked up the message on Tristan – we were monitoring every wavelength! We could have nailed the bastard who did it! Now it's too late! *Where did that missile come from, Peter?*'

'Everything was shadowy and insubstantial,' I replied. 'I'm still not sure whether I saw it happen or not.'

'It happened all right,' Brockton retorted. 'That lost Orion and her crew were not a shadow.'

'Why,' I asked, 'if the Orion was in fact shot down by a Red missile, should there be any Russian naval interest in those waters – the area *Jetwind* is now heading for? It's utterly and totally unfrequented. The last ship recorded before *Albatros* was a British survey vessel which visited the South Sandwich Islands sixteen years earlier. And the South Sandwich group is a hell of a way south from where the Orion crashed.'

Brockton's reaction surprised me. He rounded on Tideman. There was steel in his voice. 'John, you've done a hell of a lot of close listening. You haven't spoken much. I said earlier, a man could die for what he has heard in this cabin today. I don't buy your Royal Navy Adventure School story. The Royal Navy doesn't send its officers and men on pleasure cruises on yachts round the world just for them to catch a suntan. By your own admission, you've been three times round the Horn. You've also got some tough cookies here with you in *Jetwind*. You're not aboard *Jetwind* simply in order to sky-shoot your reputation as a sailor. What's the name of *your* game?'

Chapter 18

———————◆———————

Tideman reached into a pocket and threw on the desk what looked like a metal-cased slide-rule.

'As you say, Paul, men could die for what they heard in this cabin today.'

He leaned forward and fiddled with the instrument. The brass casing snapped open on a spring. A steel blade nearly the length of a man's hand shot out. Tideman clinched the brass casing between his fingers. Now it doubled as a handle for a hellish weapon. He smiled at me, a microwave smile that had no warmth in it.

'Like your plane crash, it makes no sound,' he said.

He addressed Brockton. 'Sound, or the lack of sound, is the name of my game. A yacht makes no sound. It hasn't any engines to be picked up by a sonar buoy, or by any other electronic marvel you drop from an Orion. Even with every latest listening gadget you can't hear a yacht off Cape Horn from under the water.'

Brockton said, 'I think I get it.'

'I don't,' I interjected sharply.

Tideman gestured at Brockton. 'We're in the same game. Our approach is different. Paul uses the latest sophisticated electronic techniques; I use man's oldest friend, the sail.'

'Tracking . . . what?'

'My function is to monitor the passage of Red submarines rounding Cape Horn via the Drake passage,' he replied levelly. 'The Royal Navy yachts I've sailed there have been a cover. Sonar buoys are planted in advance by R.N. ships – you remember HMS *Endurance*, which sheep-dogged the passage of the Whitbread Round the World yachts in those waters? It was given out that she was there in case the yachts ran into trouble. It was a bluff. *Endurance* and three other Navy ships belong – officially – to the British Antarctic Survey. So they have a legitimate purpose in hanging round the Drake Passage and Cape Horn. Their true function, however, is to plant secret sonar buoys which detect Red subs negotiating the Horn and relay their movements to monitoring instruments aboard Services yachts such as mine. The yacht is the perfect vehicle for the job – silent, immune from counter-detection by Red subs' underwater listening devices. Every one of the boats I have commanded has had enough secret equipment on board to make a Russian spy's mouth water. I and four sailor-paratroopers are a top secret team.' He toyed with the dagger. 'I intend to see we remain top secret.'

'I got to hand it to you, John,' said Brockton slowly. 'It's an approach we never thought about. We're comrades-in-arms, I guess.' He reached out and shook Tideman's hand. Tideman seemed slightly embarrassed by the gesture.

'The term comrades-in-arms implies an enemy,' I said. 'What you're doing seems rather less hostile – watch-dogs.'

'Never!' retorted Brockton. 'The Reds think in terms of

sea denial, we in the West in terms of sea control. The Red aim is to build a naval infra-structure round the entire world – and they're busy doing it.'

I must have looked sceptical, for he asserted, 'Let's take a look at the Drake Passage to start with. Got a chart handy?'

I indicated one on my desk. He spread it out. It was on a small scale, showing the top of South America, Cape Horn, the ocean southward to Antarctica, and the Southern Ocean as far as the Cape of Good Hope.

Brockton laid his hand across the sector south of Cape Horn.

'The Drake Passage is five hundred nautical miles wide,' he said, picking his words. 'It's what we call in terms of global naval strategy a "choke point". Narrow, easily controlled access points in the oceans – such as the Strait of Hormuz leading from the Persian Gulf to the Indian Ocean, or the Gulf of Aden and the Horn of Africa, or again the Straits of Malacca at Singapore, or the Cape of Good Hope . . .'

'All of them now Red dominated,' broke in Brockton.

'Hardly the Cape,' I said.

'No?' went on Brockton. 'Sixty per cent of the West's oil flows round the Cape. What did the United States do when the Red threat was directed towards it? Gave its tacit blessing to Marxist regimes in Angola and Mozambique with their naval and air bases able to dominate the sea-way, one of the world's most important feed routes. Pah! It makes me want to throw up!'

He looked indeed as if he wanted to throw up. But he resumed, 'The Reds gain their naval objectives by establishing puppet regimes in states adjoining strategic choke points. The way is then open for their naval squadrons – and make no mistake, there are one hell of a lot of them – to block these routes. The West is then forced to its knees and is subject to political blackmail. It's a technique they've perfected. I don't have to tell you the sorry story of each one of these global choke points – you know it already. The last one that still remains undominated is – the Drake Passage. It's a free-for-all submarine alley for American, British and Soviet nuclear-armed subs. Yet it's in mortal danger of going the way of those other choke points.'

Tideman added gravely, 'The Drake Passage is not a straight logistics problem, Peter. It's greatly bedevilled and complicated by political factors.'

'You mean Argentina?'

'Argentina is up to the neck,' he answered. 'You must get the overall picture clear. The Drake Passage is dominated geographically to the northeast by the British-owned Falklands Islands, and to the south by the South Shetland Islands, which are also British, as you know. I want you to visualize the Drake Passage problem from the point of view of deep-diving nuclear subs . . .'

'Hold it for a moment, John,' Brockton broke in. 'I'm going to get something for you two to see. If I don't come back within three minutes come and look for me with that dagger of yours, John. It's as top secret as all that.'

He jumped up and was gone. Neither Tideman nor I knew how to handle the awkward silence which followed.

Jetwind gave me the opportunity to shift to neutral ground, so to speak. The ship gave a heavy jar as the bow slammed into a wave; the sea crashed along the deck. Both of us glanced automatically at the speed log.

'Twenty knots,' said Tideman. 'I've never had her so fast as this before.'

'She must be starting to steer like a bitch,' I replied. 'I hope the wheel will hold her. She's putting her head down deep. She won't achieve her true maximum this way.'

'During the wind-tunnel tests I asked for staysails between the masts just for the sake of the steering,' he said. 'The experts all opposed the idea. Aerodynamically inefficient, they maintained. I agree with that, but it isn't the complete answer in relation to ship handling.'

'Did Kay agree too?'

'I think she went along with the majority because she couldn't argue against the scientific line-up without having the practical knowledge herself.'

'What this ship needs now is some sailoring know-how . . .' Then Brockton reappeared.

I had never seen a chart like the one he smoothed out for us to examine. It was made of tissue-thin paper with a kind of silvered backing.

It didn't need the superscription 'Zone SS 2 Top Secret' to tell me what it was all about. Undersea channels, depths, underwater mountain ranges and ocean bottom contours were all demarcated. Here and there a small cross in purple ink showed the location of an underwater electronic beacon.

It was a nuclear submarine chart of the Drake Passage.

Both men craned over my shoulder; Brockton was breathing heavily.

He traced a clearly marked channel which negotiated a maze of underwater mountain peaks. 'This is the route American subs use,' he explained. 'As you see, it runs zig-zag through the centre section of the Drake Passage. It's roughly one thousand fathoms or two thousand metres deep. It finally emerges here – near South Georgia in the east. That's the sort of route the Reds aim to seal.'

Tideman added, 'The immediate Cape Horn area is no bet for the deep-diving subs – it's too shallow, only a hundred fathoms in places. They have to stay well south to negotiate the passage, beyond Diego Ramirez Island.'

I said, 'Accordingly, that's the route your yachts took.'

'Aye,' he agreed. 'That was the route.'

Brockton pointed again, this time to a shallow area near the Falklands. 'This is the Burdwood Bank. It is ninety nautical miles south of the Falklands. Logistically, it's of great importance. It completely blocks the northeastern approaches to the Drake Passage as far as nuclear subs are concerned.'

'Why?'

'The Bank is so shallow,' Brockton replied. 'Its depth ranges from a mere forty-six to a hundred and forty-five metres. It would be straight suicide for a nuclear sub to attempt it – we've got the whole area, two hundred miles long and fifty wide, taped with electronic sensors.'

'It seems to me that, tactically speaking, the West holds all the aces,' I said. 'The entire area can be air and sea patrolled from the Falklands, or from the islands on the southern and eastern flanks.'

'I wish it were as simple as that,' answered Tideman. 'You forget that the land mass of South America at its southern tip belongs to two countries – Argentina and Chile. These two have carried on a border dispute for over a century. It flared up recently over the ownership of three tiny islands claimed by Chile which bar the eastern or Atlantic entrance to the Beagle Channel, one of the main waterways through the mass of islands near Cape Horn.'

'Tiny little islands like that can't be of any value to anyone, strategically or politically,' I objected.

'You don't know these Latin types, Peter,' said Brockton. 'They'd fight to their last drop of blood over a sombrero if that were an emotive issue.'

'The reason why those three little Chilean islands are so important is a question of principle,' Tideman explained. 'Argentina claims them according to the principle that she has the traditional right of access to the Atlantic Ocean. Chile equally claims right of access to the Pacific. Chile maintains a small naval base in the Beagle Channel at Puerto Williams – on one of the disputed islands.'

I burst out laughing. 'Puerto Williams! A naval base! What a joke! I staged south to Cape Horn in *Albatros* past Puerto Williams – it's a tin-pot little anchorage with a couple of houses!'

'That makes no difference,' Tideman said. 'It is the principle Argentina and Chile are disputing. The same thing applies to the Falklands. Argentina is strongly anti-British, as you no doubt gathered,' he went on with a slight smile. 'That white card business is one of the pin-pricks to keep the political pot boiling.'

'In addition,' said Brockton, sketching a large sector on the map, 'Argentina lays claim to all this vast area from the South Sandwich Islands in the Atlantic in the east through to the Pacific side of the Drake Passage – plus all the islands along its southern flank!'

'Think of those claims in terms of nuclear sub logistics and maybe something starts to stink,' said Brockton.

'Complete control of the Drake Passage,' I suggested.

'Exactly,' said Tideman. 'Plus the Falklands themselves with an airfield which could be expanded to take heavy maritime reconnaissance planes. You get the picture, Peter. Also, as you know, Argentina has proclaimed a two-hundred-mile territorial limit round all the islands she claims. That makes – in their terms – the Drake Passage Argentinian waters. Add to that the entire sea-passage you flew over between the South American mainland and the Falklands.'

'They can't be serious,' I said. 'It's surely nothing more than a lot of flag-waving.'

'It's a great deal more than that, Peter,' said Tideman. 'Some years ago a party of Argentinian patriots who styled themselves Group Condor staged a token invasion of the Falklands after hijacking a plane and forcing it to crash-land at Stanley. The incident was finally smoothed over diplomatically but it's left a nasty aftertaste.'

Brockton laughed. 'Just wait and see what you've stirred up by mucking about with their *Almirante Storni*, Peter.'

'Just an unfortunate accident.'

'You tell Argentina that,' he replied wryly.

'What Washington is deeply concerned about is that the Russians may attempt to instal a pro-Red Argentinian puppet regime in the Falklands. Then, with the co-operation of Argentina, a "friendly" Soviet Navy would effectively seal the Drake Passage. The last major link in their global choke point chain would then be complete. The United States and Britain would then have been totally out-manoeuvred.'

'There's a price tag to everything,' I replied. 'What is it in this case?'

'The price of Argentinian cooperation would be support by Russia for her claims to the Falklands-Cape Horn area as well as for her claims against Chile in the same region – backing for the principle of sole access to the South Atlantic by Argentina.'

'You've mentioned only Argentina,' I said. 'What about the attitude of Chile?'

'From the United States' point of view, Chile seems safe enough,' answered Brockton. 'The reactionary regime there is unlikely to cooperate with the Reds. There are no naval or air bases of any significance on Chile's western Pacific coast – it's too wild and rugged southwards – which could counter closure of the Drake Passage by the Soviet Navy.'

I eyed both men. 'Since we're putting our cards on the table, let me ask you both something. Paul, why were you so keen to travel aboard *Jetwind*?'

He hesitated a fraction of a second. 'I had to *know* exactly what *you* saw when the Orion went in.'

'That doesn't mean you had to make the run from the Falklands to the Cape.'

'True,' he answered. 'But as I said before, a crack team from Naval Securities Group Activities was specially moved from the Azores to Tristan because of a build-up of Red signals emanating from the Southern Ocean. We lost out over the Orion's deep probe. There are no ships at all in these waters, no aircraft routes. *Jetwind* is a once-only chance that something might turn up.'

'Why should it?'

'Your route stakes us right across the area we're interested in.'

'You weren't to know that when you first came aboard *Albatros*. You didn't even know then that I had been given command of *Jetwind*.'

He seemed a little taken aback by my cross-questioning. 'All I had to go on was that last sighting by the Orion of a yacht whose description fitted *Albatros*. I played it by ear from there.'

'What do you hope to learn still?'

'Who knows?'

I turned to Tideman. By hindsight later, I realized that he had had time to work on his story while Brockton was explaining his.

'John, your stamping-ground is Cape Horn, by your own admission. Every mile *Jetwind* goes takes you further from it. What do you hope to get out of *Jetwind*? You, plus four paratroopers?'

'Our Navy got tipped off by the U.S. Navy of a build-up in the South Atlantic,' he replied. 'We're even more handicapped by lack of ships and aircraft than the U.S. We're a shoestring outfit. Like Paul, I'm also taking a chance on something turning up.'

There was an imperative knock at the door.

'Come in!'

It was Arno, his face expressionless. He gave me a half-formal salute as if to underline the importance of the signal he handed to me. It was in plain language. It was from the Argentinian Navy.

TO RAINIER, JETWIND, JWXS, POSITION . . .'

I gasped – our position was stated exactly as it was half an hour before! I thought I had brushed *Jetwind*'s tracks clean!

RETURN TO PORT STANLEY IMMEDIATELY. SURRENDER TO *ALMIRANTE STORNI*. NON-COMPLIANCE WITH THIS ORDER WILL BE FOLLOWED BY APPROPRIATE AIR AND NAVAL ACTION.

I read the signal over to Tideman and Brockton. Tideman noted the position fix give-away even before Brockton.

'How the hell could the Argentinian Navy possibly know our position?'

'It tallies with the satellite navigator's read-out barely half an hour ago,' I replied. 'I mean to find out more about this.'

'Do you intend to comply with the order?' asked Brockton.

'What the hell do you think?' I retorted. 'It's a bluff. "Appropriate air and naval action"!' I snorted derisively. 'In this kind of storm? This is the sort of weather to exploit the sailing ship's built-in advantage over power. We're doing better all the time. I mean to get even more out of this ship still once I get on the bridge!'

'Good man!' Tideman said with warm sincerity.

Brockton paced the cabin excitedly. 'We'll lick these Red sonsofbitches yet – just the three of us! No goddam Soviet Fleet is going to seal the Drake Passage!'

My reply was aimed at throwing a bucket of water over his fervour.

'Both of you talk as if there's a war on.'

My remark had the desired effect on Brockton. His excitement vanished. The gravity which took its place was all the more striking by contrast. Tideman nodded agreement when he said,

'The war *is* on, Peter. It's not a shooting war – yet. It's a silent war. It's a war of move and counter-move deep under the oceans – deep as the nuclear subs run. The Drake Passage is the West's last great bastion. I am at war, John is at war.'

I indicated the Argentinian signal.

'It looks as if *Jetwind* is also at war.'

Chapter 19

A radio phone call I had put through to Thomsen in Cape Town broke up our meeting. Brockton and Tideman left the cabin, Tideman under orders to get some rest as soon as I could relieve him on the bridge.

My news left Thomsen ecstatic. He brushed aside the implications of the *Almirante Storni*. His enthusiasm was unbounded when he heard *Jetwind*'s progress and speed. There was a tough, I'll-show-them admiration in his voice when I told him the route I was taking. Fastest, but most perilous – the Trolltunga route. I cut short his congratulations. A lot could happen in 2100 miles to Gough, I told him before I rang off. What I wanted most now was to coax *Jetwind* up to her maximum.

I made for the door. As I reached it, it was thrown open as if the gale had suddenly burst its way below-decks.

It was Sir James Hathaway.

The impetus of his entry and a lurch from the ship caused him to stagger and trip over the old ship's bell on the floor which Robbie Lund had given me at Comodoro Rivadavia. Sir James stood glaring at me and the bell, as if torn between which he should curse first.

'Rainier! Why the devil do you hide yourself away? I've been trying to get hold of you all morning!'

I bit back my retort; he was *Jetwind*'s potential purchaser.

I said as civilly as I could, 'My job is to keep this ship moving. That comes first.'

Maybe he wasn't used to being answered back, but what I had to say seemed to mollify him. He reached for my hand. His grip was like a welter-weight's at a fight weigh-in.

It cost him an effort to say, 'Congratulations! You've done well, Rainier. Yesterday I couldn't have imagined myself saying that to any skipper who took over this ship.'

'Thanks.'

'Everyone on board is full of what you did to that bloody dago warship.'

'There may be more people than those aboard talking about it soon,' I said. 'The Argentinian Navy, for example.'

'The hell with them,' he rejoined cheerfully. 'The United Nations included. They'll blow it up and make capital of the incident before the international forum, make no mistake. Lots of tub-thumping from the Reds into the bargain. That's my view. Take it or leave it.'

'They won't leave it, you can be sure.'

His attention seemed divided between me and the old bell.

'Where'd you get this from? Ship's bells are my hobby.'

I was surprised that he admitted to having any weakness. I explained and he bent down and examined it.

'*Ambassador*, you say? She was a Lund ship, wasn't she?'

'It's generations since that line went out of business, Sir James.'

'Ship-owning is an ongoing business,' he retorted saltily. 'Ships driven by fossil fuels such as oil are on their way out, in the same way that coal killed the windjammer. The next phase is the genuine sail-driven, aerodynamic cargo carrier. That's why I became interested in *Jetwind*.'

'I hope you still are interested.'

He seemed to dance up and down with excitement. 'Drive her, man! Show the world! Drive this bloody ship under! What's she logging at this moment?'

'Twenty knots – but she can do better.'

'Then why aren't you doing better? How much better?'

'Three, maybe a maximum of four, if the gale rises above Force Ten. And if I'm given the opportunity to get on my own bridge.'

For a second I thought he would explode, then he grinned. 'I don't like anyone brushing me off, but this once I'll take it.'

I didn't leave immediately; I paused for a diplomatic minute or two to tell the irascible little so and so about the ship-owners' rendezvous Thomsen had arranged at Gough. He appeared wary of my softer approach. Perhaps he thought I was trying to con him.

I added Weather Routing's warning about Trolltunga.

He considered me shrewdly. 'Why don't you deviate to miss the ice?'

'If I could sail *Albatros* that way by my own devices, then I can manage it with a ship full of electronic gadgetry.'

'I really believe you mean what you say, Rainier. But that first officer of yours will let you down – Grohman.'

'He won't. He's suspended.'

'That's what I like to hear. If a man can't go along with your ideas, there's only thing.' He gave one hand a mini karate chop with his other. 'The axe.'

He seemed a man of unpredictable switches of mood. Grohman having been disposed of, so to speak, his interest returned to the old bell.

'Have it for yourself,' I offered. 'Anything aboard this ship which hasn't got a computer attached belongs to the Dark Ages.'

'I'll keep it in my quarters for good luck,' he said. He hefted it up to go. I was surprised at his strength. He reminded me again of a Cock Robin boxer. 'One always needs the luck at sea, especially in a sailer.'

I hurried up to the bridge. The sea was a wild scene. My instinct told me even before I consulted the anenometer that the wind speed was over fifty knots. It was shearing off the overhanging crests of the rollers – about ten metres high and throwing the foam and spray in streaks like a giant fireman's hose. The rollers themselves had a thudding, killer punch to them, each one a threat to the fleeing ship.

In the bows there was enough water and spray over *Jetwind*'s deck to match an anti-nuclear washdown system. The ship was steady, but lying over far – almost to her full count of nine degrees. If she were ambushed by a sudden gust she would go over on her beam-ends and never come up again.

Kay was standing with Tideman at the control consoles. He had taken the royals off her; she was down to top gallants. Kay looked worried. As I joined them, *Jetwind* put her bows far down; hundreds of tons of sea came sweeping along the deserted decks.

Kay gave me a brief smile of welcome and said, 'Peter, the slamming is slowing her down. The resistance component of the sea-way is getting bigger all the time. In spite of the wind she's not travelling faster.'

Tideman added grimly, gesturing for'ard, 'Look at that!'

The next blow against the ship's bow was like hitting a solid wall.

Sweat poured down the helmsman's face. He wore only a shirt and jeans; they had big wet patches. He compensated heavily on the wheel as the bows tried to break away.

'She's very hard to hold any more,' he panted. 'I can't keep her steady, sir. If any of the rudder controls go, the ship's had it.'

Tideman gave me an inquiring look.

'Kay,' I asked, 'what sort of thrust is there on the sails?'

'I made the calculation about five minutes ago – roughly, about forty thousand horse-power.'

'But she's not getting the full benefit of that?'

'No, she's not. She's actually losing speed instead of picking it up. If we could stop the slamming it would raise the speed. I know theoretically what's happening, but I don't know what the practical answer is.'

'What – in theory – is happening?' I questioned her with my eyes fixed on *Jetwind*'s sails. 'A converter of solar energy into thrust,' Thomsen had termed them. Here then was that process – the sea white with fury, the tearing overcast black with rage, stooping so low at times that *Jetwind*'s royal masts were lost to sight, the ocean itself raging uncontrollably.

I formulated orders – radical, unheard-of orders.

'*Jetwind* is plunging violently in a pitching plane,' she was explaining. 'That's the problem. The movement is playing havoc with the aerodynamics. As the bow falls into the trough of a wave, there is an upward component of span-wise flow on all her foresails. Then as the bow hits the solid water of the next wave, that flow is ended abruptly and replaced by a sudden downward component as her bow rises to that wave. And so on. *Jetwind* could experience a stall like an aircraft – brought about by the span-wise flow if this continues.'

I interrupted her, noting how the lower part of the forecourse was blanketed and went slack as *Jetwind* dived deep into the troughs.

'Where is the main driving force centred?'

Kay answered unhesitatingly. 'About fifteen to twenty metres above the deck.'

Jetwind crashed into a bigger roller. It felt as unyielding as the Berlin Wall.

'She can't take this sort of punishment very long,' Tideman cautioned. 'Something must go.'

'Stand by,' I ordered. 'Stand by to slack off the fore-course.'

Kay looked startled.

'No way,' answered Tideman. 'You can't slack off *Jetwind*'s type of sails. They're fitted to form a single aerodynamic unit from truck to deck.'

'The thrust of the wind so high above the deck is ramming her bows down,' I said. 'Plus the fact that there's no lift for'ard.'

'Plus no stay-sails,' added Tideman.

'What's the size of the fore-course?' I asked Kay.

'About two hundred square metres.'

'That's a lot of sail,' I said. 'It's the sail for the job of lifting her bows if we can get the wind under it and balloon it out.'

'You can't do anything with it . . .' began Tideman.

'Raise the lower yard ten degrees port and starboard as for cargo loading,' I ordered. 'There's only one way then the sail can go – out like a balloon.'

'My oath!' exclaimed Tideman. 'Whoever would have thought of that!'

Kay grabbed my arm in protest. 'You can't do it, Peter! It'll wreck the effect of aerodynamic efficiency!'

I looked into her eyes. 'There are times at sea when you have to do what the sea calls for, not the wind-tunnel,' I said gently.

I turned away from her puzzled, resentful gaze. 'Carry on,' I told Tideman.

His fingers manipulated the controls. The great yard folded upwards, halted. The heavy dacron billowed. The wind started to get underneath it.

'Give it another five degrees,' I said.

Up went the yard again. Out ballooned the great sail. The next wave rushed at *Jetwind* with the solidity of a concrete tank-trap. Her bows rose, shouldered aside the water. There was no sickening slam.

Tideman exclaimed, 'You've lifted her bows two feet out of the water!'

The quartermaster was grinning. 'That's done it, sir! She steers like an angel now!'

Kay came close and took me impulsively by the upper arms. Her laugh had some tears in it. 'You're . . . you're a magician, Peter! You're the best afloat since Woodget skippered the *Cutty Sark*!'

I wanted to kiss her, but a ship's bridge isn't the place.

I tried to laugh off her praise. 'It's just one of those things one learns at sea.'

But she wouldn't have it and pointed to the speed reading. 'She's making twenty-one knots already!'

Jetwind did better during the day. At times she nudged twenty-three knots, surfing, I suspect, a little on some of the biggest rollers. She remained dry and safe, tearing along as the wind reached Force 12, or nearly seventy knots. The earlier sickening cork-screwing was gone now that the fore-course held her bows high.

There was no sun. The twilight greyness of the storm was illuminated in a curious unreal way by the sea's surface which the harrowing of the gale had seared white. If there was growler ice about, we would never have spotted it in that streaming whiteness before it ripped open *Jetwind*'s hull. I didn't think about ice; I kept her going; and in the next twelve hours *Jetwind* had put 480 kilometres between herself and the last land.

Ahead lay nothing but Gough. And Trolltunga.

Chapter 20

I knew I was in love with Kay when I saw her death-fall from the mainyard next day.

That morning death struck three times aboard *Jetwind*.

I was on watch; it was about seven bells, 7.30 a.m.

Our speed had fallen slightly during the night, but she was still logging a splendid eighteen knots. The storm had eased but the ocean remained an awesome sight. In the grey first half light the crests seemed steeper than before. *Jetwind* was putting her shoulder into them and every time her bows went down mountains of water swamped her long, unbroken main-deck. It was the sort of situation I had foreseen when I had criticized the deck's lack of 'breakwaters' to Thomsen.

I had just spoken to Jim Yell, the bo'sun, on the intercom. Jim's quarters were aft, under the poop. The bo'sun in a sailing ship occupies a different status from a bo'sun aboard a steam ship. Jim had almost officer standing. Since Grohman's suspension and 'house arrest' a much greater burden had been put on him. I intended to use the half-hour before the relieving watch came on duty to inspect the after-peak which housed the auxiliary engine nacelle, the stern dropkeel, and the steering gear.

I arranged to meet Jim in the crew's mess, also aft near his own quarters. I passed Arno's office on my way and told him where I was going. He eased the head-phone clear of his blond hair and nodded. It was the last I saw him alive.

Kay and I almost collided as I started down the companion-way from the bridge to the main-deck. She had watched her moment with the seas coming aboard and had sprinted along the deck from her cabin in the stern. The icy cold air – contrasting with the air-conditioned interior – had brought colour to her cheeks. She was wearing sneakers and a green and white tracksuit with a loose top. It did nothing for her figure; I was not to know then its importance in the forthcoming drama.

'Isn't it enough to sprint a hundred and fifty metres along a deck without running up and down the mast as well?' I joked.

She held on to the handrail and looked up at me. I should never have let her go.

'Exercise is a sacred cow with me,' she smiled. 'If it's not milked every day, it becomes sloppy.'

'There seems to be a strictly feminine undertone to this conversation.'

She laughed and was about to reply but then exclaimed urgently, 'Watch out, Peter! Here it comes!'

The water did not reach the top of the companion-way where we were but swirled along the deck. It was cold, green, hostile. The big deck ports clanged as it flooded overboard.

'This is my moment,' I said, and started down.

I managed the deck without the life-lines. An additional

165

precaution was safety nets. I barely had time to dodge up the quarter-deck companion-way before the next roller swept the decks. I glanced aloft before making my way inside. There was ice on the burnished yards above.

Jim's cabin was the fourth down the passage. As I passed, his phone rang. I answered in his absence.

The scream of terror was Arno's. The shot was someone else's.

'Arno! Arno!'

I dropped the silent instrument and ran for Jim Yell. He was standing smoking and talking to a seaman eating breakfast.

'Jim!'

He spun round as I burst in. I jerked my thumb in the direction of the bridge. We both erupted on to the main-deck.

The nearest companion-way to our objective was on the starboard side of the bridge. But that was the weather side, the side which was shipping hundreds of tons of water. It created a waist-deep, freezing barrier. We hung on to the life-lines. There was an interminable delay while we waited for the sea to drain

'It's Arno!' I explained hastily to Jim. 'He gave a scream. There was a shot . . .'

'Now – run!' shouted Jim.

We had reached No. 3 mast when Jim grabbed me and pointed aloft.

Kay was standing on the mainyard of the next mast for'ard, No. 2 mast, the one which bisected the bridge. This was her daily run. She was far out along the yard, hanging on with one hand to a loading cable. She spotted us, gesticulated urgently forward seawards. From our level nothing could be seen but the next wall of water waiting for *Jetwind*'s bows.

'Hang on, sir!'

I made an uncompromising gesture in response to Kay. I grabbed the life-line and braced myself.

To my horror, Kay let go the cable and cupped her hands like a megaphone to her mouth.

'Ice! A growler! Right ahead! Port! Hard-a-port!'

The wave dealt a right cross to *Jetwind*'s jaw. She gave a wicked lurch, like a boxer absorbing a hay-maker. Kay grabbed frantically for her support. The yard was coated with ice. I saw her feet slip. She tried to regain her balance by tottering out along the yard. Her plan might have worked had there been no ice and no second lurch from the ship.

Kay staggered a few steps beyond the line of the ship's side, then pitched overboard.

Had she fallen from her original position, nothing could have stopped her being smashed to pieces on the deck. As it was, she catapulted clear of the ship. But a sea's surface from a height of twenty metres is as hard as a deck. She turned a complete circle in the air. It was not a quick kill fall. Even as my mind went numb, I sensed that she was falling more slowly than she should have. The wind had got under her loose track-suit top, ballooning into the loose-fitting pants as well.

It took a little less than five seconds for her to hit the water.

I followed her fall into the sea. A human body is a puny thing. It left no tell-tale splash where it hit the foam-torn surface. As *Jetwind* lifted again I caught a glimpse of a terror-struck face with staring eyes only a few metres from the ship's side.

I have no conscious memory of my actions during those brief seconds of her fall. All I know is that I had ripped a life-belt from the rail and was poised to throw it when her face showed again momentarily against the grey-white sea. Even as my mind registered the fact that she was still alive, another thought supervened: no human could live long in that icy ocean.

I hurled the life-belt. I could only pray that it would land near her. I didn't pause to think about the next flood of water sweeping along the deck. I took it up to the armpits. How I reached the starboard bridge wing within seconds, I shall never know. I threw open the door.

The bridge watch – Tideman was there now – stood frozen at my frenzied entry.

'Back the tops'ls – Numbers One and Two masts! Man overboard!'

No skipper gives an order like that in that sort of gale and sea unless he is mad or drunk. It is a life-or-death manoeuvre for a sailing ship – like pulling a Grand National steeplechaser up short while hell bent over Beecher's Brook. The ship, running off before the wind, would crash into the troughs of waves as big as hillocks. That meant she would roll – roll herself full of water, roll the masts clean off her. Even if she survived, she faced the same dangers a second time as she came round to pick up the rescue boat.

I was already shouting for a boat. 'Number Four boat – clear away! Volunteers!'

It was a small, four-man harbour runabout which was secured on the port, or lee, side of the quarter-deck.

I found Jim Yell at my elbow with two other of Tideman's men he had conjured up from somewhere.

Tideman held my eyes before obeying. He was silently asking the unaskable question – was it worth risking the ship and the lives of all aboard for the sake of one person who would already be starting to stiffen in the cold? Would it not be better rather to let her go? One life for the sake of twenty-eight? One life for the sake of twenty million dollars' worth of ship?

I never admired Tideman more than at that moment. When I did not respond, he gave the kill order steadily.

'Helm down!'

We four sprinted for the boat. Jim Yell cut it loose and in a moment we seemed to be pitching among the breaking crests. Once clear of *Jetwind*'s stern, the full fury of the storm struck us. The light was as grey as a shroud. I steered by guess and by God. Somewhere to windward Kay was gasping out her life.

It was the very greyness of the storm which saved Kay.

'Flare, sir! Thereaway!'

I was at the outboard tiller. Already the freezing metal was stripping my skin.

I got a sight of the self-igniting life-belt flare. That didn't mean to say Kay was in it. I guessed it to be a couple of hundred metres away; separating the boat from it were hills of water. I riveted my gaze in that direction.

Then – one of the men shouted. 'The ship – the ship, sir! Christ, she's going over!'

Maybe Tideman alone was capable of saving her. Nine degrees was *Jetwind*'s theoretical maximum heel before things started to give. She must have been superbly built to have stood up to twelve degrees in those killer troughs. To my overwrought senses the sail plan seemed to flatten down almost parallel with the water. Would Tideman blow away her top-masts with the ring charges? It seemed the only way to save her now.

I tore my eyes away from the sight when Jim Yell shouted. 'There! There she is, sir! It's her!'

'Is she . . . dead?'

'No – I saw her face.'

The next wave intervened like disaster itself. From its trough we had no sight of either *Jetwind* or Kay. We went deep, deep, into icy, white-lashed water.

When we soared to the crest – baling frantically – Kay was only two waves away. I hoped she could see us.

'Keep your eyes on her!' I yelled. If *Jetwind* were going to her death, there was nothing any of us could do now. Afloat in that tiny boat would be only a way of prolonging our agony. No wonder the old windjammer crews refused to learn to swim.

Jim Yell reached for an oar. 'Take it easy, Jim! You'll smash in her face if that touches her! Hold the boat off till we can grab her!'

'She'll be safe enough with me, sir!'

The flare pinpointed her position. She was slumped over, head down, arms trailing. Her mouth and nose were perilously close to the water.

'Easy, boys! Let her come down into the trough to us!'

Kay seemed to hang there at the summit, but the life-belt

169

could not have taken more than a few moments to coast down towards us.

Then – our boat cork-screwed away.

'For Chrissake!' exclaimed one of the men. 'Don't lose her now!'

I didn't though. The tiller felt ready to take my arm out of its socket but I forced the boat in close.

Kay's face was white against the scarlet paint of the life-belt. Blotches of purplish-blue were forming round her mouth and eyes.

'Handsomely, boys!'

Yell leaned outboard, a man holding his legs, and plucked Kay, life-belt and all, to safety.

I tried to steady my voice. 'Is there life in her, Jim?'

For an answer, she moaned and gagged sea-water on the bottom boards.

'Take over the tiller,' I ordered, pulling off my thick jersey and pants. I'd already shed my oilskins. 'The cold will kill her if we don't get her warm soon.'

Jim and I got rid of her soaking track-suit. We rolled her over on her face and tried to clear her lungs. The roughness of the bucking boat platform helped our life-giving massage. She coughed and gagged repeatedly.

I picked her up. She was as limp as a rag doll. Her eyes were staring; I don't think she saw me.

'She'll make it, never you worry,' Yell consoled me.

With only my oilskins now, I realized how perishing cold it was.

'It's warmth she needs,' I repeated. I held her close to me to try and absorb some of my body heat. 'There's not such a thing as a blanket aboard, I suppose?'

'No, sir. Not in a boat this size.'

'Okay, let's get back,' I said urgently. 'Head for the ship, will you?' I said to the man at the tiller.

The tillerman made a gesture which took in the waves, the wind, the wide emptiness of the Southern Ocean.

'Ship, sir? There is no ship.'

Chapter 21

There *was* no ship.

Fear as icy as the gale plucked at me. From the vantage height of the next wave-crest all that confronted us was an empty sea, its foam-covered lips snarling for vengeance.

'See anything, Jim?' I asked.

He levered himself to a standing position. He tensed, and said quickly, 'Ice, sir! Close by! A couple of hundred metres away to port!'

His warning triggered a hope. Maybe it was the same growler Kay had tried to warn me against before she had pitched overboard. If that were so, it could save us yet.

'How big?'

'Big enough, sir. A growler.'

I knew what he meant. Big enough to have ripped open *Jetwind*. Growlers never float alone. There must be others around. If the ice were reduced to growler size, it was probably because the sea was slightly warmer than I thought. Kay could live. Could we? I tried to remember what they call in Antarctica the 'wind chill factor' – how much the human body can stand at various wind speeds. All I could recall was a ridiculous phrase about face protection being mandatory.

If it was the same growler that Kay had spotted, it could provide a marker, the point from which *Jetwind* started her turn into the eye of the gale. That is, if she hadn't rolled herself into eternity. She might therefore be coming back in a wide circle to pick up the wind . . .

'Close the ice!'

'Pardon, sir,' asked Jim Yell. 'Is that wise? If *Jetwind* spots the growler on her radar, she'll steer clear of it.'

He had not carried out my order but I wasn't going to pull my rank with a sailor of his calibre.

'Okay, Jim. There's the life-belt flare. The ice will act as a mirror and give it ten times the range it otherwise would have.'

One of the other men broke in excitedly. 'There are also a couple of emergency flares in this locker, sir. We could shoot 'em off against the growler, too!'

'Good man!' I said. I tried to imagine how Tideman would act. He would have everything furled except a couple of top-gallants, just enough to keep the ship from being pooped in order to have the maximum time to search for us over the previous area. He'd have every light aboard full on in the hope that we would spot him. He'd use rockets and flares.

Jim Yell edged the boat near the growler. Kay started to shudder.

I said to Jim, 'If the ship doesn't come soon, she'll die.'

'She won't be alone, sir. The rest of us can't last very long either.'

The growler seemed almost a friend, something stable, amongst the gyrating waters. One face angled away like the shape of a radar dish. Jim threw the life-belt plus flare against its base. The unreal light made our faces look like those of sacrificial victims. Kay's was corpse-like.

'Boat flare next, sir?'

'Fire away.'

This flare was blue. It blinded us.

'Careful – keep the boat off!' I warned. 'A bang against the growler and we've had it.'

Two minutes.

Five minutes.

I was starting to shake with the cold. Sea-water Kay had gagged inside my oilskins froze on my chest.

'Try another flare, sir?'

'Not yet. Give the first one time.'

One of the men exclaimed suddenly as the boat soared to a wave-top. 'Seems like a bit of a glow – there, astern, sir.'

'Could be another berg,' I replied cautiously. 'Keep an eye on it.'

'It is something,' the man insisted. 'There – something white – square.'

Tabular berg – or top-gallant?

We strained our eyes into the murk. It was difficult to judge distances – the grim uniformity of the water offered no scale.

'Two, sir!' yelled the man excitedly. 'It's two – it's a couple of top-gallants, sir!'

'See anything, Jim?'

Yell managed to stand on the gunnel while the others supported him.

'It's them all right, sir!' he shouted. 'It's the ship! Wait – she's turning away – that growler's scared her off . . .'

'Fire another flare! Note the ship's position!'

The brilliant spurt of orange-yellow penetrated even my closed eyelids. When the flare had burned down, we fixed our eyes on the quarter where we had last seen the sails.

There they were.

'She's answering, sir!'

A brilliant white flare rose from the still invisible hull. I saw the angle of the sails diminish – she was turning towards us!

Tideman handled the rescue like a genius. In minutes the hull appeared below the burnished, streaming yards and masts which rose up out of the murk like the bright wings of an angel of salvation. We burned our last flare. The ship neared, slowed, then turned to give us a lee under the stern to bring the boat alongside. Tideman furled all sails except one top-gallant; his judgement of the balance of forces between the amount of sail necessary to keep the ship from being swamped and overshooting the boat was masterly. One false move, and *Jetwind* could never have beaten back a second time.

They threw ropes down to us.

'You and Kay first, sir!'

Kay couldn't be swung up alone for fear of her smashing

against the ship's side. Jim Yell and I roped her fast to me. We waited for the ship's roll; eager hands hauled us up and grabbed us.

'Get those men aboard – quick,' I told the group on deck. 'Then cut the boat loose. Let it go.'

'Aye, aye, sir.'

I gave rapid-fire orders for blankets, towels and hot-water bottles for Kay. Her cabin was close by, in the stern accommodation.

One of the rescuers remarked, 'You look pretty done in yourself, sir. Let us carry her to the cabin.'

'No. Just get me some clothes. Anything warm.

'Wait – a glass of hot rum too.'

'At the double, sir.'

'I'll be in her cabin.'

I laid Kay on her bunk. I stripped the soaking, icy under-garments off her. I got to work towelling her dry and warm. Her nipples were purpled and crumpled like metal foil; an old scar near her right groin had come lividly alive from the cold. Her head still lolled; her colour was a blend of grey and blue. She breathed: I could not detect any tell-tale choke-gurgle which would mean her lungs were full of water.

I paused only long enough in my life-restoring massage to renew my supply of towels and hot-water bottles. The messenger thrust a pair of pants, woollen shirt and jersey at me. I whipped into the clothes; the hot rum down my throat was worth more than any of them.

I turned Kay over on her face; she was still senseless.

I turned away to switch the heating to maximum. When I returned to Kay, she had managed to roll herself over. Her body was now pink from my rough massage. Her eyes were open and conscious. She extended her arms to me with a lead-like effort.

'Peter!'

'Kay!'

I took her under the armpits and held her to me. Her mouth was against mine; her lips were cold but her tongue was warm.

'My love, my love!'

I reached for the survival gear heaped on her bunk and chair.

Kay smiled and shook her head. 'Not that. Just you.'

I never got to her.

From down the corridor came the rattle of automatic fire.

Chapter 22

———————◆———————

Kay's cabin was the second down the corridor; there were four others between it and the crew's dining-saloon at the end. I yanked open the door and sprinted. Cordite smoke was wisping from the last doorway – Brockton's cabin.

I rushed in.

Brockton's body had been almost cut in half at shoulder level by the blast. He lay sprawled, face down, over the black brief-case he had had at his feet on the flight from the Cape to the Falklands.

My impetus almost impaled me on two stubby barrels of skeleton-butted UZIs. I grabbed the finning under the nearest one to save myself from falling. It was hot. The man who held it swept it free savagely. I found myself looking into Grohman's face.

Before I could say anything, the muzzle of the second sub-machinegun was jammed into my ribs from the other side. The cabin was full of the bitter smell of death, cordite, and the kill-sweat of the two men. In a flash I recognized Grohman's companion as one of the men I had seen on the Falklands plane. Crew additions, Grohman had called them to Tideman.

'Back!' snarled Grohman. 'Get back! Keep away from me!'

I started towards the door; Grohman waved me against a side wall.

'No tricks! Don't try and escape!'

The shock of Brockton's murder had left me moment-arily speechless. Now the sight of the bullet-ridden body with blood starting to stain the carpet loosened my tongue.

'You stinking murdering bastard, Grohman! I'll see you hang for this!'

His gun-barrel had more warmth than his laugh. 'The great Captain Rainier,' he sneered. 'The man who kicks my country's Navy up the arse!' His swarthy face contorted. 'Shut up, or I'll kill *you*!'

The corridor was filled with shouting men trying to see what was happening. Grohman said something in Spanish to his bully-boy. The man went at the crowd like a hooker in a rugby scrum, leading his charge with his UZI.

'Brockton!' I shouted. 'You killed Paul Brockton! What had he ever done to you!'

Grohman kicked Paul's body from where it lay across the attaché case.

'A filthy American spy!' he rasped. 'Look!'

The hard-fabric case, which I had seen Paul open several times for customs inspection, obviously had a false bottom. I caught a glimpse of electronics, a mini speaker, and what could have been a tiny transmitter.

'Do you know what that is?' demanded Grohman. 'It is called a Racal Datacom Portable Cipher Terminal – special to the United States Navy. That is a pocket cipher unit – there's a fragment of the signal he was transmitting when I got him. There is also an acoustic coupler and power supply . . .'

The thought crashed through my mind – had Brockton revealed everything about himself to me? What else beyond what he had told me had led him to insinuate himself aboard *Jetwind*? Now I winced thinking of Tideman. He was in the same game as Brockton – did Grohman suspect him too?

'Grohman . . .'

'Captain Grohman to you now, Rainier.' His grin was a death's head. 'One false move from you and you'll join your friend. Shut up and listen. This ship is now under command of Group Condor. I am the leader. The bridge and other key points have been occupied by my men.'

There was a renewed commotion at the door. I heard an oath from the thug with the gun and an angry voice.

'What the devil is going on here? I demand to know . . .' It was Sir James Hathaway.

Grohman said, in English, to the guard, 'Don't hurt that man, he's worth a million dollars.'

Sir James would not have got as far as the entrance had it not been for that warning. He thrust himself inside, livid-faced.

'A million dollars? What!' He stopped in his tracks at the sight of Brockton.

'Group Condor will ask a million dollars' ransom for you,' Grohman said in a sinister voice. 'If it is not paid . . .' He indicated the dead man. 'Take him away,' he added to the guard. 'Lock him in his cabin. Get the girl. Bring her here – by force, if necessary.'

The man started to frog-march Sir James away. My concern was not for him.

'Leave Kay Fenton alone!' I snapped. 'If you touch her, I'll kill you with my own hands.'

My tone stopped the guard. He looked questioningly at Grohman.

I went on. 'She's half-drowned. She needs care, and above all rest. You'll kill her if you disturb her at this time.'

'It was a very touching rescue,' Grohman sneered. 'Very romantic, very brave. Just the sort of thing I would expect the great Captain Rainier to attempt against all the odds.'

'Cut out the sarcasm,' I retorted. 'We're dealing with someone's life.'

'A life that is precious to you?'

I gathered myself to jump him. My intention must have been obvious. He aimed the UZI at my chest.

'You'll never reach me, Rainier,' he warned. His fellow hijacker also switched his aim to me.

'Your gallant rescue cut right across the beginning of our

operation,' continued Grohman. 'You nearly sank the ship in the process.'

Arno's last agonized cry now came back to me. 'You killed Arno,' I said. 'That makes two murders.'

'Arno could have lived, but he wouldn't cooperate. He was a key man. In his position he could have endangered Group Condor.'

'Is that what you call your group of murdering hijackers?' I retorted.

He flushed. '*Puerio*, sooner or later you will understand. Group Condor . . .'

Then, thinking perhaps that by arguing I was playing for time, he ordered bluntly, 'Take that old goat away! Lock up the girl, too, for the moment. She's worth more to us than he is.'

'She's only the sail-maker!' I expostulated.

'Ah!' he echoed. 'Only the sail-maker! For what sails!'

His jeer reduced me to silence. What other game might Kay also be playing? I simply could not believe it.

'Clear the passageway,' Grohman ordered as the thug marched Sir James out in front of him. 'No one is to leave their quarters from now on – understood?'

Jim Yell, I thought, wasn't the sort of man who would take kindly to being pushed around. Nor any others of the crew. They were paratroopers, trained to kill.

'The rescue crew must be cared for,' I intervened. 'They've taken a beating.'

'We'll see that they don't come to any harm,' said Grohman maliciously. 'Now – get on the phone. Check with Tideman on the bridge. And no tricks!' He gestured at the UZI.

I stepped past Brockton's body. I noted in the cipher terminal case that there was a plug connection to link with the telephone. It certainly was sophisticated equipment.

'John?' I said when I had dialled the bridge.

Tideman's voice was full of suppressed tension. He said, obviously marking time, 'You got Kay all right?'

'She's going to be fine, I think. I'm in Paul's cabin in the stern.'

'Yes?' I could imagine that neutral reply being forced out of him with a gun at his back.

'Paul is dead.'

Grohman made a silencing gesture. 'I am on my way to the bridge. With Grohman.'

Tideman's voice was without inflexion. 'I've got problems here.' In other words, the take-over was complete.

'Everything functioning – shipwise, I mean?'

'Aye.'

'Keep her like that until I come.'

'I'll do that.'

'Discretion is the better part of valour,' Grohman sneered further. 'First, the bridge. Then you'll enjoy my own recent experience of being confined to quarters. I am going to lock you up in the sick-bay – you'll be safer there. I want your cabin. Come!'

Jetwind was running like a greyhound newly back in its stride. Tideman was carrying a press of sail. What puzzled me was that Grohman made no move to interfere. Maybe that was why Tideman had been left alive, to handle the ship.

We made our way along the life-lines to the bridge via the radio office, Grohman behind me, UZI at the ready. Arno's chair was now occupied by one of Grohman's gang. Several alarms were buzzing away unanswered.

'Landajo! Who the devil wants us?'

'One of them is the radio-telephone, the other is Weather Routing's call-sign,' answered the operator.

'You expecting a call?' Grohman asked of me.

'Possibly Thomsen from Cape Town,' I replied. 'You can explain this situation, Grohman.'

'Let them buzz,' he told Landajo. 'You are not to reply to anyone – total radio silence.'

'Very good, comrade.'

Comrade! Brockton's warning about the Red threat in the Southern Ocean had become very real. Real enough for him to have paid with his life.

'This is to be the only signal – send this in our code,

179

Landajo . . .' Grohman switched into Spanish. The message was brief, but I recognized the phrase, 'Las Malvinas son nuestras.'

'You won't get away with this,' I told Grohman. 'International terrorism doesn't pay.'

I did not appreciate how near the limit he was. He struck at me with his open hand, but I ducked. Before I could counter-punch, he had stuck the automatic in my stomach.

'Don't try that again, you bastard!' he rapped out. 'When that signal is received a new era will begin! The Falklands will be ours again, after a century and a half of British oppression!'

I kept a contemptuous silence. Then he snapped, 'We've wasted enough time!'

Tideman and the helmsman were on watch. A trigger-happy hijacker stood guard at the rear of the bridge brandishing an automatic like Grohman's. He started nervously when we entered.

'Las Malvinas son nuestras!' Grohman's catch-phrase relaxed the man immediately. It must have been the gang's password for the hijacking.

'Tideman!' said Grohman. 'Put the ship on automatic! Face this way. You are at the wheel, keep your eyes ahead! If you turn, you die!'

Tideman manipulated the controls, then turned and came to us. For all he knew, he was about to be blasted into eternity.

'What is all this about?' he asked coolly.

Grohman indicated the UZI. 'It is all about this.'

'Do as he says, John,' I warned.

Tideman gave me a quick glance. I could see the meaning behind it – did Grohman know his background?

'Stop!'

The other gangman moved so that both he and Grohman had clear fields of fire.

The slightly hysterical note returned to Grohman's voice. 'This ship is now under my command. You and

Rainier will be locked up. Any attempt to escape and you will be shot.'

I could see Tideman's tension ease. Grohman wasn't wise to him!

'Yes.' Tideman's tone was completely neutral.

Grohman ordered the guard. 'Search him! I'll hold your gun while you do it!'

The two of them were as wary as if hunting leopards The passing of weapons between them was so quick it was almost sleight-of-hand. There wasn't a chance of jumping either of them.

The man frisked Tideman; from a pocket he pulled out the slide-rule which concealed the lethal blade. He raised it inquiringly to Grohman.

Grohman said, 'It's for navigation. Put it back. It can't hurt anyone.'

When the search was over, Grohman returned the gunman's automatic. Then he backed to the ship's intercom, keeping his own weapon levelled on us. Bitchbox, Brockton had called it. The recollection was like a stab to the heart.

'Grohman speaking,' he said. 'I have taken over command of *Jetwind*. I am now the captain. The ship is in the hands of Group Condor.' His voice rose. 'We are liberation fighters. The Falkland Islands – the Malvinas – have groaned under the British yoke for a hundred and fifty years. We, Group Condor, have come to liberate the oppressed populace. This is a great hour for my country. The capitalist-colonialist regime is about to end. The islands will be returned to my people. An Argentinian regime based on equality for all will be installed under my leadership. Argentinian justice will replace the colonial tyranny which has suppressed the people for so long. Las Malvinas son nuestras!'

'Is that why you shot a harmless American reporter?' I said derisively when he had finished at the instrument.

'Brockton was a spy!' he shouted. 'We caught him sending off a signal which would have wrecked our enterprise. That was his death warrant. He had to die!'

'Enterprise? That's a goddam funny word for murder and piracy.'

Grohman shrugged and went on in his hectoring tone. 'When Argentina freed itself from the colonial rule of Spain, the thieving British saw their opportunity in the upheaval which followed and stole the Malvinas from us. One American life is nothing beside that.'

'How can you and four gunmen hope to seize such a spread-out group of islands?' I asked. 'You might perhaps get away with it for a while in a little place like Port Stanley. Also, think of the international stink you'll create . . .'

Grohman seemed amused. 'You'll see, in a few days' time.'

'It will take more than a few days for *Jetwind* to beat back to the Falklands into this gale,' I replied. 'A few weeks, more likely.'

Perhaps Tideman felt that his continued silence was playing the situation a little too dumb.

He said, 'I'll back that up, as a sailor.' The emphasis was on sailor.

'Shut up, both of you!' retorted Grohman. 'Don't argue with me. I'm in command, and what I say goes. You are the enemies of Las Malvinas. Consider yourselves lucky that I do not shoot you out of hand. But I will let you live – provided you behave – for a few days.

'Until we reach Molot.'

Chapter 23

Molot was the riddle which bugged our long day in captivity in the ship's sick-bay. The 'hospital' was situated underneath the port wing of the bridge – in exactly the same position but on the opposite side of my captain's suite. It had two curtained-off cubicles and a minute double 'ward' containing two surgical beds. A glass partition separated the sick-bay itself from an outer reception office, designed for a medical orderly. The sick-bay did not seem to have had much use except as a junk room for ship's odds and ends. One of these was a survival suit stored on a hanger which, Tideman explained, was used in icy seas for inspection of *Jetwind*'s drop keels.

'Molot?' I asked Tideman for the hundredth time. 'Where the hell is Molot?'

'It must be the base from which the attack on the Falklands will be launched,' he replied. 'That's about all I can guess.'

'But Grohman is heading *away* from the Falklands,' I pointed out. 'He's kept *Jetwind* going like a bomb all day. *Away* from his objective. There is no land – whatsoever – between the Falklands and Gough Island.'

'Perhaps Molot is a place we know by a different name – like Malvinas,' suggested Tideman. 'Even then, I don't get it. Grohman is holding *Jetwind* on the course you selected for Gough.'

'He's not doing it too badly either.'

'There's nothing wrong with his sailoring,' replied Tideman. 'He's sailing by computer. Maybe we could get an extra knot or two out of her manually.'

'The only possibility of land is the South Sandwich group,' I went on. 'But they're far to the south of our present course.'

'South Sandwich it might be,' said Tideman. 'But that doesn't mean much. Most of the islands are volcanic. They're all coated with ice being so near Antarctica. I've heard that the only way to land is by helicopter. They would be totally unsuitable as a base. What if Molot is another name for Gough?'

'No, John. Gough is a South African weather station. It's important – it's the only weather station in the central part of the Southern Ocean. Group Condor couldn't take it over without provoking a massive retaliation.'

'The same objection applies to Tristan da Cunha which is only a couple of hundred miles northwest of Gough,' he answered. 'If Group Condor occupied either of them, it would prejudice the Falklands attack in advance because the secret would be out. Also, any assault force would then have to cross twenty-one hundred miles of ocean in order to reach the Falklands.'

'Poor Paul!' I said. 'I wonder if he got wind of Grohman's plans?'

'I'm in the same boat as Paul,' Tideman replied quietly.

'Grohman doesn't suspect a thing,' I reassured him. 'If he had, you wouldn't be here, John.'

'You're also living on borrowed time, Peter. Until Molot, Grohman said.'

It all came back to Molot. When night came, we were no nearer an answer.

Suddenly the outer sick-bay door opened.

'Kay!'

I jumped up to go to her.

'Keep back!' Grohman appeared behind her threatening with the UZI.

Kay and I looked at one another for a long moment. Her eyes told me everything. She was still pale but smiling. The guard warily pitched her suit-case inside.

Grohman looked strained. Holding down a crew of twenty-eight could not have been easy.

'She's to stay here,' he said briefly. 'It's not for the pleasure of your company, let me assure you. It's because I can't spare one man solely to guard her.'

'What do you expect me to say to that?' I asked.

'Listen, Rainier,' he said angrily. 'You and Tideman are expendable, understand? The final decision does not rest with me or else you'd have been overside already. This woman is not in the same category. She is valuable to us. Just as in another way Sir James Hathaway is valuable to us. A million dollars will help finance Group Condor's operations.'

I deliberately tried to rattle him. I would have been prepared to risk the second gun if I could have grabbed his automatic. Tideman, I knew, would back me to the hilt – the hilt of that wicked dagger, which he had managed to keep.

'You're going back to the Malvinas, you say – but you're heading in the opposite direction!'

Kay broke in. 'What possible use can I be to Group Condor! Who'll pay a million dollars for me?'

'You are an expert in sail aerodynamics – that is why you are valuable,' replied Grohman.

'Sail aerodynamics!' she exclaimed. 'What has that to do with killing and murder and unsuspecting attacks?'

'You play the innocent well,' said Grohman. 'But it doesn't wash. At Molot you will be transferred to Soviet protection. I have been notified that afterwards you will be transferred to Kyyiv in Russia itself where secret experiments are being conducted into sail aerodynamics.'

I was stunned; Kay was speechless. If Grohman got wind of Tideman's connection with the Schiffbau Institut's tests, he was a dead man.

Grohman looked triumphant. Perhaps it was his paranoid temperament which compelled him to boast of his superiority – in the face of murder.

'I have been to Kyyiv,' he said. 'We admit that the Schiffbau's experiments are ahead of ours. This ship proves it. You will be a valuable asset to our research team.'

'Kyyiv! *Me*! I won't go!'

Grohman stroked the finning along the UZI's barrel. It was a cat-like, sinister gesture.

'The decision is not mine whether to force you or not,' he said. 'That rests with Command at Molot. But I advise you not to push your luck too far.'

'Soviet Command, you mean?' I asked.

He looked surprised. 'Who else?'

'Nothing will make me go to some secret test ground in Russia under threat!' Kay burst out.

'You have about three days to think it over before we reach Molot,' replied Grohman. 'Think about it well, Señorita Fenton. You will be treated well if you cooperate. Otherwise . . .' He shrugged.

'You bastard!' I said. 'You crazy bastard!'

He swung the automatic on me. For a moment his eyes

went kill-blank. Then he relaxed. 'Three days – that is all *you* have, Rainier!'

He backed out of the sick-bay; the guard took up his previous position behind the glass partition.

I felt as if I had been kicked in the stomach. For fully a couple of minutes we all stood rooted. Finally, I broke the silence.

'I'll put your case in a cubicle, Kay – any particular choice?'

'The closer to you both, the better.'

I started to pick up the case and she said, 'They let me bring my transistor radio. It might help pass the time – until Molot.'

She was close to tears. 'What is Molot? Peter? John?'

'I wish we knew,' replied Tideman. 'We've been racking our brains all day.'

She went into her cubicle. I followed. Inside, there was no need to say anything. She came into my arms. I could feel the dry sobs from her throat through her breasts against me. Her lips were a warm pulse of agony and denied ecstasy, wet with tears.

'Just when I've found the man I want, I'm to lose him!' she whispered brokenly. 'Why didn't you just let me go this morning? It would have been better all round. Oh, my love, my darling!'

I held her close and said those things which can only be said in the presence of new love. Finally her sobs quietened.

I said, more to comfort her than with any plan in mind, 'Three days is a long time, Kay. Anything could happen before we reach Molot.'

'Molot!' she echoed. 'How I hate that name already! What is it? What does it mean? It has an evil ring, like Trolltunga.'

'It's Russian, that's for sure. What it means is as much a mystery as where it is.'

Then we joined Tideman in the main 'ward'. He was listening to Kay's radio, turning it every way to try and improve reception.

'I had the Cape Town news,' he said. 'It reported concern because no signals had been received from *Jetwind* for a day. There was an interview with Thomsen. I couldn't hear clearly – something about no contact with the ship.'

Kay voiced the concern uppermost in all our minds. 'John – Peter – why should the Russians be interested in me? I haven't any secrets!'

Tideman switched off the radio with a significant gesture. He said gravely, 'You have, Kay.'

'I? Secrets?'

He waved us into a couple of hard chairs round a low table. He opened a drawer by his bed and produced a pack of cards, obviously provided for patients. He nodded towards the watching sentry.

'If we hold a discussion in the ordinary way I'm sure we'll rouse his suspicions,' he said quietly. 'We'll pretend we're playing cards. I'll explain.'

Kay's hand was shaking when Tideman dealt the first round. 'Secrets?' she repeated incredulously.

'Aye, secrets, Kay. Remember when the Schiffbau Institut was making the final wind-tunnel tests of *Jetwind*'s sails and masts?'

'Sure – I was there!' she exclaimed. 'You were there, too. That's where we met.'

'I was – at the invitation of Axel Thomsen himself. He'd heard of my runs round the Horn as a member of the British Services Adventure Scheme and thought I might be able to contribute something practical to the theoretical tests.'

'I stressed the same thing to Thomsen,' I interjected.

'That's what probably made him interested in you as a skipper – your practical experience in *Albatros*.' He looked anxiously round the sick-bay. 'I take it this place isn't bugged, is it? If so, we might as well say goodbye in the light of what I'm going to say now.'

'Grohman hasn't had any opportunity,' I replied.

'Here goes, then. Both of you know, of course, that *Jetwind*'s sails are made of dacron, not canvas.'

He stressed his statement so carefully that Kay said, 'Of course, John – but that's no secret.'

'Dacron is tougher and smoother and therefore more aerodynamically efficient than canvas.'

Kay was staring at him, and he warned, 'Try and keep your eyes on your cards, Kay.'

She gave a little shake of her head, half reproach, half incredulity.

'Dacron is also far more expensive than canvas,' Tideman went on. 'Therefore it is worth protecting in a way canvas need not be. *Jetwind*'s sails alone cost a fortune.'

'*Albatros*'s dacron sails at the end of my run were as thin from sun damage as the Ancient Mariner's ghost ships,' I said.

'That's it – sun damage!' he went on. '*Jetwind*'s designers realized that to prevent sun damage from infrared and ultra-violet rays the sails would have to have a plastic coating. You realize the problem this poses – what plastic could stand up to the continual flexing, reefing, furling and endless changes in wind pressure? There was also the problem of cracking and flaking. The protective coating would have to withstand that also.'

Kay said, 'I remember the headaches that caused. But the Schiffbau team came up trumps in the end.'

'It was brilliant inventiveness,' Tideman went on. 'The specialists evolved a completely new plastic in the polymer group – the same chemical group as dacron itself. It was named polyionosoprene. The day we tested the new plastic and found that it absorbed infra-red and micro-waves was sensational.'

I threw down a card at random on the table. It was the top ace in the pack.

Tideman gave value to the pause, gathering up the pack and riffling the deck like a professional card-sharp. The guard beyond the glass partition was lolling, disinterested.

'That absorption was due – we believed though we couldn't prove it – to an unknown chemical reaction occurring between the dacron and polyionosoprene.'

'That doesn't sound too dramatic, John.'

'I was there,' Kay added. 'Everyone seemed quite pleased but not over-excited at the discovery.'

A slight smile broke the seriousness of Tideman's explanation. 'It was in fact one of the biggest strategic breakthroughs of the satellite age.

'Infra-red and micro-waves are the basic elements of American and Russian spy satellites. However, infra-red rays are strongly absorbed by water vapour, with the result that a spy satellite cannot "see" through cloud, which means restricting their use to cloud-free days.' He slapped down a card. 'Now – here is polyionosoprene, an artificial substance which similarly absorbs these rays.'

Kay looked dumbfounded. 'I never guessed it was that important.'

'Micro-waves can actually penetrate water vapour – cloud, for example – but the deeper they penetrate the poorer becomes the resolution of the sensor image,' continued Tideman.

'I still don't quite get it,' I said.

'In the latest Nimbus series of satellite using micro-wave instruments, resolution is of the order of two hundred to three hundred metres. In other words, any object with a distinct water mass, say, an iceberg, with dimensions smaller than this will not show up on the spy satellite scan.'

'I still don't get the connection with *Jetwind*,' I said.

'The combination of heavy cloud cover and poly-ionosoprene-coated sails renders this ship undetectable by spy satellite,' said Tideman.

He gathered up the cards as a token gesture and reshuffled them.

'Polyionosoprene-coated sails also deflect most of what we call PECM – passive electronic counter-measures – which are used in the multi-sensor module installations of the latest American and Russian high-altitude spy-planes.' He dealt the cards.

'*Jetwind*'s secret makes her of top strategic significance in today's world.'

Kay still seemed dumbfounded. 'Remember, John, when they told us in Hamburg that polyionosoprene was a big commercial secret and we were not to talk about it? I never dreamed it was anything as momentous as this.'

'Now then,' Tideman went on. 'You, Paul and I discussed the importance of the Drake Passage as an anti-submarine choke point. We shall never know how much Brockton was in on what I am about to tell you now. When I learned the facts about polyionosoprene, I immediately thought of the Drake Passage, where cloud cover is total for twenty-five days in the month. A ship protected by polyionosoprene in those waters is almost undetectable by spy satellites. Even under light cloud cover conditions, *Jetwind* would show up on spy satellite instruments only as an amorphous white blob, indistinguishable from innumerable icebergs. In fact we have the biggest anti-surveillance breakthrough since the first spy-in-the-sky went into orbit.'

Kay made a helpless gesture. 'They simply referred to the danger of industrial espionage.'

'What did you do about it?' I wanted to know.

'I got back to London as fast as I could make it. After top-level discussions the Navy decided to keep the tightest security watch over *Jetwind*'s proving voyage, which was then scheduled to take place from Montevideo to the Cape.'

'How does Mortensen's murder tie up with what you're saying now?' I asked.

'My guess is that Grohman's Molot Command ordered him to kill him when the Soviet Navy lost track of *Jetwind*.'

'Lost track? There was no secret about her position! Her journey was publicized throughout the world!'

'Lost track – from the sky. Satellite track. I think something happened which sent a powerful shock through the Red Fleet.'

'But why?' Kay asked.

'This ship had to be stopped from going anywhere near this Molot place, in case the alleged Soviet base was exposed.'

I said ruefully, 'And I, too, unwittingly headed for Molot from the Falklands.'

'I suppose that's why *Jetwind* was hijacked. She had to be stopped because she was invisible to Red spy satellites. Grohman knew he was safe in the Falklands – that's why he holed up there after Mortensen's death. Then you came along and threw a spanner in the works. He never bargained you would get past the warship which was meant to detain *Jetwind* – orders for which originated, no doubt, right back at Soviet Naval Command HQ.'

'God, what a mess!' exclaimed Kay.

'Keep your eyes on the cards,' Tideman warned again.

'John,' I cut in. 'Don't you think you exaggerate the whole situation? Grohman is just a puppet whose strings are being manipulated. Suppose he is to lead an attack on the Falklands. There's no way he can count on a force of any size. All he can do is lead a small group of terrorists against Stanley and occupy the place. It would be a demonstration, a gesture – not an operation of international scope such as you have in mind.'

'Unfortunately, there's more to it than that. The Navy's anti-submarine specialist team decided that if *Jetwind* proved herself, a fleet of five *Jetwinds* would be built. Their true purpose would constitute the newest and most novel form of anti-sub weapon. The projected fleet has even been given a name, the Cape Horn Patrol.'

There was a long silence. We threw down the cards mechanically, unseeingly.

'The operational area of the Cape Horn Patrol would be the Drake Passage and its ocean approaches. It has one overriding assignment – to monitor the passage of nuclear submarines. Drake Passage presents a unique problem in tactical detection which no major navy has yet mastered. It is impossible, because of the bad weather and lack of bases, to monitor the passage of nuclear subs by conventional means. If any navy attempted warship patrols of the Passage, they would be detected within hours by satellite. Powered ships are heat-emitting. They are easy game for infra-red sensors. In addition, engines make a noise –

a give-away to counter-sonar tracking by submarines. Submerged subs are out of satellite reach. Never forget that a nuclear sub is a noisy machine, that is its Achilles' heel. The latest Soviet Titanium class is, fortunately for the West, the noisiest of the lot.'

'What can *Jetwind* do that they can't?' Kay wanted to know.

'*Jetwind*, being wind-driven, is the silent stalker, the silent killer,' he said. 'In Southern Ocean conditions she is fast – faster than most warships can travel safely. She also offers what no powered vessel can – a *stable* operations platform. Her sails hold her hull down on the water.

'So you see,' he said, '*Jetwind* is in fact a fast, silent, satellite-undetectable weapon against nuclear subs in an area which also happens to be a naval choke point of major global strategic significance.'

I said slowly, 'Now we have it, John.'

He shook his head. 'At present something else alarms me – rather, did alarm me.'

Kay and I waited anxiously.

'I was afraid that after the hijacking Grohman might turn back to the Falklands,' he said. 'That would have put paid to *Jetwind*'s major proving test.'

I felt my stomach muscles cramp.

'Is there more?' asked Kay, now even more alarmed.

He nodded. 'I told you, I'm pretty sure the Reds panicked when they couldn't pinpoint *Jetwind* by satellite. The United States Navy and Britain have arranged a similar sort of test. The U.S. Navy is diverting one of its latest Seascan spy satellites to check on *Jetwind* at a given place and time, roughly four hundred miles southsouth-west of Gough. A little over three and a half days from now *Jetwind* must pass at a point directly beneath the line of the Seascan satellite. This nadir position will offer the best test of her undetectability.'

'Why select that particular spot in the Southern Ocean?' I asked.

'Because drifting icebergs and ocean and weather

conditions are very similar to the Drake Passage,' he answered. 'The location was very carefully chosen.'

'And if *Jetwind* doesn't show up?'

For the first time in many fake deals Tideman lifted his head and looked squarely at Kay and me.

'The Seascan is in transit from one secret destination to another – I don't know where,' he replied. 'It is the once-only time and place for the test. No *Jetwind* at the rendezvous, no Cape Horn Patrol. It's as simple as that. The sailing ship will be dead – for ever.'

'How much did Paul know of this?'

'I wish I'd had time to find out,' he answered. 'Remember his intense interest in your so-called hallucinations? They were supposed to have occurred roughly in the Seascan rendezvous area.' He paused and added, 'And that's where the Orion crashed.'

'I have something to add,' I said, 'something I didn't mention even to Paul in regard to my "hallucinations". To this day I'm not sure whether I saw it or not.'

Tideman leaned forward; his elbows banging on the table.

'Okay, say it now – what was it?'

'I thought I saw a submarine. She wasn't moving. She was at anchor, moored. Loading something. Then she was swallowed up by the mist.'

Chapter 24

'We've got to retake the ship!'

I was saying next morning to Tideman what I seemed to have repeated a hundred times since the evening before. Tideman's revelations about *Jetwind*'s value as a space-age weapon had left me with a feeling of bewilderment. I had slept badly. It was before breakfast in the sick-bay, and we were waiting for an early Cape news bulletin. Radio reception on Kay's little set was improving. The deduction was that we were shortening the distance to Cape Town. There was no way of establishing our position, even roughly. Tideman and I had speculated about it as frequently as I had reiterated my determination to recapture the ship. We were aware that *Jetwind* hadn't altered course and was still following my planned route to Gough. We were also able to estimate her speed to within a couple of knots; Grohman kept her going like a train.

The strain of his long vigil was telling on our guard. He would fidget in his seat, then take a pace or two up and down the outer glass-partitioned office, keeping himself alert until his relief arrived.

Tideman nodded in his direction. 'To get at him, we have somehow to get past that glass partition. As things stand, we have no hope of a surprise.'

'They hold all the trumps,' I agreed.

'All but one,' he answered. He thrust his hand into his 'slide-rule' pocket. 'This.'

'Keep that hidden, for Pete's sake!' I said. 'We've got to find or create the opportunity to use it. It's not only our lives that are at stake. There are all the other consequences. I'm also desperately worried what they'll do to Kay.'

'I don't like the sound of Kyyiv either,' he replied. 'If they got their hands on her at Molot, I fear she's done for.'

'Meaning?'

He side-stepped a direct answer. 'It was better she should know *Jetwind*'s secret. If the pressure becomes too great, she could always break down and confess. Not knowing and playing the genuine innocent might only lead to something worse.'

I got up and made for the partition like a lion trapped in a cage. Up came the sentry's automatic.

'Peter! Leave it! Here comes the Cape news!'

It took a great effort to pull myself away.

'There is concern in Cape Town shipping circles regarding the whereabouts of the missing sailing ship

Jetwind, which began an attempt on the Falklands-Cape record some days ago,' said the suave tones of the woman newsreader. 'All attempts to establish communication with the ship have failed. The owner, Mr Axel Thomsen, told our news staff this morning that he is worried about the safety of the ship, which encountered a storm of hurricane proportions shortly after leaving Port Stanley. Weather satellite photographs confirm that a storm of unusual intensity is still raging along the route Captain Rainier decided to take to Gough Island. Captain Rainier had been warned by weather experts not to follow this course . . .'

'I can't stand this holier-than-thou, I-told-you-so crap!' I exclaimed angrily. 'If they only *guessed* what was going on!'

'No one could guess, Peter,' replied Tideman.

I tried to defuse my frustration. 'This amounts to the fact that Grohman is keeping radio silence, doesn't it?'

'Wouldn't you, in his shoes, with the stakes involved?'

The bulletin went on: –

'Mr Thomsen adds that South African Naval Headquarters has informed him that the area where *Jetwind* was last reported is well outside the range of long-range maritime reconnaissance aircraft. Nevertheless, if nothing is heard today from the missing ship, the South African research vessel *Agulhas*, which is now on a routine replenishment voyage to our weather station on Gough Island, may be diverted to search for *Jetwind*. The *Agulhas* is equipped with two helicopters, which would enable a wide area of ocean to be covered . . .'

There was an interruption. Grohman had arrived in the outside office. With him was the guard's relief, looking the freshest of the three.

Grohman, carrying his automatic, unlocked the door. He was strained and unshaven. If I was short on sleep, he was shorter.

Kay emerged from her cubicle.

I said, 'You just missed an interesting news bulletin,

Grohman. Everyone is getting pretty worried about *Jetwind*.'

'The people who matter aren't worried,' he retorted.

I went on, trying to needle him. 'Your radio silence is proving counter-productive. You didn't hear what the radio had to say.'

'Don't play games!' he snarled. 'Landajo tapes all the main news bulletins. I can hear them at my leisure.'

I kept silent. His nerves were too ragged to take it. Finally he snapped. 'Out with it – what did the news say?'

'If nothing is heard today from *Jetwind*, the *Agulhas* will divert from Gough and search the Southern Ocean – with helicopters.'

'You lie!' he exploded. 'You are making this up!'

'You can check – it's on tape, you said so yourself.' I pushed home my verbal attack. 'That means that they'll locate Molot, Grohman. What will your bosses in the Soviet Fleet say when they find out you've blown their cover? The eyes of the world are already focused on this section of the Southern Ocean because of *Jetwind*. You haven't been nearly clever enough!'

'I should shoot you!' he snarled.

'It's too late,' I replied with more bravado than I felt. 'You've started something you can't reverse. Searchers will be here soon like a swarm of bees.'

I felt Grohman was against the ropes, psychologically speaking.

He said defensively, 'If I had sent a Mayday, they would have been here in any event.'

'You should simply have carried on as if nothing had happened,' I persisted. 'Just pretended you were me. I doubt whether if you'd tried it Thomsen would have fallen for a yarn about a second *Jetwind* skipper having died by accident.'

'Don't mock me, you bastard! There is still time to put the search off the scent.'

'Go ahead,' I said. 'You're the skipper.'

'Rainier,' he said in a way which was more sinister than his histrionics, 'Molot Command has instructed me to deliver you – unharmed. It might be a lot easier for you if I could tell them you had been cooperative. As it is . . .' He shrugged.

Kay broke in. 'Get this clear – I will not cooperate under duress or any other way. I go along with Peter and John – whatever.'

'Those are very big words,' sneered Grohman. 'We shall see – at Molot.'

We knew what had been in his mind regarding the search for *Jetwind* when we heard the lunch-time news bulletin.

'There is news at last of the sea drama being enacted in the Southern Ocean around the space-age windjammer *Jetwind*. Naval Headquarters at Silvermine, Cape Town, reports that a faint, garbled radio message was picked up this morning from the ship. It appears that she has been partially dismasted and that there have been casualties as a result of the accident . . .'

'Casualties – accident!' expostulated Kay.

'The signal stated that the ship was in no immediate need of assistance and gave her position as fifty-two degrees south, thirty-nine degrees west, near the island of South Georgia . . .'

'South Georgia!' exclaimed Tideman.

'The island of South Georgia is approximately seven hundred miles eastsoutheast of *Jetwind*'s starting-point in the Falkland Islands, which means that the ship must have been driven considerably off-course by the hurricane which damaged her. At this stage no further details are available.'

'What is Grohman up to?' Kay asked.

'It's a red herring to stave off a possible search,' I said. 'He hopes it'll give him the breathing-space he needs to reach Molot.'

'The experts won't be put off by a fake distress signal like that, surely? Won't they smell a rat?' asked Kay.

'In the light of his assurance that *Jetwind* is in no immediate danger, no one is going to mount an expensive, dangerous search far away from the main shipping lanes,' I said.

'Peter, John! We must do something! We can't just let the situation slide! We can't go on like this, waiting, just waiting!'

'Keep calm, Kay,' said Tideman gently. 'The guy who wins in a hijacking is the one who can keep his nerve the longest.'

Just how corrosive that tension could be, we discovered throughout the interminable afternoon. There was nothing to do, nothing to read. We played what Tideman called 'silly-buggers card games' – inconsequential time-wasting which we tried to enliven by wagering impossible sums. The attempt was not a success. The nightmare of Molot overshadowed everything.

We could not wait for the main dinner-time news bulletin from Cape Town:

'No further messages have been received from the missing sailing ship *Jetwind* making for South Georgia,' it reported. 'Shipping experts believe that the vessel may try and reach the sheltered harbour of King Edward Cove where the old Grytviken whaling station is situated. This is now occupied by the British Antarctic Survey. So far all attempts by the Survey's radio ZBH to contact the damaged vessel have failed. Until some positive information is received, the survey replenishment ship *Agulhas* will continue to Gough Island as scheduled without mounting a special search as was originally planned.'

'Grohman pulled it off!' I exclaimed. 'There goes our last outside chance!'

The bulletin continued:

'Mr Axel Thomsen, *Jetwind*'s owner, was interviewed today on the fate of his unique attempt to reinstate the sailing ship as an ocean cargo carrier. "This is the second mishap which has hit *Jetwind*," he said. "I think the ship must be jinxed." Mr Thomsen added that he would remain in Cape Town until specific news had been received about the ship and would then return overseas. He added that he was bitterly disappointed at the failure of *Jetwind*. If the ship could be repaired, he added, he would decide whether or not to sell it. "That is, if there is anyone left who is still interested in sailing ships," Mr Thomsen said.'

High overhead, the towering aerodynamics of Thomsen's space-age marvel thrust her along at seventeen knots through a Force Eight gale and dark confused sea towards her goal.

Fate – or Molot?

Chapter 25

It was Molot.

It was the most colossal spectacle I have ever seen.

Grohman's arrival on schedule was a tribute to the magnificent way the automatics had handled *Jetwind*, although he had been lucky with the wind. It was the afternoon of the third day of our captivity.

Perhaps it was mainly Tideman's diagnosis that the winner in a hostage snatch was the one who kept his nerve the longest that kept us going. That, and our endless – and sometimes futilely impractical – plans to retake the ship which we formulated and reformulated as the hours and the guards' presence leaned on us. The worst aspect was that we had nothing to keep us occupied. An adjunct to our plotting – like prisoners of war doing mental mathematical calculations to prevent them from going mad – was our attempts to estimate *Jetwind*'s speed, course, and destination. The gale had fluctuated between Forces Seven and Nine. Neither Tideman nor I needed instruments to judge that. Only once did *Jetwind* slow. There was a curious hiatus one afternoon when the wind fell to a light northwesterly breeze and the ship rolled heavily in the rough swell. Then the wind backed strongly and *Jetwind* put on her seven-league boots again. The course was the big poser. We knew *Jetwind* still headed eastnortheast from the sun's position through the porthole. Often, however, it was obscured by cloud.

World interest in *Jetwind* became progressively less as the days passed. At first there was some comment on the radio bulletins about the lack of further information. However, a report that the British Antarctic survey ship *RRS John Biscoe* would shortly be leaving South Georgia and would traverse the area from which *Jetwind* had supposedly radioed, seemed to kill the drama in the media's eyes.

Our guards had remained super-vigilant but we saw almost nothing of Grohman. On one of his rare visits I had tried to rattle him by accusing him of throwing the bodies of Brockton and Arno overboard. His reply had been, had he the discretion, he would have done so. As it was, they were being kept in deep-freeze 'for clinical examination' at Molot. This answer had started new trains of speculation. Clinical examination postulated a base with facilities.

Now – it was late in the afternoon watch. Kay, Tideman and I were trying to kill the unkillable time.

Suddenly Kay exclaimed, 'What's happening?'

A second guard had entered the glassed-off section. The sentry himself seemed surprised. The newcomer gestured in our direction. He was strung about with spare UZI magazines and there were two grenades at his belt.

He opened the door.

'Come!'

The two hijackers conducted us along a passageway leading to the navigation and chart offices and finally to the bridge.

There I paid no attention to Grohman: I had eyes only for what lay ahead of the ship.

'By all that's holy!' exclaimed Tideman softly.

In *Albatros*, it had been a hallucination, a dream; now it was a living nightmare.

The entire ocean was a fantasy in foggy blue, white and pearl with no clear demarcation between green-grey sea, pale horizon and grey overcast. The misty reality was the same as before; the two groups of piled-up icebergs were the same. So was one great isolated berg which rode alone and whose resemblance to a Cunarder had made me doubt my senses when I had sighted it from *Albatros*'s cockpit. The two assemblages of bergs tumbled together to form a kind of gigantic gateway to what lay behind – undefined as yet, vast, murky, secret.

'Molot!'

Grohman was amused at our thunder-struck silence.

'It's not on any chart,' I said doubtfully.

Chart or no chart, it was engraved in my memory. It was there, out to starboard, inside the huge entrance, that I had seen the Orion vanish into a no-world of water vapour, ice and sky. Further in still, I had sighted the submarine.

Kay found her voice. 'Molot – what does it mean?'

'Hammer,' replied Grohman. 'The hammer . . .'

'. . . and the sickle,' added Tideman.

Grohman chuckled. 'Molot is on the chart – if you have the right chart.' He brought one out from under his arm. He'd obviously been waiting for the question – the typical need for exhibitionism of the paranoiac.

I did not need to understand the Russian lettering. It was the Soviet Fleet's nuclear submarine chart of the Southern Ocean. Tideman gaped.

Grohman indicated a position. I could not follow the Russian scale; at a guess, the place was about six hundred nautical miles southsouthwest of Gough Island.

'Molot!' he repeated. He waved to the spectacle outside as if to underscore what he was telling us. 'Molot!'

'There *is* no land!' I expostulated. 'There can't be! It would have been discovered years ago!'

'It is not land,' answered Grohman. 'It was not land we were after. Molot is a seamount, a series of shallow-water shoals. It is the shape of a huge triangle – the sides measure thirty-one by twenty-nine by eighteen kilometres!'

'No one has ever suspected that such a place exists!'

'Of course they haven't – except the Red Fleet,' Grohman retorted contemptuously. 'What do you think was the true purpose of years of patient oceanographical research carried out by Soviet ships in the Southern

Ocean? Whales? Plankton studies? No! The purpose of our search was strategic, and we found what we were looking for – Molot.'

Tideman and I had our attention focused on the chart; we did not see what caused Kay to utter a further gasp of amazement.

Some freak of cold air interacting with warm vapour drew aside the mist curtain for a moment.

A single monster iceberg stretched from horizon to horizon. It blocked our entire view of the ocean to port as far as the eye could reach. It had the characteristic tabular shape of the Antarctic iceberg, but I had never seen anything to approach it in size. It towered some five hundred metres out of the water. Although this giant was the centre-piece, the rest of the panorama was equally breathtaking. Groups of smaller bergs, giants in themselves but puny by comparison with the monster, scattered the ocean ahead and on both sides of *Jetwind*, now moving under reduced sail. The barrier of ice was already having a taming effect on the swells at the approaches to the bases.

Grohman said, 'It is the biggest iceberg ever seen in the Southern Ocean.'

'Trolltunga!' I exclaimed.

'Yes, Trolltunga,' he repeated.

Kay stared at the great berg as if mesmerized and shivered. I remembered her premonition of evil when she first heard the name Trolltunga.

'You're seeing Trolltunga only in old age,' Grohman continued, repeating what I had already heard from Brockton. 'It was first spotted by an American satellite in the Weddell Sea as long as fifteen years ago. Now, it is only about half its original dimension. Trolltunga has taken all those years to drift north from the main Antarctic ice shelf and it has lost size as it passed gradually into warmer seas. Now, as you can see, it is fast.'

'Fast?' exclaimed Tideman. 'What do you mean – fast?'

'The nearest comparison to Molot I can make is the Burdwood Bank off the Malvinas – your Falklands,' he answered. 'There, every season, are gigantic accumulations of icebergs which have grounded in the shallow water after breaking free of the Antarctic pack. Don't forget, Molot's present position is still within the limits of drifting pack-ice. Trolltunga has rested stationary here for years. It forms the entire southwestern barrier of the base.'

It prompted the question which had been in my mind ever since the day in *Albatros* I had imagined I was suffering from hallucinations.

'How is the fog formed? The icebergs themselves are not enough to generate it.'

'I told you, Molot is a seamount,' said Grohman. 'It is a section of a highly unstable ocean-floor volcanic pattern which stretches southwestwards from the vicinity of Gough towards the Horn. You remember that some years ago Tristan da Cunha was almost destroyed by a volcanic eruption. Molot has the same characteristics, except that its volcanic crater lies just below the sea's surface. We have established that it is alive, but it is not active in the sense that it is liable to blow up at any moment. The underwater volcanic action in contact with the cold sea surrounding the icebergs causes the fog.'

'You keep saying we – do you belong to the Soviet Navy?' I ventured.

While he had been explaining the physical features of Molot Grohman's earlier hectoring, paranoid attitude towards us had abated. Now my question seemed to fuel it afresh.

'I am a patriot, an Argentinian,' he snapped. 'I am going to recapture the Malvinas – the Falklands – for Argentina.'

'That's a tall order,' I observed.

'You think so?' he sneered. 'Listen. For years I have led Group Condor, which began purely as a patriotic society. Under my leadership it became a para-military body, then finally a military strike force. But alone we could not mount an attack against the Malvinas. So we grouped ourselves with the super-power most likely to help us – the Soviet. From Molot here I will lead my assault force against the Malvinas.'

A warning bell rang at the back of my mind. 'Why are

you telling us all this, Grohman? It is top secret information.'

I didn't like the way he laughed. 'Why shouldn't you know? You will never live to tell. That goes for Tideman as well. As for the woman, I think Kyyiv is about as security-safe as Siberia.'

I decided to play further on his deep-seated mania in order to elicit more information. 'How does *Jetwind* come into all this?'

'There was the danger that on her run from Montevideo to the Cape she would divert and discover Molot.'

'So that is why you murdered Captain Mortensen?'

Tideman added, 'Anyway, the Great Circle course from Montevideo passes hundreds of miles away from here.'

Grohman's eyes went from Tideman to me. They were merciless. 'You are only tiny pawns in a big game. So was Mortensen. His life didn't count for a damn beside the big issues. There was a danger that he might go south into the Molot area to look for better winds. I was planted aboard *Jetwind* in the first place – a long time ago, when she was building – to hold a watching brief, just in case. It proved to be a very wise precaution.'

I recalled Tideman's guess that the Soviet Navy might have suspected that *Jetwind* was not merely a new type of sailing ship but a vessel of strategic significance.

Grohman's next words bore it out. He said in a quiet, sinister voice, 'This ship has a secret, and we mean to find it out.'

I went cold inside. Had *Jetwind*'s picture after leaving Montevideo – as we had speculated – indeed failed to register on a Red spy satellite sensor because of her polyionosoprene-coated sails and in consequence precipitated the order to Grohman to kill Mortensen and take the ship to safety in the Falklands pending the Group Condor attack? The jigsaw seemed to fit.

What Grohman added made me certain. It also frightened me.

'The woman knows what it is,' he said. 'At Kyyiv, we will extract it.'

Kay went white. 'I'm only a sail-maker!' she exclaimed.

'Only a sail-maker!' he mocked. 'We shall see! There are ways of extracting the unextractable, señorita!'

'There is nothing to know, Grohman!' I snapped.

His face suffused with rage. '*You* tell me that! You! Listen – you interfere in everything! You nearly caused the entire attack plan to abort! My orders were to wait in Port Stanley in *Jetwind* until the main body of Group Condor arrived for me to seize the place. Just to make sure, my country sent the *Almirante Storni* . . .'

I laughed. He swung on me so violently I thought he was about to use the UZI.

'Laugh – while you have the time!' he snarled. 'Soon you will regret what you did to the *Almirante Storni*!'

Tideman stepped in to try and defuse the tension. He played on Grohman's illusions of grandeur.

'The Soviet Navy's oceanographic ships have combed the Indian Ocean for years,' he said. 'Likewise, they must have charted every seamount and shoal in the Southern Ocean, from what you say.'

It seemed as if Tideman had pressed the right button. Grohman calmed down.

'Have you asked yourself why?' he asked rhetorically.

'Obvious. Safe routes for nuclear subs,' replied Tideman.

'As you say, the obvious deduction,' Grohman retorted with an air of contempt. 'It is what we wanted the West to think.'

'What else?' I interjected.

He asked obliquely, 'Have you ever heard of jellified fuel?' He did not wait for us to venture an answer. 'The Soviet Fleet uses it. It is a type of fuel ideally suited to submarines. It minimizes vapour pressure and is easily relinquished. It does away with all need for the elaborate array of fleet replenishment tenders and refuelling points in mid-ocean which are subjected to monitoring by spy satellites and spy planes. Stored underwater in a base which is secure, shallow and cold, jellified fuel gives the submarine – the Red submarine, that is to say – a range without limit.'

'Molot!' I exclaimed.

'Yes, Molot!' he said triumphantly. 'Supply ships dump large plastic containers of jellified fuel which are cached away at Molot safe from detection beneath the surface. The shoals of this seamount could not be bettered for our purpose. Our submarines are guided to the dumps by means of underwater electronic markers. Once the fuel is scooped up by a submarine, the process of reliquification is easy. By having this base, the way is open from Molot to choose our point of attack anywhere in the Southern Ocean – the Drake Passage, the Cape oil route, the Malvinas, anywhere we wish. The Malvinas is the initial operation to be mounted from Molot. The first anyone will be aware of it will be when the attack squadron with Group Condor appears in The Narrows.'

I knew now that the submarine I had seen from *Albatros* had been no hallucination. Grohman's words told me what it had been busy doing – refuelling with jellified fuel. The secret was so momentous that the Orion had had to pay with its life merely because of its presence near Molot. Brockton had been in deeper waters than he had suspected.

Molot was safe from detection by virtue of its remoteness and the wildest seas and weather on the face of the oceans. No ship-master in his senses would risk approaching that protecting screen of icebergs, even if by some off-chance he should be so distant from all recognized sea routes. Most valuable of all to the Red Fleet was that canopy of foggy vapour. It effectively created an impenetrable screen to spy satellite surveillance.

Molot was the dagger aimed at the heart of the West.

Chapter 26

The blade of that dagger lay unsheathed when *Jetwind* rounded Trolltunga's ice head-land as high and impressive as Cape Horn itself.

It was a Soviet naval squadron.

It was a gut-roiling exhibition of the iron fist.

I spotted the submarine. The shape of its elongated fin was the same as I had sighted from *Albatros*. Now, in addition, I was aware of its strange camouflage colour – bluish mauve, with the hull darker. It was the colour of the Antarctic half-night. It was (so Tideman told me later) a radar picket sub, a Whiskey Canvas Bag class. The odd name sprang from the way the Soviet Fleet had tried to mask the conning-tower from the eyes of Western observers by means of a coy canvas cover.

Moored alongside was a big, deadly *Kashin*-class destroyer. Even at our distance from the warship the gaggle of four twin missile surface-to-air launchers plus four other single launchers was clearly visible. She mounted heavy guns as well; the snouts of quintuple torpedo-tubes bared their teeth over the ship's side.

Sheltering under this formidable weaponry was the vessel responsible for the discovery of Molot itself – the oceanographic survey ship *Akademik Kurchatov*. Her eight heavy masts made her quite distinctive. One was in the bow, two immediately for'ard of the bridge, another immediately abaft with a mass of heavy gear and aerials. Others were sited at various points, but a triangular, gantry-type with a big derrick rigged on heavy cables left no doubt that the *Akademik Kurchatov*'s work was in the ocean deeps.

Dwarfing the squadron, however, was a massive, square-looking vessel – over thirty thousand tonnes, I reckoned – with a huge steel gantry running athwartships between an armoured, enclosed super-structure over her bow and stern. Her sloping steel anti-splinter upperworks, tall lattice mast for'ard strung with sophisticated search and firing radar antennae, twin SAM missile launchers, and eight 57 mm and 30 mm guns left no doubt that the *Berezina* could defend herself as well as fulfil her purpose, which was to act as fleet replenishment unit to the Red Navy.

Hundreds of men appeared on the super-structure of the *Berezina* when *Jetwind* came in sight – Group Condor.

'Shorten sail! Topsails only!'

It seemed that we were about to join the fleet at anchor. I could not fault Grohman's handling of *Jetwind*. Operating the consoles' controls was Jim Yell, the bo'sun, who had helped me rescue Kay. He had obviously been dragooned into the job at pistol-point: he was new to it, all thumbs. Grohman's automatic at his back wasn't a help.

Yell's handling was not quick enough for Grohman. He gave an oath at the bo'sun's awkwardness, waved him aside with the gun barrel, and took over the manoeuvre himself.

Jetwind edged past the ice cape.

Four explosions rang out.

Grohman and the other hijackers' nerves must have been shot to react so violently. Both dropped into a firing crouch. The shots originated from the ice head-land we were passing. I saw spurts of ice chips fly.

Our escape plan from Molot did not come to mind fully fledged, as had *Jetwind*'s plan to elude the *Almirante Storni*. However, the sound of the explosions, the sight of a small naval pinnace moored at the foot of the iceberg, and the formidable array of Red sea-power riding at anchor in the stormy, uncertain light, were the ingredients of the mix. Consciously, it was a daring impossibility; subconsciously, my mind began to free-wheel.

In retrospect, I was not aware of my thought processes. All I noted at the time was a small group of men in heavy clothing emerging from a tent on the summit of Trolltunga and making for the site of the explosions.

'That's quite a hero's welcome for you!' I told Grohman derisively.

He straightened up truculently. 'I can't be too careful. They must be testing something up there.'

Landajo, the radio operator, appeared on the bridge and spoke excitedly to Grohman. Grohman spoke into the ship-to-ship radio microphone. I presume he used Russian. He conversed haltingly and finally nodded.

'Up helm! Back the fore and main! Stand by to let go the anchor!' he ordered.

I made a quick check of wind, sea and the nature of the mooring in case I was returned to immediate captivity. The wind had more south than southwest in it. This meant it was blowing almost straight into the Molot entrance. *Jetwind* had not penetrated far enough into the holding ground to get the full benefit of a lee from the ice cape, situated to port. However, the fleet anchorage, protected by the bulk of Trolltunga, was snug enough. The ice made a huge semi-circular arc, forming an embayment. The place was shallow, as Grohman had outlined – the secret of the jellied fuel dump. *Jetwind* lay about three kilometres from the fleet. Banks of fog, into which the warships merged and reappeared, drifted across my line of vision. The eastern flank of Molot – the side away from Trolltunga – was obviously the clear-way to the open sea. For at least half a dozen kilometres I could make out small stranded buoys during the momentary fog clearances. They provided natural markers through the shoals like channel buoys.

'Let go!'

The anchor cable roared out.

'Señorita!' Grohman's eyes were hard. 'You will come with me!' He addressed me. 'You and Tideman will stay here. I have ordered that if you make any attempt to interfere with the controls you will be shot. Is that clear?'

'Peter!' Kay appealed desperately to me.

It was blind rage – and love – and I lunged at Grohman. Maybe he'd been expecting this. The blast from the automatic seemed to go off in my face. I felt the cordite grains sear my left cheek. I spun round, stunned, caught a glimpse of a finned barrel clubbing at my head, and then everything went black.

I don't know for how long I was out. When I came round Tideman was propping me up. I felt as if the whole of *Jetwind*'s top-hammer had clouted my head. The bridge was empty except for Grohman's stooge with his finger on the trigger of his gun.

'Kay! Where's Kay?'

'Take it easy, Peter,' said Tideman. 'That was a stupid thing to do. You're lucky to be still alive.'

I felt sick and dizzy. 'John! Where is she?'

Tideman hefted me to my feet. 'There!' He pointed to the fleet.

The agony in my head was nothing to the sight of *Jetwind*'s boat heading towards the *Akademik Kurchatov*, which was moored nearer *Jetwind* than the rest of the squadron.

He said quietly, 'I think you should make up your mind to the fact that you won't see Kay again.'

I staggered to the starboard wing of the bridge and watched the disappearing boat.

'Did she finally give in?' I asked at last.

'She fought like a wild-cat. They had to rope her to get her into the boat.'

Now I had only a distant sight of her receding into the fog. The way to Kyyiv. The way to hell.

'There are four of them in the boat,' I remarked.

'Yes. Grohman took another of his gang along. The fourth is Sir James.'

The mists swirling across my brain resembled those about the fleet. Like them, there were clear patches.

'Worth a million dollars.'

'Grohman has gone for orders from Molot Command We can only wait and see when he returns.'

Another round of small explosions reverberated from Trolltunga.

'What the hell are they doing!'

'Explosion seismology is the name for it, Grohman said after consulting HQ,' explained Tideman. 'A party of Red scientists are using small charges to measure acoustically the thickness of Trolltunga below the water level.'

I spotted one of the group leaving the pinnace with an armful of fresh charges.

The idea tugged at the back of my mind. 'How far is that pinnace from *Jetwind*, John?'

He eyed me. 'Three cables, a trifle more, maybe.'

'Five hundred metres?'

'About that.'

'Explosion – seismology.' I turned over the words slowly, thoughtfully. Tideman watched me, waiting for an explanation. As yet, my plan was too nebulous to formulate in words.

As we stood, the sun suddenly broke through the storm clouds. The sunset mist swirled and flowed and ebbed like pink foam from a lung-shot. Molot became even more unreal. The ice was blue-white; the grey lengths of the warships were tinged with red, the colour of their ensigns. Soon the long Antarctic summer night would begin, a night which never really got dark.

The boat with Kay vanished behind the *Akademik Kurchatov*.

'The sub's moving!' exclaimed Tideman.

His keen eye had spotted the narrowing of the sail's angle against the white back-drop of Trolltunga.

'She's coming out,' he added.

'No,' I replied. 'She's heading for the fleet replenisher.'

The sub edged towards her big sister. Which warship housed the faceless Molot Command?

The sub neared the *Berezina*.

'The gantry – look!' exclaimed Tideman.

My muzziness was passing; I could focus again. The cut from Grohman's blow was small and did not bleed much but the bruise felt the size of Trolltunga.

A section of the *Berezina*'s prominent athwartships gantry slid out of its housing to reach over the sea like a horizontal crane. Then, cables with massive hooks attached spilled into the water.

'Watch!' said Tideman excitedly. 'This is something no

Westerner has ever witnessed! The fleet's fuelling! They're bringing up the jellified fuel from the undersea dump!'

Tens of thousands of hectolitres of jellified fuel! Each massive container in itself a bomb big enough to sink a ship! Molot itself – the whole anchorage – a more gigantic bomb still! It only needed a trigger to detonate it!

And then my plan was born: I knew how I would attempt it.

But it would kill Kay.

That was the thought which lacerated my mind for the next hour while Tideman and I stood viewing the fleet begin its refuelling operation. The soundless process was punctuated at intervals by the detonation of more seismic charges from Trolltunga. The mystic half-light of the Antarctic twilight, the swirls of mist and cloud, the ice skyscrapers brooding over the Red Fleet's secret base in an ocean as remote as the moon's Sea of Storms, made the scene as unreal in its own way as the one I had witnessed from *Albatros*. Progress was much slower than I had anticipated. Floodlights sprang up aboard the *Berezina* and *Akademik Kurchatov*. Strange reflections flickered off the ice and the blue-grey hulls of the squadron. The artificial light added a further dimension of unreality to the macabre scene – a mother suckling her brood with dragon's blood.

The time to strike was when the babes were at the fuelling teats. Tonight!

But Kay! What about Kay!

I jumped off my stool in agitation. By now I had largely shaken off the effects of Grohman's blow. The sentry followed my movements with his automatic.

'Cool it, Peter!' warned Tideman in a low voice. 'Don't attempt anything again!' He broke off, staring at the warships.

'What is it, John?'

'*Jetwind*'s boat – it's coming back!'

'There are several more men in the boat than Grohman left with,' added Tideman.

The craft sheered off its course and made for the

scientists' pinnace at the foot of Trolltunga. Then one of Grohman's crew made his way laboriously up to the tent party above. It seemed to take an excruciating time for him to reach the summit. Finally he returned to the boat.

'They're coming our way! It looks as if Kay and Hathaway are coming back!' exclaimed Tideman.

The boat finally tied up alongside *Jetwind*. Now I could go ahead! With Kay back, I would set match to fuse of my plan the moment Grohman stepped on *Jetwind*'s deck.

Kay climbed aboard under guard. Her progress to the bridge along the main-deck took a light year to my impatient senses.

Then she was with me. When a person walks in from the dead, words are not enough. Grohman had no need to guard us at that moment. I did not even notice him.

I came to earth when he ordered abruptly, 'Take them away – lock them up!'

He snapped something further in Spanish at the sentry, who had a half-smoked cigarillo between his lips. The man sullenly ground out the smoke with his foot.

Grohman addressed us. 'No smoking – even at this distance from the fuel. Orders from Command. One spark, and up would go the ships. Is that clear?'

Too clear, Grohman. It is the heart of my plan.

He added, 'Molot Command has even stopped the scientists firing their charges during the operation because of the risk.'

'The ships are taking their time about it,' I remarked.

'Just you hope for the sake of your skins that it goes on for long,' was his comeback. 'Make no mistake, you're not coming along with Group Condor.'

He cradled the gun and spoke briefly to the guard. You couldn't call it a smile which crossed his face. He went on, 'If the English capitalist has his ransom paid, it will be a condition of his release that he keeps his mouth shut.'

'We have seen the operation, Tideman and I,' I pointed out.

His reply sent my stomach nerves into a spasm. 'Dead

men tell no tales. The rest of *Jetwind*'s crew will be given the option of cooperating with us and keeping their mouths shut – or else. You two have got till the fleet has finished refuelling.'

'How long is that?'

'Why shouldn't you know?' he asked cynically. 'Operation Molot has been advanced – the squadron sails tomorrow morning. After the stir over *Jetwind*'s disappearance, Command considers it unwise to delay. The fleet dares not risk detection; there is still the possibility of a chance interception. The attack must and will come like a bolt from the blue. If there is local resistance, the *Almirante Storni* will support Group Condor in crushing it.'

Kay took a step towards Grohman. 'You can shoot me along with Peter and John!' she blazed. 'I'd rather die than play along with terrorists who are planning to murder innocent civilians and seize their homes!'

Grohman said speculatively, 'I believe you mean what you say, señorita.'

'You can do what you wish, I will not cooperate!'

'You are a fool, señorita,' retorted Grohman. 'Do not love a man like this. Let him go. There are plenty more men. You can save your life – have a good life, even, at Kyyiv.'

'That's my business,' Kay answered hotly.

'Take them away!' he snapped. Then he added something in Spanish to the guard. There was no mistaking the threat in his voice. Nor the way it cowed the man.

He repeated it in English for our benefit.

'I have warned him that if any one of you attempts any funny business, he will be shot tomorrow with you.'

Chapter 27

'This is my plan.'

Kay, Tideman and I were back again in the sick-bay. I waited only long enough for the guard to settle behind the glass partition before sitting the others down at the table. The pretence of playing cards was agonizing. Guillotine victims did it with more aplomb. But they had no hope of escape.

'We are going to escape,' I added. 'Tonight.'

Kay's fan of cards trembled. Even Tideman's iron control cracked.

'How?' he demanded. 'For pity's sake, how?'

'It is tonight or never,' I answered. 'Our one big chance – our only chance – is while the fleet is occupied fuelling.'

'Peter!' Kay started to remonstrate.

'Try to remember you are supposed to be playing cards,' I reminded her. 'You know what to expect if that gorilla out there suspects us. It's his neck as well as ours. I intend it to be his.'

'Go on,' said Tideman quietly.

I made a pretence of trumping a card.

'I intend to blow up the fleet.'

Tideman's incredulity, backed by the authority of a naval officer, was shattering.

Kay broke the ensuing silence. Her tone said everything. 'I have never seen so many guns or so many men as there are in the squadron. Group Condor alone must number five or six hundred. Peter, what you propose is totally and wholly impossible.'

'Even if you weren't imprisoned,' added Tideman.

I tried to muster my words calmly despite my excitement.

'Soon every ship will be engaged in refuelling,' I said

'The fleet will, figuratively speaking, have its pants down. Never will it be more vulnerable. The ships will be surrounded by tens of thousands of hectolitres of highly explosive jellified fuel. Molot Command itself is nervous – no smoking even here aboard *Jetwind*, kilometres away. No seismic explosions allowed on Trolltunga, either.'

'What's in your mind, Peter?' asked Tideman.

'Molot anchorage is one gigantic, ready-to-detonate bomb. One match would do it.'

'You could escape that way if you had a kamikaze death-wish. But you'd go up in smoke, too,' answered Tideman.

Nevertheless, I thought I detected slightly less scepticism.

'Aboard the pinnace is the scientists' supply of explosive charges,' I went on. 'I intend seizing the pinnace. I will set the charges on a time fuse. I will direct the boat at the fleet. The charges will blow. Up will go the fuel – up will go the fleet.'

'*I* am not going to stand by and watch you commit suicide,' protested Kay.

I smiled, despite my tension. 'The pinnace will be unmanned. I will aim her at the fleet by locking the tiller. A bull's-eye isn't called for. A target that size is too big to miss. A flash anywhere near the fuel container will do the trick.'

'It's a good idea, Peter,' said Tideman. 'But it remains only an idea – there are far too many practical steps in-between that it doesn't take account of. The principle is excellent, your logistics are non-existent.'

'What steps?' I guessed what was coming.

'Let us assume for the sake of argument that somehow you managed to escape from the sick-bay – past a guard with an automatic weapon, past another similarly armed on the bridge, past Grohman himself . . .'

Kay added, 'Grohman brought two extra men back with him from the fleet to reinforce those aboard *Jetwind*. That makes six guards plus himself.'

'You've got to get from *Jetwind* to the pinnace. How?' Tideman resumed. 'By boat? Their automatics would cut you and the boat in half before you got clear of the ship. Also, the pinnace is within range of the AK-47 rifles the new guards have – they have the power, even if the UZIs don't. Forget it, Peter.'

'I wasn't thinking of using a boat, and besides they wouldn't dare shoot because of the danger of an explosion.'

'Please, Peter, this is just talking!' Kay said agitatedly. 'It's simply killing time. Listen to John's advice – forget it.'

I went on. 'I need you two to win control of the bridge for as long as it will take me to climb up to *Jetwind*'s top-gallant masts. We'll work out the precise time. Then – ' I addressed Tideman ' – I want you to fire the chicken button on the bridge and blast away Number Two top-gallant mast directly overhead.'

'Ring charges – the ultimate emergency!' he exclaimed.

'That's it,' I replied. 'The ultimate emergency. Those charges are meant to blow away *Jetwind*'s top-hamper if ever she went over on her beam-ends in a storm. I intend using them for another type of emergency.'

Kay looked horrified. 'And you – where will you be, Peter?'

'Inside the crow's nest – above the site of the charges. The detonations will project the mast and me clear of the ship – the same principle as a pilot's ejector seat. The way the ship's head is lying at present and the direction of the wind will pitch the mast towards the pinnace. The mast is hollow so it'll float for a while. I'll reach the pinnace from it – you know my plan from that point onwards.'

'You'll be killed!' protested Kay. 'The blast inside the confined space will kill you!'

'Self-destruct charges like that are precisely calibrated to do their job and their job only,' I answered. 'In this case, it's to chop off the mast at a given point and throw it clear. The force of the explosion will be directed outward, not inward where I will be. The structure of the crow's nest in itself will be an additional protection.'

'This is plain crazy!' went on Kay. 'I won't let you do it, Peter! No experiments were ever carried out to establish how far the masts would be thrown by the ring charges. It's designed purely as a last-throw emergency!'

'I'll have to take the risk, Kay.'

'I'd like to hear what else you have in mind, Peter,' said Tideman speculatively. 'Before you do so, however, you might remember something else – the sea temperature, especially close to Trolltunga, is close to freezing point. You won't survive for more than a couple of minutes in it after the mast blast-off, even if the rest of your plan succeeds.'

'Deal another round of cards,' I told him. 'Don't either of you look up in surprise when I speak. The next step in my scheme is probably the most crucial of all. It's the way I aim to break out of the sick-bay.'

Kay gathered up the cards like a sleep-walker. Tideman dealt.

'In the sick-bay there's that anti-exposure survival suit for inspecting *Jetwind*'s drop keels and underwater propeller nacelle. We moved it into the cubicle next to Kay's – it's hanging there still. That's what I intend to wear to overcome the problem of the near-freezing water.'

Tideman gave a silent whistle through his teeth. 'You half convince me, man!'

'The anti-exposure visor will protect my face and eyes against flash from the ring charges,' I continued. 'The suit is foam-lined, which will help give me a soft landing when the mast hits the water. I'll swim from the floating mast to the pinnace, fuse the charges, and send the boat on its way to the fleet. Then I can swim back to *Jetwind* in safety – it's not far.'

'It might just work, Peter – it just could work!' Tideman's sceptical questioning had changed to a vibrant, excited undertone.

'We must be careful not to betray ourselves to the guard by any action or gesture,' I warned.

'He's the joker in the pack.' There was a near-sob in Kay's voice. 'We can't get past him.'

'We can,' I said. 'This is how. Again, the survival suit is the key. I've often accompanied you to your cubicle, Kay.

The guard is accustomed to it. Now – as soon as we've fin·shed this discussion, you and I will go there. John will stay here, pretending to be listening to the radio. There's only a curtain between your cubicle and the empty one. We slip next door. You help me into the survival suit. It takes less than a minute, you said, John. Back you go into your cubicle, Kay. Then, after a while, you join John at the radio. I'll be missing. After a time the guard is certain to wonder about me. You can leave your cubicle's outer curtain drawn so he can see for himself that I'm not there. The idea is to draw him into the sick-bay.'

'Where will you be all this time?' asked Kay in an anguished tone.

'Where the survival suit always hangs – up against Number Two cubicle wall,' I said. 'Arms outstretched, just like a suit on a hanger.'

'The guard will see your face – he must!' protested Kay.

'No. Before you leave you will pull the helmet right down over the visor, which normally leaves only the nose and eyes visible. It will restrict my range of vision, but I can't help that. In addition, I'll hang my head. The rest of the suit is so shapeless that the guard won't suspect that it's occupied.'

'Then?' Tideman demanded.

'I'll want your slide-rule dagger,' I said as matter of factly as a man can when thinking of a sudden knife-thrust to an unsuspecting victim's heart. 'The suit is unwieldy so I'll have only one chance to finish the guard in the cubicle. After that it's up to you to grab his automatic and cope with him further, if necessary.'

'Any chance shots will bring the rest of the gang at the double,' said Tideman. 'Action must be silent at that stage.'

Kay shuddered and glanced involuntarily at the sentry. He was staring the other way, probably yearning for a smoke.

'I won't be able to move fast in the survival suit,' I continued. 'John, you've got to take the bridge guard by surprise. You must keep control while I get up aloft to the top-gallant mast.'

'This is not going to work,' said Kay emphatically. 'You're both assuming that the bridge is the only place which is occupied by the gang. With the reinforcements Grohman brought there are now three Group Condors in the stern keeping watch over the crew. There's another in the engine room. Then there's Grohman himself – where will he be? As soon as shooting starts on the bridge, the gang will converge on it. John against – how many? He won't stand a chance.'

I had earlier realized the discrepancy of forces involved. I had rather pushed the risk to one side when thinking through the logistics and split-second timing of the operation.

'That's part of the risk . . .' I started, but she stopped me.

'The odds are too long for success.'

'What do you suggest?' I asked.

'I'll give you a more sporting chance.'

'*You*, Kay?'

'I want to rush the bridge with John.'

I was about to protest, but Tideman interjected. 'I agree.'

'While John is . . . accounting . . . for the guard, I'll make for the hydraulics control panel . . .'

'Kay,' I said impatiently, 'the hydraulics can come later.'

Kay's eyes were bright. She went on. 'Let's run over the position of various members of the gang – three in the stern, one in the engine room, another on the bridge, and finally our sick-bay guard. Grohman could be anywhere, but let's assume he will be in your cabin, Peter, when our attack goes in.'

'At the slightest sound of trouble he'll be out like a rocket – plus UZI,' I remarked.

'I intended stopping all of them from getting into orbit, like a rocket or anything else,' she said.

'What's in your mind?' demanded Tideman incredulously.

'*Jetwind* is practically unsinkable,' she replied. 'She has the most elaborate system of watertight bulkheads in case of damage – bridge, stern, engine room, the accommodation, the hull . . .'

'The hull's in no danger!' I exclaimed.

'The captain's and officers' quarters can be isolated in an emergency,' she went on. 'Your soundproof cabin doors double as bulkheads. As you know, all emergency doors are held open magnetically until they are released by a master switch on the bridge. One touch and the whole ship can be sealed off.' She emphasized her words. 'Sealed off. Equally, sealed in. The gang can be effectively sealed in.'

'Good girl!' Tideman exclaimed excitedly. 'Heavens, what a brain-wave!'

'Kay,' I said. 'You're wonderful! You've levelled the odds in our favour! We're going to make this operation work. It will, I hope, catch everyone off-balance. We'll play the detail by ear as we go.'

'So far, so good,' said Tideman. 'Let's assume we're in command of the ship and your part of the plan is working – you've aimed the pinnace loaded with the fused-up charges at the fleet. What next?'

'Your job, John, is to have *Jetwind* poised to high-tail the moment I get back aboard. Cut the anchor free, if necessary, manoeuvre ready to take off – you'll have the time while I'm making my way back from Trolltunga.'

'A lot depends on how fast the pinnace travels,' said Tideman. 'If our own craft of the same type are any criterion, it will cruise at something like seven or eight knots. Which means in turn it will take roughly fifteen minutes to reach the Red ships. Once I start to move *Jetwind*, the fleet is sure to spot her. We know Grohman has orders not to move. They'll suspect the hijack has misfired. The Reds are trigger-happy. A couple of 76 mm shells from the *Sposobny* or a missile will put paid to *Jetwind*.'

'The fleet has castrated itself already,' I answered. 'No ship dare fire. The flash would detonate the fuel in the same way that the pinnace will.'

Tideman riffled the cards in his excitement and repeated my words. 'We're going to make this operation work!'

'I want *Jetwind* pointing northeast when I get back aboard from the pinnace,' I went on. 'She's lying roughly facing south now, head to wind.'

'Northeast?' echoed Tideman. 'Past the fleet? What will be happening to it at that stage? It's too risky, Peter. Rather head south, altogether clear of Molot. We don't know the location of Molot's shoals, remember.'

'The stranded icebergs will guide us. They mark the main exit channel to the open sea.'

'But . . .' objected Tideman.

'It's a waste of time to attempt to beat the wind,' I went on. 'If it holds as it is now, *Jetwind* will enjoy her best point of sailing the way I aim to go.'

'Why the hurry?' demanded Tideman. 'The fleet won't be able to chase us, if everything goes according to plan.'

'There *is* need for hurry,' I said.

'What do you mean?'

'Tomorrow *Jetwind* has an appointment with Seascan!'

'You still intend to keep the rendezvous? I'd overlooked that!' Tideman exclaimed in amazement.

'Of course. Then *Jetwind* has another appointment at Gough with Thomsen's party of shipping tycoons. With any luck I'll keep both.'

Tideman forgot himself as far as to throw down his cards and stare at me.

'You're a devil for punishment, Peter!'

Kay asked quietly, 'When do we start?'

All three of us had now put down our cards. The guard still lolled aimlessly. The UZI, sinister and black, lay on the table only as far as his reach.

'Now,' I replied. 'Give me the dagger, John.'

Chapter 28

I do not clearly remember Tideman palming me the lethal slide-rule from his pocket, or my leaving the sick-bay. The nerve-stretched take-off to the operation produced a kind of amnesic blank in my mind. I surfaced in Kay's cubicle with her lips and her body against mine. She was shaking with emotion like a loose back-stay in a gale.

'Darling, my darling!' she whispered. 'I can't let you, I won't let you! This is plain suicide! You're not even seeing me, you're so preoccupied! I love you, I want you – I'm going to lose you!'

I kissed her, tried to soothe her. 'Even kamikazes have their moment of glory, my darling.'

Her mouth sought mine; it was salty with tears. 'There's no glory in a burst from an automatic,' she sobbed.

'What's the alternative?' I asked. 'Being led like sheep to the slaughter?'

Her head fell on my chest. 'What chance did our love get?' she asked brokenly. 'A week? A fall overboard? Being imprisoned together with this awful shadow hanging over us? And now . . .'

I kissed her fair hair and combed it back past her ears with my thumbs.

'There was no time, my darling – either then, or now.'

A final convulsive sob shook her body. Then she took control of herself. She eased me away from her. 'Don't kiss me goodbye,' she said, her head turned aside. 'I can't handle it. And it is – goodbye.'

I said nothing. Already part of my mind was focused on the guard.

The survival suit hung like a crucified monster on its hanger. It had big ungainly boots which were integral with the legs. The suit came in one size only and it was made of a

223

substance called foam neoprene, the latest in survival gear. Tideman had told me that the manufacturer claimed one could get into the suit in half a minute. Key feature of the outfit was a sealing zipper which had been developed for the United States space programme. Silently I handed Kay the dagger, indicating that she should not meddle with the blade release. The suit certainly bore out the maker's claims – with Kay's assistance I was into it in what seemed seconds. Almost immediately the insulation made me sweat; perhaps fear of being surprised by the guard also had something to do with it. The visor and cap came last. By pulling the cap forward and tilting my head, my face was hidden. In that position, however, I could see nothing of anyone above waist-level.

Finally, Kay clasped my fingers round the dagger. They were as ungainly as bandaged bananas. I wondered whether I would ever be able to trigger the blade release. My success depended on one lightning-quick stroke before the guard suspected the suit had an occupant. If I fumbled even for a second, I was done.

Then Kay was gone.

I maintained the hanger pose – slumped, head down, arms out.

Time ceased to pass.

My sole clock to mark the passage of the minutes – or was it hours? – was the drip of my sweat. The suit became a sauna.

I could not hear because of the waterproof cap; I dared not raise my head in case the next moment found the guard there.

The next moment he was.

My sight of him was like a cut-off television camera shot – a trigger hand, a finned barrel, a pair of legs, a firing crouch. The muzzle held steadied on the suit. On me.

I waited for the shot. A blob of sweat chased itself inside my neck, down my chest, past my stomach. I felt every millimetre of its progress. No shot.

The guard's torso swung away. Feet followed. His boots were a boxer's ankle-hugging type.

Now!

My fingers inside the glove were slippery with sweat. I flexed them for the stroke.

The guard's toes swivelled. A boxer dodging a knock-down punch couldn't have matched their speed. They pointed straight at me. Had the gunman heard? Had he seen? I froze – if that was the word in a bath of sweat.

Maybe he had caught, animal-like, some vibration of my rolling tension. Perhaps he even smelt my fear. I kept my head low, my eyes unsighted. Slowly, slowly, I watched his knees ease their tension. Slowly, slowly, that on-target barrel shifted away from my guts.

I did not know how long I could keep every muscle tight as a fence-wire without one making an involuntary give-away ripple. Sweat cascaded down my knife-fingers.

The guard's toes pivoted ninety degrees. His back was towards me.

Now!

Perhaps the switch-blade gave a click on release. Perhaps my body movements beat it by a milli-second. Or perhaps he only sensed rather than heard anything. Whatever it was, he was already turning, left shoulder following the UZI round, when I lurched at him.

There wasn't time for the orthodox overhand dagger thrust. The clumsy suit would not have allowed it. It was a low, savage up-and-under to the heart.

The jar up my arm could have been a glance off the UZI's breech, or the bone armour of his rib-cage.

I fell on him, enveloped him – a crude parody of a rugby smother-tackle. My knife hand skewered him. If he screamed or uttered any sound, I did not hear it. We cannoned off a partition wall, pitched into the main sick-bay, carrying the curtain with us.

I had a momentary sight of the UZI being snatched up by another hand – Tideman's. The guard and I lay face-to-face, I on top. I was grateful for my visor. The man's mouth was contorted. Tell-tale pink sprayed from it, blurring the Perspex.

He gave a final convulsion and was still.

It was Kay with shaking hands who freed my cap. Tideman knelt a pace away with the automatic's barrel trained on the guard's head. There was no need. He was dead.

'Quick!' I rapped out. 'The bridge – both of you!'

There was no direct access to the bridge from the sick-bay. The wheel-house, radio office, chartroom and pilot office were all situated on the floor above us. The route from sick-bay to bridge was along a corridor running athwartships, flanked by officers' cabins. At the far end was the captain's suite. There were twin upward companion-ways, one to port, the other to starboard. These ladders debouched from our level into a central well immediately abaft the wheel-house itself. This well was bisected by No 2 mast, which I now intended to climb via the servicing door which Kay and I had used during our first ascent. The whole of this well area could be isolated in an emergency by means of watertight bulkheads. In short, the central well was the junction of all routes to the bridge.

Tideman and Kay started to the sick-bay door.

'John!' I said. 'In ten minutes – no sooner, no later – you will blow the mast charges. Is that understood?'

'Aye,' replied Tideman. 'Whatever.'

'Good luck!'

The two sprinted off.

I ballooned along the corridor in their wake. I felt like a grotesque carnival figure. That is where the resemblance to fun ended. The knife was bloodied to the hilt.

I lost Tideman and Kay at the first ladder to the mastwell. I negotiated it with the nimbleness of a baby elephant.

I found myself in the well itself. The mast towered in front of me like a burnished lift-shaft. The access door was shut. It had a type of fancy quick-release press-catch. My banana fingers fluffed it. I shifted hands with the dagger, tried again. I felt it yield, open. Sound poured down from the floor above – a burst of automatic fire.

Then – shorter, staccato.

The mast was relaying the sound of the bridge action.

One – two – single shots.

The UZI seemed to appear from the direction of the captain's suite before the man. A seeking black muzzle, the unmistakable heavy finning, a hand on the trigger. Grohman!

Why didn't he blast me? I shall never know. He could not have missed, at less than four metres. I think it must have been the sight of the ludicrous apparition which froze his finger. Or perhaps it was the sight of that bloody dagger,

In that moment of arrested time I realized that Kay had failed in her part. She had not reached the hydraulics console in time to throw the vital bulkheads switch which would have caged Grohman and the other Group Condors. Those last isolated rat-tat-tats from above could have been her epitaph.

My savage despair at the attack's misfire gave me the courage to stand there facing my killer for a split-second long enough to ensure that he would come up the mast after me.

I slammed the door shut. A siren-like whoop reverberated everywhere. Emergency alarm! Kay *had* managed the bulkhead switch!

But it was too late.

Grohman had escaped the trap.

I fumbled with the lock of the mast door. Against it from outside came a savage battering. It wasn't done by hand. It was a magazine full of 9 mm shells.

The emergency siren told me that my part of the plan was still on. I had to get aloft – climb with feet like snowshoes, a suit the size of a hangover, and mittened hands I could scarcely feel through! The visor and cap I left loose against the nape of my neck. It would only take a second to zip them into place when the mast blasted off.

I couldn't climb with my weapon hand encumbered. So I put the dagger between my teeth and hefted my leg on to the first rung.

The confined space rang with two or three concussions. Grohman was trying to shoot open the lock, carefully aiming individual shots.

I levered myself up the ladder. The going was tougher than I had expected. Until I managed the rhythm of lifting the feet and understanding their non-feel against the rungs, I was certain Grohman would pick me off before I reached the level of the lower mainyard. All he would have to do, once he had blasted open the door, was to fire straight upwards. I presented the perfect target against groups of lights fitted for servicing purposes at the juncture of each yard with the mast. The first group was at the lower mainyard. I had to reach them before Grohman broke in the door.

I fought my way up.

There was another rattle of shots from below. Heavy slugs began to tear through the door and were banging about at the foot of the ladder.

Grohman wasn't inside yet.

The group of four naked electric bulbs was close. I threw myself up at them. One foot slipped, and I hung on by my right hand.

The mast door crashed open. I glanced down. Grohman brought the UZI to his shoulder. I was clambering directly above him, like a bird waiting to be picked off a branch.

It is difficult to fire straight overhead. My position allowed him no angle, however slight. He would either have to lean completely backwards or lie on his back to aim.

In that brief interval while he gathered his aim, I made the remaining rungs to the lights.

I swiped madly with my heavy paw. There was a crash of breaking glass, a blinding flash of short-circuiting electrics. Then everything went dark. A general fail-safe switch tripped out the rest of the overhead lights inside the mast.

I hurled myself up – fumbling, slipping, panting.

There was an ear-ripping jangle of sound. The blackness below was polka-dotted with red malice. The interior of the mast seemed full of ricocheting bullets.

Grohman was firing wild. He was hoping that the lethal spray would somehow find its target but the shots were all landing below me. He wasn't getting his angle of fire.

The shattering sound cut off. I guessed the magazine

228

was empty after that prolonged burst. To change it would give me a few precious moments.

Up! Up!

Jetwind's yards were spaced at five equal intervals of ten and a half metres up the mast. The mast itself towered fifty-three metres above the deck. I had now covered the first ten and a half metres. The mast was divided into three sections; the lower mast, the top-mast, and the top-gallant. It was this latter which contained the ring charges at its juncture with the topmast thirty-four and a half metres above deck. The interior profile of the mast was elliptical and diminished progressively the higher one went.

At the point where each of the six yard-arms joined the mast there was a servicing compartment. Apart from a maze of pipes and valves, the main feature of these compartments was a pair of massive vertical rollers, each ten and a half metres in length, on which the sails were rolled in along tracks like a giant roller blind.

The bottom compartment, whose lights I had just smashed, was the largest. It measured about two and three-quarter metres long and was about half that broad. A steel cat-walk extending from the main ladder enabled technicians to stand and work.

I hesitated for a moment on this cat-walk. Its open grille provided no protection against a volley from underneath. There was a metallic clinking from below. What was Grohman up to? He hadn't fired off the UZI's full forty rounds. There was another snap and click, then – unmistakable – the clack of a magazine being rammed home.

I knew enough about the UZI to realize that the big forty-rounder was too heavy to climb with. He had substituted for it a smaller twenty-five rounder. That still didn't account for all the delay. Another series of clicks reached me. He was probably unhitching the skeleton butt, converting the weapon into a compact, manoeuvrable automatic pistol. He was taking his time – he was very sure of me, pinned without hope of escape inside an ever-narrowing field of fire.

I could see faint Antarctic night-light filtering in through the chinks through which the sails rolled and unrolled. Urgently I looked for some weapon.

From the heel of each roller projected what looked like an old-fashioned car crank. I'd seen these before – manual back-up cranks in case the power-driven mechanism failed by which the sails were furled. I wrenched it from its socket and peered down. Below was darkness. I could not see Grohman's position but I heard faint movements.

I dropped the heavy bar and leapt upward again. There was a thud and a savage oath. For an answer, a shot whanged and whined from side to side inside the mast. The initial impact of the slug was much too close for comfort. I deduced from this that Grohman could now raise the automatic to a deadlier elevation.

I hadn't gone more than a couple of metres when the thought crashed home on me – at the next yard-arm bay I would have to stand and fight! It was the last bay before the juncture of the top-mast and top-gallant where the ring charges were sited. How much was left of the ten minutes until Tideman fired them?

I hurried upwards.

Grohman hadn't fired again. I suspected that he was holding back until he thought I was trapped at the crow's nest and the top.

If I were going to use the dagger, I would need elbow room, provided just above my head, in the cat-walk of the next bay.

I hauled myself on to the next set of steel gratings. Now my second enemy was the light coming through the gaps between the sail rollers. I blocked some of the light by standing back against it, but the upper section still emitted a give-away glow. How to fool Grohman into believing that I was still climbing? Perhaps if I pitched another crank-handle – but I was afraid that if I moved he would see me against the light. While I stood still where I was, I was tolerably safe.

The automatic clanked against the ladder.

God! He was close! I even thought I could hear his rapid breathing.

I felt round desperately. My hand touched something metallic that felt like a small dumb-bell. It must have a function in snugging home the sail into the roller. I tried to insinuate myself between the two sail rollers in the same way, as according to Grohman's lies, Captain Mortensen had died. Perhaps the 'dumb-bell' was the blunt instrument whose mark the London pathologist had detected.

I tossed the heavy metal thing carefully through the cat-walk ladder opening. At the same moment I thrust myself, back first, between the two sail-covered rollers.

There was a cry, an oath, a scrabbling of feet and a jangle of gun against rung. From the sound of it, Grohman must have slipped and fallen a few rungs. I could plainly hear his rasping breath.

This time he did not waste ammunition. The silence that followed was more gut-tearing than noise. I could picture the man in the darkness, steadying up, getting a grip on his fury before elevating the UZI into a firing position. The gun would have to be held well above his head if he didn't want to blind or maim himself.

The volley came – a cut-off six-rounder. It crashed and screamed through the confined space. There were also noises high above. Some slugs must have travelled all the way up to the masthead. If I had been on the ladder, I'd have been ripped apart from backside to neck.

There were more flashes of flame from the muzzle – I could almost reach down and touch them!

I took the knife from between my teeth and got a firm grip of the haft. My moment would come as Grohman came into the bay at cat-walk level. There the UZI's handiness would be at its most limited.

The light was dim, elusive. The grating poised criss-cross like a steel trap waiting for Grohman's head. Red-painted stop-cock valves glowed danger signals. Copper hydraulic tubes writhed like disembowelled viscera.

I waited.

It wasn't Grohman's head that came first. I heard a grunt, then his right hand clutching the UZI swung up and over on to the cat-walk. He wasn't much more than a metre from my funk-hole.

My reflexes were swifter than my thinking.

In a flash I was out. I stamped on the UZI, pinning the gun-hand to the gratings.

They'd been right in choosing Grohman to lead Group Condor. He was tough; he could take it.

That booted foot must have hurt like hell. He didn't make the mistake of releasing the weapon. Instead, he used my ankle to lever himself into a fighting position. His head and body seemed to explode out of the opening. Crank and bull-whanger had done more damage than I thought. Blood was pouring from a long gash across his head.

With his free hand he swept my other foot from under me. I crashed beside him on the gratings. He rolled sideways, with cat-like agility. I followed, with survival-suit agility. Now the gun was under him; equally, the knife was trapped under my own bulk.

I pawed at him with a right fist, but even a punch-drunk palooka could have dodged the blow. Grohman jack-knifed on to his hunkers. The UZI must have been heavier than I guessed, or else my first savage stamp must have damaged his wrist more than I – or he – thought. He hadn't the strength in his right hand alone to raise the barrel fully to aim. It wavered, wandered off-target. A target bigger than a house.

The split second more he needed to get his left round to heft up the UZI to fire was too long. I threw the knife. It stuck out from his Adam's apple.

He just knelt there with the UZI raised to blast me, with that obscene brass haft projecting from his throat.

Then he pitched forward through the ladder gap.

I heard the body hit the bottom of the mast and the single shot that went off. He must have hung on to the trigger, even in death.

I crouched on the cat-walk, gulping air. I seemed to be

swimming inside a suit of sweat. My muscles kicked from reaction.

Time! The ring charges!

Twenty-one metres, seventy feet to go!

I threw myself at the rungs. The anti-blast cap! I stopped, jerked cap and visor over my head and face. Securing the sealing zipper with my outsize fingers seemed to take a year.

Up!

I was still scrambling feverishly, blindly, in darkness on the upper mast-head side of the top-gallant bay, heading for the crow's nest, when the charges blew.

My first thought from the concussion's hammer-blow was that I had slipped and fallen the entire length of the mast.

Pilots who eject to safety are heroes; circus human cannons have a soft ride compared to mine from *Jetwind*.

The cap and visor saved my ear-dreams from blast, my eyes from flash, and my lungs from compression. All I knew was that one moment I was battling upwards and the next I felt a vertebrae-ripping punch in the back. The detonation pinned me like a fly against the steel rungs. The detached mast cartwheeled high into the air.

The water was to be my cushion on splash-down; I will never believe it provides cosmonauts with a soft landing. The jar when the tube of light alloy hit the sea was certainly almost as bad as take-off. Between the two, there was a merciful time-warp of oblivion.

I became aware of water glinting inside the floating mast. A circle of light showed at the severed end. It was filling fast. I knew I had to get out – faster – before it sank.

I crept towards the opening on all fours through icy water which deepened at every pace.

Then – I was out.

Chapter 29

There was no horizon. Everything was a neutral white. I panicked. I thought irrationally that I had been blinded by the mast charges.

Then I realized the reason for my white-out vision: ahead and above me towered a skyscraper of ice five hundred metres high.

I had been catapulted so near Trolltunga that I had to turn on my side to get a view of the top.

I trod water, got my bearings. The lighted fleet was to my right, *Jetwind* at my back. Ahead was the pinnace, perhaps a hundred metres away – an easy swim. The water was icier than a mortuary slab. Without the survival suit, I would have been gasping my last.

I started for the pinnace. I had gone only a few clumsy dog-paddle strokes towards my objective when a search-light stabbed out from the *Sposobny* towards *Jetwind*. The bulk of the *Berezina* sprang into silhouette in front of the light. The searchlight, inhibited in range because of the fogginess, picked out a splash near *Jetwind*'s bows – the anchor had gone!

Tideman was wasting no time. I almost ceased paddling, the sight of the sail-setting was so beautiful. An ethereal quintuple bank of white mounted up on *Jetwind*'s fore-mast, clean as a swan's breast against the blue-white night. Sail on four other masts followed – not on the ship's full number. Tideman wasn't risking the structure of Number Two after the ring charges blast.

Then – the fore-yards went aback: Tideman was emulating the manoeuvre I had used to spin *Jetwind* round in Port Stanley.

Like an angry hornets' nest coming alive, beam after beam leapt out from the fleet, spotlighting the lovely fabric of the sailer. They had heard the concussion of the ring charges – what now?

I propelled myself towards the pinnace. The whole anchorage was ablaze with hostile light. I felt sure someone would spot my give-away splashing.

My hand grabbed the pinnace's gunnel. I yanked my clumsy body aboard and my head came up. On the summit of Trolltunga a group of men were gesticulating and yelling, although I could not hear the sound. It wasn't at the searchlights; it was at me.

How long would the fastest of them take to race down the cliff? Would he have a gun?

The thought goaded me. I crawled on all fours to a locker in the bows. I fumbled at the latch – I was about as nimble as a whale stranded on a reef. I finally managed to open it.

There it was! There was no mistaking the characteristic box – explosives!

Time fuses were already mounted in the heads of the charges. These were about the size of half a brick. Each fuse setting had a pointer, a gnarled rotatable screw, and numbers punched at intervals.

I read: *FUMS. ASXX. 01. 02. 00 (03). 10/9.*

What the devil did it mean?

I dragged out the box. The Trolltunga men were slipping and sliding down the cliff like cross-country runners.

I took a blind guess as to how to set the fuses on six charges I set aside. On two of them I would set the firing pointer to the first digit; on the next two to the second, and on the final pair to the third. What if I blew myself up?

I set my teeth, turned the first pointer to 01. Nothing happened. I fused its twin charge. Rapidly I followed with the other four.

Now!

I yanked the starting-cord of the engine. It was an inboard type. I prayed that it wasn't too cold. It fired first time.

I unmoored the pinnace and motored clear of the cliff at low throttle.

Jetwind had almost completed her turn and her bows now pointed slightly at an angle to the fleet. That was our escape direction – northeast!

I manoeuvred the pinnace to aim at a gap between the *Berezina* and *Sposobny*. I hauled the explosives box well into the open to ensure maximum flash effect.

I stopped in my tracks.

A boat was being lowered from the enclosed stern section of the *Berezina*. I caught the reflection of gun barrels as a party of men jumped from the deck overhang into the boat.

Would the cutting-out party reach *Jetwind* before my fire-craft slipped in among the fleet?

I jammed the pinnace's throttle wide and threw myself into the sea. I paddled frantically for *Jetwind*. I willed Tideman to break out without waiting for me – he could not have failed to see the boarding-party. As if in response, *Jetwind*'s after yards also were backed in order to mark time waiting for me.

I thrashed and flailed onwards. Then I was against *Jetwind*'s side and a rope was in the water beside me. I snatched it up, snicked the loop under my arms. On the rail above, Jim Yell was grinning and gesturing. Once he was certain I was secure, he raised an arm to the bridge. That was the signal Tideman had been waiting for.

Even before Yell had dragged me inboard and freed me of my suit I could feel the sternway come off the ship and the beginning of headway take its place.

'You were great, sir!' Yell burst out. 'We'll lick 'em yet!'

I ran to the rail. Without the suit, I felt as light as a disembodied ghost.

'Where's their boat?'

It was there, all right. But it was not coming at *Jetwind*. It was heading towards the pinnace!

I stared in disbelief and anguish. I was brought to earth by a muffled tat-tat from *Jetwind*'s stern.

Yell spun on his heel. 'The gang is still fighting it out aft – I've got to help.'

I sprinted up a bridge ladder. I saw Kay first. For the eternity of one second our eyes locked. Neither of us said anything. There was no need.

Tideman stood at the control consoles. The bloodied mess that had been the bridge guard lay in one corner.

'Course as ordered, Peter? Same route?' Tideman asked without any show of agitation.

'Aye. Get the sails on the damaged mast also.'

'Think it will take it?'

'We need all the speed we can get. You've seen the boat party?'

'I have.'

'They've sheered away from the pinnace! They're coming this way!' exclaimed Kay.

I guessed what had happened – when the boarding party had got close enough and seen the pinnace unmanned, they had decided on *Jetwind* as their primary target. They knew – as we knew – that with all the fuel about they dared not risk a long shot.

'Oh, Jesus!'

I was accustomed to Tideman never raising his voice under almost any provocation: his breathed imprecation was as shattering as a close-up burst of automatic fire.

'Look!' he exclaimed. 'Look at the sub!'

The blue hull with its blue-mauve sail was swinging at its mooring near the destroyer. Its snout was turning deliberately, menacingly, slowly pointing towards *Jetwind*.

'She's going to fire!'

'She can't risk it . . .'

'Compressed air has no flash,' Tideman replied. 'Torpedoes are fired by compressed air.'

It took *Jetwind* twenty to thirty seconds to set sail. The damaged Number Two mast sails were in the process of slotting home; the other backed yards were swinging into position to pick up the wind on *Jetwind*'s starboard quarter. As yet the ship was barely under way. With half

237

one mast missing, perhaps we accounted for the maximum scheduled time of thirty seconds.

They were not thirty seconds; they were thirty years.

Jetwind seemed to hang. The sub's nose swung at her, round, round. There was a faint quiver through the hull as the wind gripped the aerofoils. Was *Jetwind* moving – *at all?*

'There!' Tideman pointed.

There was a white burst at the sub's bows. She was chancing a shot in a surfaced position. Perhaps the torpedo-men were over-eager, perhaps the skipper had miscalculated the running depth in Molot's shallow waters.

As it was, the silver-white tube leapt into the air. Then it plummeted back again in a flurry.

Tideman said unemotionally, 'Shooting is tricky when they run shallow like that.'

Half my mind noted one fact – *Jetwind* was moving! The other half seemed paralysed, fixated on the torpedo's progress.

'Give her two points of starboard helm!'

The long gleaming menace leaped clear of the water again. It shimmied, nose-dived. That leap gave away its target course. It would, I saw, intercept *Jetwind* a little onwards as she gathered speed. What a sub commander could not know was a windjammer's power to brake.

'Back the foremast! All aback!'

Tideman threw the toggle switches. *Jetwind* stopped as if held by a drag parachute.

The torpedo's trail streaked under *Jetwind*'s bows. Now it headed straight for Trolltunga. It seemed to flash over the intervening distance I had laboured across in a matter of seconds.

It detonated against the ice cliff.

It was not the concussion of a warhead filled with torpex TNT, cyclonite and aluminium powder which stunned and raped our sense of hearing. It was Trolltunga.

Years of drifting, years of Antarctic weathering attrition,

years of Southern Ocean corrosion, had shaken the interior architectural structure of the monster iceberg. Perhaps the final deep-down pummelling on the iron-bound tips of Molot seamount had also contributed to its inner break-up. Perhaps that very disintegration had been the reason why the Red scientists had been eager to probe its secrets.

Whatever it was, the torpedo completed the process. It was its *coup de grâce*.

The warhead's explosion was a puny thing compared to what followed.

Trolltunga split, rolled, buckled, fell apart, in a thousand fragments, each tearing at the other like cannibal killer whales. There was a stupendous broadside of sound as the iceberg writhed in its death-agony – heaving, twisting, convulsing, ice platforms the size of islands clumping and inverting as if activated by vast unknown sources of energy. Only the last few kilometres of iceberg were visible to us – it was anyone's guess what was happening to the main body out of sight in the fog.

I tore my eyes from the sight – the sub!

The world might be falling apart, but that Red skipper knew his job. His target was *Jetwind*, and he meant to get her. The submarine's blue-mauve bows steadied on target. This time he did not mean to miss.

'Brace those yards – quick!' As I shouted the order I wondered if the sound of my voice was audible to Tideman only a metre or two away.

Even as I got out the words, I knew it was too late. I had halted *Jetwind*; she could never gain enough way in time to evade the next shot.

The cutting-out boat broke clear of the fleet. What the torpedo didn't do, the boarding party would finish. The light of the searchlights was reflecting off their weapons.

Kay's fingers bit into my arm.

'*Look!*'

The pinnace's sparkle of orange flame in the heart of the fleet was insignificant compared to the tumultuous spectacle of Trolltunga.

Molot exploded.

One moment there were ships and men, living things, moving, plotting, aiming; the next they all stood still in death in front of our eyes. The world of Molot gave a single hideous orgasmic jerk and then stopped like a movie freeze. Everything pulsed in blinding relief for one explosive moment. Then the flames reached up into the overcast.

I had sense enough to remember the danger of *Jetwind*'s sail plan being exposed to a whirlwind blast of concussion.

I scarcely recognized my own voice.

'Get the sails off her! Furl everything!'

The shockwave passed like a wind out of hell. It arrived moments before the minor tidal wave Trolltunga threw up. I thought it would roll the masts out of the ship before I dared risk setting a couple of steadying top-gallants.

The burning fuel on the water drew a merciful curtain of thick black smoke over what was happening to the trapped ships. As *Jetwind* edged past the blazing holocaust to the escape route there was a brighter stab from amongst the blackness, and we saw Catherine wheels of exploding ammunition cartwheeling high into the air. *Jetwind*'s crew on deck heard screams from the men of Group Condor from deep inside the flames, they told me later, but on the enclosed bridge we were shut off from them.

'Course nor'east,' I ordered Tideman. 'Follow the iceberg channel.'

His face was grim and withdrawn; he operated the console switches like an automaton.

Kay came and hid her face against my chest. She did not speak; her dry sobs said everything.

Then the fuel-oil smut on the bridge windscreen cleared, and the wind came clean and fresh.

Jetwind was free.

Chapter 30

◆

'Captain on the bridge!'

The harsh voice of the intercom rasped through the gathering taking place in the crew's day-room, which was situated over the stern. The summons was from the substitute radio operator, one of Tideman's men named Greg. Jim Yell had been left temporarily in command on the bridge; everyone else who could be spared from their duties was attending the get-together. Both Kay and Tideman were present; the self-appointed master of ceremonies was Sir James Hathaway.

It was the morning after the Molot break-out. There was enough flying overcast down-horizon astern to blot out the last traces of the pall of smoke over the secret base. *Jetwind* was making a fair fifteen knots in the racing seas. I was pushing her hard, carrying everything I could, but *Jetwind* wasn't at her best. The missing mast which had catapulted me clear had created an imbalance in the sail plan aerodynamics. It had also affected the steering: she needed watching all the time to prevent a maverick sheer when a bigger-than-usual wave boiled under her counter.

Jetwind wasn't at her best, nor was I.

A bitter, self-reproaching reaction had set in once *Jetwind* had skated clear of the last of the shoal-marker icebergs and the flaring pyre had dimmed astern to a glowing pink and, finally, to a sooty blackness indistinguishable from storm wrack. The clearing-up of Grohman's corpse and those of the two guards had been the final straw. The rest of the gang had surrendered. I could not help thinking, eyeing Grohman's contorted face, that perhaps he had died easily compared to the hundreds of others I had sent to a fiery, diabolical end with my own hands. In war, my action would have been justified, but this was peace – of a kind. Those who might have escaped the fire would have been mortified by the ice. I could not decide which was worse. I, I alone, was responsible.

Kay tried to talk me out of my mood; even her warmth and love were not enough. The reality was like coming back to earth after a high: I could not share the smiling euphoria of everyone on board.

I had reminded Tideman when he, too, had come to my rescue that the Molot death-or-glory break-out might have saved our skins and secured the Falklands flank of the Drake Passage – but who would ever know, or believe, the implications? Neither Argentina nor Russia would admit that Group Condor had ever existed. Who but Grand Admiral Sergei Gorshkov, head of the Soviet Fleet, and his staff would be aware of the loss of two warships and two fleet auxiliaries? Molot had been a victory as secret as the wild wastes where it had taken place.

My slough of despond bit keenest over Seascan. I reproached myself for failing to make the rendezvous when the spy satellite would be at nadir – overhead – to prove beyond all doubt that *Jetwind* was invisible to infra-red and micro-wave surveillance. The rendezvous was still an impossible near half-day's sail away at *Jetwind*'s maximum speed. Perhaps the way I was flogging the guts out of the ship now was symptomatic of my sense of failure, because I knew in my heart that unless *Jetwind*'s protective secret were sealed and delivered by actual observation test, there would never be another ship of her kind built. No Cape Horn Patrol. No commercial fleet either. After what he had been through Sir James would, I felt certain, be only too glad never to set eyes on a sailing ship again.

For these reasons, I had stalled off signalling Thomsen in detail about the happenings. I had merely despatched a cryptic message saying the ship was safe and on her way to Gough. For the rest, how much or how little should I tell him? If officialdom got word of *Jetwind*'s exploits, the questions would become intolerable. What, too, should I do with the bodies of Arno, Brockton, Grohman and the two guards? Bury them at sea on the basis that their secrets

242

would remain safe until the sea gave up her dead, or continue to convey them to the Cape in the sick-bay where now they all lay shrouded? I dodged the question by telling myself that *Jetwind* could not afford the time to stop for a mass sea burial because, by some extreme of luck, there was still an outside chance that *Jetwind* might make the Seascan rendezvous, and while that chance existed I meant to keep her going. In my heart, however, I knew she never would.

I had been so withdrawn from the general life of the ship that I missed the preparations which must have preceded the ceremony I was now confronted with. The fact that it was in the crew's day-room meant that Tideman had not organized it. Less than twenty minutes previously I had been astonished on the bridge to have been handed a written invitation by one of Tideman's paratroopers – one of the men who had finally disarmed the last of the Group Condors.

The invitation read: 'Sir James Hathaway and the officers and crew of *Jetwind* request your presence without fail at a function in the crew's day-room, to be held at 10.30 sharp.'

I had been more astonished still at the sight which had greeted me on arrival. The day-room was a kind of recreation room above the afterpeak adjoining the crew's mess. Big portholes gave a splendid sight of *Jetwind*'s creaming wake. Beneath them a table had been arranged. Its centre-piece was Robbie Lund's old ship's bell. Presiding like a chairman at a board meeting was Sir James, flanked by Kay and Tideman. There was a burst of applause as I entered; it was led by a smiling Sir James, who came forward and conducted me to a seat next to Kay. If my mood had not been so black, I would have realized that I had never seen her look so lovely.

Perhaps Sir James had got to the top because he was something of a showman as well as a business-man. He reached for the bell, which had been hastily mounted between two wooden blocks, and struck it with the clapper.

At that moment, as if on cue, the bitch-box came alive. 'Captain on the bridge!'

However, Sir James was not to be put off. He gestured me back into my seat as I rose to go.

'This is more important – the bridge can do without you for a couple of minutes.'

There was a burst of applause from the men. My reaction said, the blood is on my hands, not yours.

Sir James resumed his showman's attitude. 'Gentlemen – and Kay Fenton.' They were in the mood to laugh, and they laughed at his singling out Kay. 'There is no need to tell you why we are gathered here, but for the record I want to say that all of us – yes, each one of us – owes our being here at all to the super-human courage and personal effort of Captain Rainier. That means, in fact, our lives.'

I couldn't handle it. I wanted to excuse myself, get away from the grins and acclaim.

Sir James silenced his audience with another stroke on the bell.

'This bell hung for many years on a windjammer wreck near Cape Horn,' he said. 'It is a relic of the days of sail when Cape Horn was one of the great ocean routes of the world. From the time it ceased to be until *Jetwind* took the water, the sailing ship was a thing of the past.'

I speculated what might be coming.

'You all know that this voyage was to have been the acid test of whether the sailing ship was to make a come-back in the twentieth century, whether it could become a viable economic proposition when bunker fuel has made power-ship operation a highly questionable one.'

Sir James wasn't the man to lose his captive audience in their adulatory mood by giving them a lecture on ship economics.

He turned to me. 'I – and this audience – have had no time to arrange a formal presentation, but we ask you to place this old Cape Horn bell in a place of honour in *Jetwind* as a token of our admiration, and a symbol of the reopening of the once-great ocean route.'

Neither I – nor anyone else – fathomed his meaning. He was aware of it. But he was, as I have said, a showman. He waited long enough to let our puzzlement take root, then he drew a sheet of paper from his pocket.

He addressed me. His eyes were sparkling by contrast with the formality of his words.

'Captain Rainier, I wish to request official permission to have this signal transmitted.' Before I could respond, he went on. 'It is addressed to my ship-owner colleagues aboard the *Agulhas*. I quote the contents. "Propose immediate formation fifty-million dollar consortium for construction fleet of aerodynamic sailing ships based on design and peformance factors *Jetwind*. I personally am satisfied . . ."'

I couldn't believe my ears. I found myself on my feet. Sir James was pump-handling me; Kay and Tideman led the congratulatory queue.

The bitch-box cut in imperatively. I was startled out of the mood of the ceremony by the note in the operator's voice.

'Captain on the bridge, sir! Urgent! Radar sighting! Plane, forty-five miles, bearing red zero-zero-nine degrees, coming up fast! Heading our way, sir!'

It was there, all right. There was no mistaking the decisive blip on the big Decca radar screen when Tideman, Kay and I reached the bridge at the double.

'What do you make of it?' I asked Greg.

'She's big and she's stuffed with electronic gear.'

'How do you deduce that?'

'She started transmitting like the clappers a minute back,' he replied. 'She must have picked us up on her radar.'

'Radar?' Tideman interjected.

Greg laughed deprecatingly. 'I'd say, a lot of other sophisticated gadgets as well.'

'What is she signalling?' I demanded.

'Can't say, sir – code. All I know is that that sort of sending isn't commercial.'

I asked Tideman, 'Calling up the other dogs for the kill, do you think?'

'Greg,' asked Tideman, 'is there anything to suggest that the plane is in contact with a ship nearby?'

'A warship?' I added.

The faint green of the screen with its revolving range-finder washed across Greg's face. He concentrated a while and then said, 'She's changing course a little, sheering off.'

'Sniffing the bait?' I asked Tideman again.

Kay said quietly, 'I thought we'd finished with all that.'

Greg manipulated his instruments. 'There's another transmitter coming in!'

'Range?'

He listened carefully again before answering. 'It's coming a long way, that's for sure. That's all I can tell. It's in code too.'

'What's the plane's range now?' I asked.

He checked against the calibrations. 'Twenty-three nautical miles.'

I had a sudden thought. 'Can you establish the altitude?'

'Low – very low. Under a hundred metres.'

'I don't like it, Peter,' Tideman said. 'If it were a long-range search plane looking for us it wouldn't cruise at such a low altitude because it'd be guzzling fuel. It would stay high until it picked up a surface contact and only then descend.'

'Unless it comes from a carrier. Perhaps that's where the code answer is coming from.'

Kay formulated the fears which were in both our minds.

'Perhaps it's a plane looking for . . . for . . . Group Condor and the Red squadron.'

'It can't be that,' I replied. 'The plane would know the exact location of Molot and wouldn't need to search.' I spoke to Greg. 'What's the direction of approach of the aircraft?'

'Northnortheast, sir.'

The adrenalin which had seeped out of me after the Molot debacle was back in my veins. Maybe *Jetwind* hadn't won, after all.

The screen with its regular blip exercised a kind of

hypnotic effect. The four of us went silent. The target came closer, closer.

At twelve miles, it hesitated, moved sideways.

The hunter sniffing the trap further?

Who was the hunter?

Greg broke the silence. 'She sees us, for sure.'

'Visually – surely not!'

'I mean, by means of whatever fancy equipment she's using. She's casing us.'

'Twelve miles – that's beyond immediate sea-to-air missile range,' murmured Tideman. 'She's playing it very carefully.'

'Any way of contacting the plane?' I asked Greg.

'If she speaks, I've got all the taps ready open.'

Silence again washed through the radar office on a background wing of electricity.

Then I was startled by a voice. It was so loud, it seemed right at my elbow.

'This is a T-3 Orion of the United States Tracking and Control Group speaking. Identify yourself. Immediately. Use this wavelength. I warn you not to try any tricks.'

I activated the UHF microphone we used for ship-to-ship conversations.

'Sailing ship *Jetwind*. Captain Rainier speaking.'

'Rainier! Well I'll be goddamned to hell!' The voice lost some of its suspicious, offhand note. 'You're Rainier! The guy who's been giving us the runaround all over the Southern Ocean!'

'Are you from Naval Securities Group Activities?'

The pilot clammed up. 'What do you know about NSGA?'

'Paul Brockton was my friend.'

There was a short silence. Then the pilot answered in a different, friendly voice. 'Mine, too. Yeah, this ship's from NSGA. Put Paul on the line, will you?'

'He's aboard. But he's dead.'

'Paul – dead!'

'I killed the man who killed him, if that helps.'

'It doesn't. Paul was a regular guy.'

247

I was still too raw over Paul's death and the other killings to want to talk about them. Instead there were a hundred questions unanswered about the presence of the American long-distance maritime search plane.

'What are you doing in these waters?'

He replied tersely with one word. '*Jetwind*. Half the world wants to know what's happened to you. So does the othe half – the boys behind the scenes.'

'What do you mean?'

'If you were Paul's friend, I guess he told you something.'

That bridged a lot of conversational gaps. 'I get you,' I replied, 'but I don't understand why you should come searching here. A position signal was sent off from *Jetwind* days back saying she was dismasted and in no need of assistance . . .'

There was a snort of derision from the pilot. 'You can't dipsy-doodle NSGA with a decoy signal, fellah. We weren't born yesterday. The Group on Tristan was on full alert . . .' So Paul had got enough of his secret signal away to sound the alarm before Grohman's burst had killed him! 'That kind of half-Mayday didn't decieve us. Whoever sent it was a fool. The transmission time was long enough for us to get a position fix. When we compared that with where *Jetwind* claimed to be, we smelt stinking fish. To NSGA, the stink was to high heaven. It wasn't you who sent that corny signal, I guess?'

'No, it wasn't me. But why the time-lag? Why didn't the Orion come sooner? You could have saved a lot of lives.'

'Lives?' he echoed.

'Lives,' I repeated. 'That part of the story will keep for the present. Why didn't you come?'

'The logistics for mounting a search take time. So do the decisions. NSGA had to be convinced. It took a few days to arrange after *Jetwind* failed to respond to our signals. You're also a helluva long way from anywhere. This plane has been airborne since yesterday. I've flown all the way down the Big Pond. Thousands of miles.'

'From Lajes in the Azores?'

'You were Paul's friend, so I can tell you secrets. Yes. From Lajes. Refuelled Ascension. They had to send an aerial tanker ahead specially to have the gas waiting for me. Maximum load. TACDIFIPS missions.'

'Translate, please.'

'Temporary active duty in a flying status involving operational flights.'

'Operational?'

The pilot's reply was terse. 'This flight is operational, fellah. I'm armed with every sort of goodie in case of trouble. I'm coming in now for a visual intercept.'

'I also want to see you. I'm changing over to the bridge mike. I'll let you know when I sight you.'

'Okay.'

'Come,' I told Kay and Tideman. We went to the bridge. I opened a window in front of the wheel and took the microphone from its hook.

'There's the plane!' exclaimed Kay.

Visibility was medium; Kay spotted the T-3 emerging from a cloud to the northeast. I imagined it approached watchfully, as if the pilot still did not wholly credit *Jetwind*'s bona fides. I recalled his remark about the punch of 'goodies' the Orion packed. The wires in behind-the-scenes secret counsels must have burned over *Jetwind*'s disappearance.

The pilot exclaimed suddenly, 'I see you! Say, you're beautiful, *Jetwind*!'

'Don't touch me or I'll scream.'

I liked the way the pilot laughed. Then he added. 'Say, you're also damaged – you're missing part of a mast.'

'I was in a fight.'

'When Paul was killed?'

'No – later. What I tell you about it, I'd like to be on the record. Can you tape this conversation?'

The pilot laughed without humour. 'This flight's operational, top secret. Everything you've said already is on the reel. You're important. Tristan is monitoring us as a back-up. Now tell me about your blow-off.'

'Blow-off?'

'That fight.'

I couldn't think where I should begin. I tried to muster the facts. I said, marking time, 'I have five dead men aboard.'

The pilot's voice held admiration. 'Who else was on your shit list, fellah?'

'A Soviet *Kashin*-class destroyer. A Whiskey Bag sub. A fleet replenishment vessel. An oceanographic survey ship. An assault force of about five hundred men named Group Condor . . .' I gave him a brief rundown on Molot. I went back to *Jetwind*'s hijacking and the plan to seize the Falklands. I sketched Paul's death, and how we had escaped the *Almirante Storni*. I explained how I had sacrificed *Jetwind*'s mast.

When I had finished, the pilot exclaimed in an awed voice, 'Sweet Mother of Jesus! All this and Molot too! *Dosvidanya!*'

'What's that supposed to mean?'

'It's Russian for goodbye.'

Dosvidanya! It was as good an epitaph as any for that blazing hell of burning liquifying fuel which had been Molot.

There was a silence. Then the pilot said, 'Got a fix for this place Molot where you played clinker boy? I'd better go check and see if there's anything left.'

'Aye. Here it is.' I had made a special point of fixing the location of the secret base by means of *Jetwind*'s satellite navigator as the ship had broken clear of the last of the shoals. 'I don't expect you'll see much, though. The fire must have burned itself out by now . . .'

The pilot's voice cut me short with a shout. 'Sub! Sub! Sub! Sub! Action stations!'

I froze. Kay shrank against me. 'Dear heaven, no! Not now! Not after what we've been through!'

Tideman leapt as if galvanized to the bridge windows, searching the surrounding sea.

The pilot's voice rose. 'She's surfacing! Alongside you! To starboard! I'm going in after her!'

Brian Callison

There can be no better adventure writer in the country
today.' *Alistair MacLean*

One of the best writers of modern sea stories.' *Daily
Telegraph*

A FRENZY OF MERCHANTMEN   £1.50
A PLAGUE OF SAILORS   £1.50
TRAPP'S WAR   £1.35
TRAPP'S PEACE   £1.00
A WEB OF SALVAGE   £1.50
THE JUDAS SHIP   £1.25
THE AURIGA MADNESS   £1.50
THE SEXTANT   £1.65

FONTANA PAPERBACKS

Fontana Paperbacks: Fiction

Fontana is a leading paperback publisher of both non-fiction, popular and academic, and fiction. Below are some recent fiction titles.

- ☐ SO MANY PARTINGS Cathy Cash Spellman £2.50
- ☐ TRAITOR'S BLOOD Reginald Hill £1.95
- ☐ THE KREMLIN CONTROL Owen Sela £1.95
- ☐ PATHS OF FORTUNE Susan Moore £1.95
- ☐ DAYS OF GRACE Brenda Jagger £1.95
- ☐ RAVEN William Kinsolving £1.95
- ☐ FLOODGATE Alistair MacLean £1.95
- ☐ FAMILY TIES Syrell Leahy £1.95
- ☐ DEATH IN SPRINGTIME Magdalen Nabb £1.50
- ☐ LEGION William Blatty £1.75
- ☐ A CROWNING MERCY Susannah Kells £1.95
- ☐ BLIND PROPHET Bart Davis £1.95
- ☐ ALL THINGS IN THEIR SEASON Helen Chappell £2.50
- ☐ A CRY IN THE NIGHT Mary Higgins Clark £1.75
- ☐ SUNRISE Rosie Thomas £1.95

You can buy Fontana paperbacks at your local bookshop or newsagent. Or you can order them from Fontana Paperbacks, Cash Sales Department, Box 29, Douglas, Isle of Man. Please send a cheque, postal or money order (not currency) worth the purchase price plus 15p per book for postage (maximum postage is £3.00 for orders within the UK).

NAME (Block letters) _____

ADDRESS _____

_____